Captain William ... **looking straight** ... **when their eyes** ...

That was enough for Flora. When a member of the gentry not only got you talking but then kept smiling at you for no good reason it meant only one thing. Trouble.

Flora fixed her eyes straight ahead and pursed her lips. She would have to forget all her silly fantasies about the handsome hero. Allowing his charms to work on her was a sure way to disaster.

She must have none of it—her mind was made up. For the moment, at least. . .

Born in Somerset, **Polly Forrester** has been writing for as long as she can remember. Her working career began with twelve years as a humble office clerk, eventually escaping to combine her love of history and the countryside in a new career as a writer. She now lives in the depths of rural Gloucestershire with a cat, a dog and a flock of very eccentric poultry.

CHANGING FORTUNES

Polly Forrester

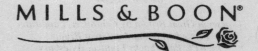

*First published in Great Britain 1997
Harlequin Mills & Boon Limited,
Eton House, 18-24 Paradise Road, Richmond, Surrey TW9 1SR*

© Polly Forrester 1997

ISBN 0 263 80126 8

*Set in 10 on 11½ pt Linotron Times
04-9705-83269*

*Typeset in Great Britain by CentraCet, Cambridge
Printed and bound in Great Britain
by BPC Paperbacks Limited, Aylesbury*

Chapter One

Flora froze with fear. She had spotted a trespasser—crouching just the other side of the bank of rhododendrons that she was hoping would hide her.

This is what I get for being too nervous to go straight to the kitchens to start work, she thought as her thundering heart tried to escape from her ribcage. Oh, why on earth did I try to waste time with a walk? The rustle of starch in her new uniform and the unfamiliar button boots would make a silent escape impossible. Flora would simply have to stand where she was, as quiet as a mouse, until the intruder had moved away.

Her muscles taut and every instinct urging her to fly, Flora still managed to make herself study the intruder. Mr Grimes the gamekeeper would need a full description of the trespasser as soon as Flora had managed to escape.

If I can escape, she thought with another shiver of apprehension.

The intruder was at the lakeside, with his back toward her. Dressed only in vest and trousers, his braces were hanging loosely from his waist and jingling as he worked intently at some task.

Suddenly he stood up—turned—and caught sight of

Flora cowering behind the threadbare limbs of the rhododendrons.

She was rooted to the spot with horror. Taking advantage of her confusion, the stranger reached her in two strides and quick as a striking snake caught at her wrist.

'Well, hello!'

His voice had a predatory sophistication about it that matched the expression in his sea-grey eyes. Flora wanted to scream, but the breath recoiled in her throat. All she could manage was a choking sob of terror. She had recognised the type of clothes he was wearing, and the immaculate creases in his trousers. His dark, thick hair showed the recent work of a barrack-room barber and his heavy boots shone with a mirror-like glow that would have impressed any sergeant major.

'I've had breakfast. I'm not going to eat you, you know!' he chuckled in a low, confidential whisper.

Flora gathered up every last vestige of her fast draining courage.

'Let me go.'

She must have managed some kind of authority because to her great astonishment he did let her go. Flora was so surprised that she forgot to seize her chance and run to raise the alarm.

'What are you doing here?' she risked asking, and fortunately he met the interrogation with a grin.

'A soldier has a duty to keep himself and the equipment issued by His Majesty clean, neat and ready for inspection at all times!'

He gestured toward the billy can that he had been scouring at the water's edge. There was no apology, no explanation of his trespass on Alvoe land.

Flora's initial fear began to harden into annoyance. Her new employers had lost two sons in the Great War and they didn't deserve to have their land trampled by trespassers. This flippant survivor ought to be taught a lesson.

'My husband was a soldier. He was killed on the Somme,' she said with quiet dignity.

It did not produce the usual rush of apologies. The soldier continued to study her, his brow creasing in concentration.

'That must be. . .three years ago?'

He spoke as though it had been an exercise of memory. When Flora gave no reply other than a flare of her delicate little nostrils he tried to revive the exchange.

'It *was* in 1916, wasn't it?'

His uncertainty only added to Flora's growing fury.

'The date should be engraved on the heart of every real soldier. I suppose you were one of those with a nice safe job, well away from the action? A clerk who only sent out the black-edged telegrams? If indeed you were a soldier *at all*. Perhaps you're just one of those who have picked up a uniform somewhere and now use it to whip up sympathy and cash on your travels,' she finished bitterly.

'I did my share in the war.'

Flora continued to stare at the trespasser, wanting him to feel the guilt about her widowhood that she could not. He ignored her silent reproach and turned back to the billy can.

'There's been some trouble with the trains. I didn't get into Bristol until nine o'clock last night. By the time I'd got to this place, it was too late to go rousing decent people so I pitched camp where I was.' He gestured towards a little summer house nestling beside the ornamental lake. 'I was about to make myself a cup of tea. Would you like one?'

The question was totally unexpected. First fear had stopped Flora escaping, then annoyance had made her stay. Now curiosity about this barefaced trespasser with the laughing eyes was threatening to get the better of her.

It took Flora a moment to remember her position as a respected part of the Alvoe household, and his as a trespasser. With that in mind there could be only one answer.

'No, thank you. Certainly not!' she managed with a little more force, taking another step back towards the rhododendrons. He folded his arms and watched her with amusement.

'I'm not an escaped lunatic or a mad murderer, you know!'

Flora hesitated.

'I'm only a soldier. Like your husband,' he persisted.

Flora knew all about soldiers.

Far away a muffled gunshot blew a riot of rooks cawing into the air. That was it. The spell was broken. Flora bolted like a frightened rabbit, the intruder's laughter still echoing in her ears.

She didn't stop running until the sandstone bulk of Alvoe Court came into view through the trees. Then she remembered the dignity that her new position accorded her and with a last petrified glance around the deserted woodlands she tried to convince herself that she had left the intruder far behind.

Out of breath and plagued with a savage stitch in her side, Flora slowed to a walk. Without a looking-glass she had to rely on touch to check her appearance. An auburn curl had escaped from the starched severity of her cap. She poked it back in hopefully, straightened her apron and checked that her white cuffs were still spotless. When she saw Mr Stacey, the head gardener, it was with relief, rather than the suspicion with which a more experienced cook would have viewed such a traditional enemy.

'Oh, Mr Stacey? There's an intruder inside the estate. A suspicious-looking character, loitering around the lake.'

Mr Stacey took one look at Flora's face and could see everything that she was trying so hard to conceal from him. A flush in the face that was usually as pale as alabaster and the fevered brightness in her normally calm green eyes. Instead of the slightly scornful disdain which Mr Stacey had always harboured for the previous cook, he now felt only concern. He hurried off to round up the garden boys and track the intruder down.

Flora continued to the kitchens, knowing that work would have to take her mind off her shock. There could be no excuses, and no time to be nervous on her first full working day at Alvoe Court. There was to be a big party that evening in celebration of the return of Ralph Morwyn, the Duke of Alvoe's son, on leave from the army.

If I'm going to start at the top I might as well begin as I mean to go on, Flora had thought to herself. She was very good at her work, but had no illusions about the way she had been chosen for the position of cook at Alvoe Court. When the Great War had taken away all the menfolk, women had soon discovered that they were in demand to do jobs that were more glamorous than domestic service. Great houses like Alvoe Court had been left to struggle on with a skeleton staff made up of those too young or too set in their ways to find employment elsewhere.

It was rumoured that when their old cook had died the Duke and Duchess of Alvoe had been reduced to eating meat paste and margarine sandwiches prepared by a scullery maid!

That would explain why they had suddenly started to accept every available invitation to dine away from home. When they had wheedled themselves a dinner at Falgrave Manor, their host, Sir Hubert Wilson, had been only too proud to show off the skills of his treasure of a cook—and her young assistant, Flora.

The following day a note had arrived by carrier, asking if Flora's employer would 'lend' her to Alvoe Court. Sir Hubert, a self-made man in awe of anyone who came from what he called an 'old family', was overwhelmed with pride and only too delighted to be in a position to do a Duke and Duchess a favour. Flora had been allowed to take up the position of cook at Alvoe Court, when she was not yet twenty-one.

Flora smiled to herself. She might be young, but the Alvoe family were certainly going to get something a bit better than a scullery maid's meat paste sandwiches for their party tonight.

As soon as she stepped into the kitchens that were her workshop, time began to race. She tried to immerse herself in her work, as there was still plenty to be done for the celebration dinner that evening. She couldn't afford to think about her fright over the trespasser. The appearance of another soldier in her life had revived fears that she had hoped were deeply buried.

The trouble was, her mind would not let go of the intruder's image. A picture of his tall, strongly built body with its tanned and smiling face kept shouldering its way to the front of her consciousness. On one occasion the distraction almost proved disastrous. Her usually nimble fingers stumbled over the task of making cutlet frills. It was a job she normally could have done in her sleep, and what made it even more annoying was that she was teaching Ivy — one of the kitchen maids — at the time.

The truth was that a feeling of gnawing guilt was trying to overtake Flora. It was a feeling that had often kept her awake at night, but had never been allowed to cast a shadow over her days before. It had taken a trespasser in a soldier's uniform to make her confront her darkest thoughts — that one terrible secret she had been trying to suppress for the past three years.

She had been glad that Alfred Westbury had not come home from the war.

It was an awful admission. Sinful. *Unforgivable.*

But it was true. Flora could not bring herself to feel the genuine grief for Alfred that other widows were suffering for their husbands. His death had freed her — given her another chance in life and one that she was determined not to squander. When the telegram had arrived she had put on a show of distress for the sake of her family. It had been expected of her.

That had been when the guilt had started, feeding on the lie of Flora's grief.

Flora didn't realise that it had been Alfred himself and his behaviour that made her feel differently from other widows, not the honesty of her feelings.

All those other widows had lost good men.

Everyone had known about Alfred's quick temper. Nothing but summer storms, they had always called his outbursts. His moods soon passed, then he was all smiles again.

That was what his drinking companions thought, but Flora had soon seen a darker side. In the short time between their wedding and the day Alfred left for the war, Flora had learned how easily his temper could be inflamed. Savage words had soon turned to savage deeds when the nearest target was his wife rather than a lad of similar strength and build.

Flora had experienced marriage like a servant, waiting on the whims of an unpredictable master. Creeping about in his shadow, afraid of what the smallest word or action might incite.

With Alfred's death had come freedom from all that terror. Flora had started to live again, resuming her job as assistant cook at Falgrave Manor, safe in the knowledge that her money would no longer end up flowing into Alfred's pint glass at the Porter Stores. At long last her post office savings had begun to grow again, ready for the time when her father became too old or infirm for farm work. She hoped to have improved her own situation by then. Her own little bakery with rooms attached, so that her father could live with her and she could earn money enough to support them both.

Flora had to shake off these private thoughts. I've got more than enough to do at present, she told herself sternly. This isn't the time to let old fears rise up and swamp me. She could have cursed the good-looking trespasser who had taken only a few minutes to bring to razor-sharpness what three years had hardly dulled.

Leaving Ivy to make the rest of the cutlet frills unsupervised, Flora tied on a clean white apron and began her proper work. She sent Mary, another of the maids, for the kitchen book then set about concentrating solely on the task in hand. The Marquis of Dayle's celebration dinner.

Nearly every one of the several dozen ingredients she had listed in the order book had a satisfying tick beside it. All that remained outstanding was the fishmonger's delivery and for Mr Stacey, the head gardener, to send the fruit and vegetables up from the kitchen garden.

She checked the menu yet again. Tartines de Caviare as a savoury, followed by the last of the salmon and the first of the oysters. September was such an awkward time of year, between seasons, but the Duchess had stressed that no expense was to be spared.

Glad to be free of the penny-pinching that had gone on at her last job at Falgrave Manor, Flora had indulged herself on behalf of her new employers. The seafood course was to be followed by soup, then lobster creams, veal and grouse, a choice of hot or iced puddings then cheeses and a selection of bakery, sweets, fresh fruit and coffee.

Flora thanked her lucky stars that Cook back at the Manor had taught her to keep well ahead of herself. The birthday pudding had already been steamed for eight hours and would only need a couple more hours of reheating that evening. Slices of bread had been drying off in the bottom oven all night for the caviare savouries. The salmon and oysters would need only the briefest preparation when they arrived.

If they arrived.

Flora forced herself to stop worrying. They would be here soon enough. Meanwhile she reassured herself that the piece of veal sent over from the home farm was the finest she had ever seen, and that the grouse had been hanging in the game larder for long enough to be tasty without being too rank.

All she had to do now was to ensure that everything was prepared to the highest possible standard.

In between working and instructing her staff, Flora had to introduce a routine and supervise the deliveries that arrived by pony and trap at intervals during the morning. She was about to go out into the courtyard

and introduce herself to the fishmonger when a flurry
of excitement rippled through the kitchen.

Much to the giggling confusion of the female staff, a
short, slight young man in a soldier's uniform had
entered through the door that led from the main part
of the house. He had sandy hair, freckles, and wide-set
blue eyes that raked his appreciative female audience
before catching sight of Flora. He advanced with a
smile.

'Mrs Westbury?'

Flora bobbed a curtsey obediently.

'I'm Ralph Morwyn, Marquis of Dayle. The Duke's
son. I hear you're in charge of the rations around here
now.'

'Yes, sir.' Silently, Flora thanked heaven that all the
cooking was going according to plan—so far. 'I think
you'll find that we'll be able to provide something a bit
better than army food, sir—' she began, then stopped
dead as she caught sight of another arrival at the
kitchen door.

It was the stranger that she had taken for some
common trespasser.

He had changed from his army uniform into a smart
riding outfit of breeches, boots and one of the brightly
patterned knitted jumpers that were so fashionable.
Flora found herself thinking that it suited him even
better than the uniform, until she realised what she had
done. With a sinking feeling in the pit of her stomach
Flora wondered how on earth she could have mistaken
this tall, handsome stranger with the roguish smile for
anything but a member of the gentry.

She looked down quickly to avoid the rebuke she
expected to find in his eyes. Ralph Morwyn noticed the
movement.

'This is Captain William Pritchard, everybody. One

of the friends of mine who will be staying here while we all take a bit of a break from India.'

India? So *that* was why this Captain Pritchard had asked about the date of the Somme battles. Flora had already heard that Master Ralph had been away in the East for the duration.

She found herself drawn to look up into the eyes of Captain Pritchard again. His tanned, wolfishly hand-some face was alight with silent laughter. With renewed terror Flora realised that this Captain Pritchard held the power to make a fool of her in front of Master Ralph and the whole kitchen staff. Just when it was so important that she should be impressing everyone with her ability to take charge, this *soldier*—it was the worst slur Flora could think of in her panic—was about to make her a laughing stock.

'If Mrs Westbury is as good a cook as she is guardian of your family's estate, Ralph, you should have no worries. No worries at all.'

White, even teeth flashed against the rich colouring of Captain Pritchard's skin and not for the first time Flora saw a predatory edge to his amusement. He was too clever to relinquish the hold he had over her immediately, but Flora was in no doubt that he would think of a way to use it to his own advantage.

She was quite sure of that.

Heat rose within her in such burning waves of embarrassment that Flora was sure both men would be able to feel its warmth, despite the gulf between them.

'What do you mean, Will?' Ralph Morwyn looked up at his friend, puzzlement clouding his pale eyes. In reply William Pritchard smiled, raising the dark arc of one eyebrow as he continued to study Flora.

There was a pause. William Pritchard's beautifully cruel eyes were holding Flora in an agony of expectancy. He was able to keep the attention of the whole room, yet Flora was the only one who knew he was holding the power to influence the success or failure of her career at Alvoe Court, too. No one would respect a girl who sent the outdoor staff on a wild-goose chase and, worse, had mistaken one of Master Ralph's friends for a trespasser.

'As I arrived at the front door of Alvoe Court this morning the outdoor staff were searching for some rascal that your new cook had discovered billeted in a summer house. I told them that a wicked-looking fellow had indeed been walking along their drive, and they rushed off to look for him.'

Flora's eyes opened wide with surprise. The cheek of it! In a voice rich and smooth as honey this scoundrel was acting as though the whole affair was some sort of private joke between the two of them. Flora was incensed, but there was not a single thing that she could do about it. There was still no place in a grand household for a servant—however talented—who spoke her mind in front of her betters.

She tried to quell her own rage by turning it on Ivy, the kitchen maid who was dimpling and dazzling in a way that Captain Pritchard all too clearly appreciated. It's bad enough knowing that he has a hold over me without seeing the effect he's having on the rest of the staff, Flora thought furiously.

'Fetch me the dish of apple and custard left over from last night, Ivy. It's been put away in the sweet pantry.' Flora nudged the maid into doing something useful. Ivy backed away, still smiling at the Captain, but Flora was determined to prevent anything untoward starting up between a master and maid in her kitchen.

She smiled directly at Ralph Morwyn, trying to get rid of him and his overbearing friend.

'We're always very busy here, my lord. I haven't had time to have any breakfast yet.'

Her ploy worked only too well. 'Oh, you poor little thing!' Ralph said with concern, throwing up his gloved hands. His friend was not so easily impressed.

'I hope she'll have time to make sure everything goes well this evening,' Captain Pritchard said with an edge of warning behind his feigned amusement.

The hint that she might not be equal to the task stung Flora, but she could not let it show. She hid her clenched fists in the folds of her skirt and smiled, but only at the Marquis.

'Of course I shall, my lord.'

'Come on now, Mrs Westbury! Call me Master Ralph. Everyone else does.'

'Yes, Master Ralph.'

'Any chance of one of those frozen dessert things tonight?' Ralph went on with almost childlike enthusiasm. 'They're my favourite.'

'I know, Master Ralph. The Duchess informed me. There will be apricot and raspberry bombe available as well as a birthday pudding.'

Ralph laughed, but the eyes of Captain Pritchard were thoughtful. 'That sounds almost *too* fearfully brisk and efficient, Mrs Westbury.' He looked to his friend. 'I hope working in your place here will soften her up a little, Ralph.'

Ivy arrived with a dish from the sweet pantry. Taking a tin spoon from the table drawer, she placed it and the dish on the kitchen table, managing both tasks without once taking her eyes off Captain Pritchard.

He was ignoring her, but Ralph's gaze had shifted from Flora to the cold pudding.

'What's that?'

'Apple and custard, Master Ralph.'

'Custard? I thought custard was white and bubbly.'

'Custard sauce made with fresh eggs and milk is, Master Ralph,' Flora explained patiently. 'This is Downstairs custard. For the staff. It's made with powder, from a tin.'

This intrigued him, and he leaned forward to pick up the spoon.

'May I?'

Flora could do nothing but nod her acceptance of this liberty. Her annoyance showed only in the merest flicker of a frown as Ralph scooped up a healthy spoonful from her dish. There was a lull as he savoured it fully.

'I might as well give you the message I've been trying to give your mother.' With evident reluctance Captain Pritchard tore his attention away from Flora and Ivy and turned it full upon his friend. 'The Reverend Mr Standish says he would be delighted to make up the numbers for dinner this evening, Ralph. I was trying to find your mother to tell her myself, but the staff say that she has asked not to be disturbed.'

Ralph had finished his first two mouthfuls of Flora's breakfast and took another one. He compounded this sin by speaking with his mouth full.

'I don't think Ma took too kindly to Pa telling you to go over and invite your Reverend friend in the first place. She likes to be the one offering the hospitality.'

William Pritchard smiled at Flora again. She looked down and saw Ralph removing another large spoonful of her breakfast.

'What do you reckon to this, Will? It's what they eat down here. Have a taste.'

He held out a good helping of bright yellow custard to his friend.

Flora winced, expecting the lofty Captain Pritchard to refuse such common fare. Instead there was a pause as he savoured the custard, then a chink as he replaced the spoon in the bowl.

When William Pritchard spoke again it was with wistful longing.

'Bird's custard?'

Flora was staggered. To find that Captain Pritchard knew all about Downstairs custard was a shock almost as great as his arrival in her kitchen had been. She looked up quickly, to see him taking another helping.

'I haven't had any of this for years,' he was saying in a thoughtful tone.

Ralph was intrigued. 'You've had this stuff before?'

'At home. Mrs Fielding used to let me scrape out the saucepan on Saturday dinnertimes—' He grinned quite openly at Flora. 'Sorry, Ralph, that's what they call "luncheon" below stairs. She always made Mr Fielding a great steamed jam pudding with lashings of Bird's custard on Saturdays. Best food of the week.'

He was still laughing, but although the words were directed at his friend the amusement was not. Flora clenched her hands until the nails bit into her palms, wishing that she could tell Captain William Pritchard exactly what she thought of him and his way of scrutinising the kitchen staff as though they were exhibits on display.

Ralph Morwyn took a final mouthful of Flora's apple and custard then pushed the dish away. There was barely a spoonful left for her.

'That was a bit of all right, but there's no sense in spoiling my appetite for luncheon, or dinner, or what-ever it's called down here.' He pulled a face at his friend. 'Little Mrs Westbury should be supplying us guns with a good-sized picnic.'

William Pritchard pushed his hands into his pockets and for once looked serious.

'That's another reason I came to find you, Ralph. Mr Standish has asked me to go back and have lunch with him today. Would you mind if I missed the shoot?'

'Oh, Will!' Ralph grimaced. 'I was looking forward to showing you around the old place as much as I was looking forward to picking off a few pigeons. Ring him up. Say you can't go back today.'

'Not everyone has a telephone, Ralph.' Captain Pritchard laughed despite Ralph's sour expression. 'I shall have to ride back to Branxmere myself to deliver the message. It wouldn't be polite to send a boy. By the time I've travelled all the way over there and back again, then changed and got up to the shoot, you'll be lost in the excitement of trying to bag more pigeons than the next man. You won't even notice if I'm not there.'

'I shall,' Ralph muttered, heading for the door. 'I never thought you'd be the sort to treat a good host badly, Will.'

'The Reverend has been a very good benefactor to me in the past, Ralph,' William Pritchard persisted. 'Today is the first time we've actually met face to face. He was so pleased to see me at last. I can hardly disappoint him now, can I?'

Ralph shrugged. He accepted the explanation but with bad grace. William Pritchard must have been used to such displays of truculence, for while the kitchen staff watched in nervous silence he went to the kitchen door and flung it open.

'Come on, Ralph. You could always ride along with me for a while if you're so desperate for my company.'

He held the door open but it was some time before Ralph's expression softened. Strolling forward at last, he struck his friend companionably on the arm.

'All right. Standing your ground has worked again, Will. You win. We'll cut across the fields. It'll be quicker than using the roads and I can show you a couple of the best coverts on the way.'

The two men left the kitchen, easy conversation absorbing them as they disappeared back into the depths of the house.

Mary could hardly contain her excitement. She skipped straight over to Flora's side, the vegetable knife in her hand still dripping water.

'Did you see the way that chap said he wasn't going shooting? I can't imagine how anybody could refuse Master Ralph anything! Oh, and isn't he good-looking? So much taller than Master Ralph, and that smile. . .' The kitchen maid shook her head slowly in wonderment.

Flora sent the girl back to the vegetables with a flea in her ear. She could only wonder at it all, too. In her imagination she could still feel the cool, vice-like grip of William Pritchard's hand on her wrist. He had deliberately kept his identity a secret then, letting her think that he was a trespasser. Flora tried to remember what she had said to him, all the time dreading the reason why he had decided to keep his hold over her by not revealing her mistake.

There was an easy answer to the question of why a member of the gentry should do that. Flora knew full well what it was. She also knew that as long as William Pritchard was in residence at Alvoe Court she would have to watch her step very carefully indeed. She could not afford to take any chances. There must never be the slightest chance that their paths would cross again. Upstairs and Downstairs should not mix.

'I wish that William Pritchard had talked to me,' Ivy muttered dolefully.

'He'd only be after One Thing if he did,' Flora rebuked her.

'Oh, I wouldn't mind that, miss. Chance would be a fine thing, anyway.'

Flora sent the girl off brusquely to help Mary with the vegetables, but she couldn't banish the truth quite so readily. Ivy had only said what the other kitchen girls would be thinking.

When William Pritchard had tired of using his power on Flora, he would start working the same dubious charm on her kitchen maids. She looked across at Ivy, Mary and the other girls, giggling away together over their work. She could guess what, or rather who, they were talking about. Some of them were so young— barely fourteen. They would be even less able to resist Captain William Pritchard's charms.

Suddenly, Flora felt her stomach contract. What on earth was she thinking? She shouldn't be allowing herself to find him charming at all! Quite the opposite.

It was as though Captain Pritchard had insinuated his way into her very soul, persuading her from within. The fact that he was a paid-up member of His Majesty's army made it even worse. An army uniform was no guarantee of good behaviour.

She had learned that lesson well.

There was only one sure way of preventing Captain Pritchard's dangerous charm from getting to work on her. She decided to think of his handsome, laughing face contorted above her in the sweating, grunting efforts that had so obsessed Alfred.

Memories of that could still make her feel sick, even now. All the swearing. All the shame.

She could not face going through all that again. If only she could prevent the other girls from ruining their lives in the same fashion. To judge from the whispering giggles still entertaining the kitchen maids, such good intentions were the last thing on their minds.

Chapter Two

The rest of the day was filled to overflowing with work. Final preparations for the celebration dinner were a priority, but in addition normal meals had to be prepared for Those Upstairs as well. There was also the added complication of packing hampers for the shooting lunch.

It was this last job that proved the most difficult. Flora had planned ahead to prevent panics but Ivy was determined to be in the right.

'But they *always* have cold cuts in the shooting hampers, miss!'

Ivy slid a glance around the rest of the kitchen staff for support, but Flora was determined not to be deflected from her working plan.

'Well, they aren't having cold cuts *today*, Ivy. I'm not having the Duchess think I have to resort to cold meats, pickles and cheese for the shoot because I'm overcome by feeding the house and preparing a grand dinner at the same time.'

'It's true that the men always seem to like the cold cuts, miss,' Mary chipped in. 'The old cook, Mrs Wells, used to give the guns the same thing every time. When the hampers came back they were always near enough empty.'

Flora knew she could not allow the girls to worry her into changing her plans. She had calculated everything so carefully. It just *had* to work.

'This time the hampers are going to come back *completely* empty.' She tried to sound convincing. 'There will be a choice of a hot or cold main course, so that the gentlemen may please themselves.'

The shoot was taking place on a tenanted farm at the other side of the estate. Picnic hampers were to be despatched by pony and trap at eleven o'clock that morning. The hot dishes of braised beef, vegetables, potatoes and apple dumplings were packed up in hay-boxes to continue cooking until lunchtime. Cold game pie and salad, fruit cake and cheese and biscuits were available for the hardy types who preferred cold food at luncheon.

Flora had arranged that everything could be eaten easily enough with one hand. She had watched Mr Grimes, the gamekeeper, putting the Duke's shooting dogs through their paces during her first visit to Alvoe Court, earlier in the week. From what she had seen the guns would each need a free hand to fend off the greedy, energetic animals if they took a fancy to the sporting lunch.

'Are you sure that I shouldn't put a bit of ham in the hampers as well?' Ivy said as the pony and cart was led up to the back door.

'No.' Flora went down the kitchen steps to make sure the gamekeeper's sons packed the hampers in the right order. 'Hot food at the back, cold at the front. Then those that can't wait till lunchtime can start on the cake. The hay-boxes can be pulled forward when everything is unpacked and the gentlemen can eat at the tailboard, if they like.'

Ivy muttered her disapproval but Flora was too absorbed in her work to care.

To her relief, the rest of the working day went like clockwork. Finally, at well past nine o'clock that evening, the desserts and cheeses were sent up to bring the grand dinner to a close. It was the signal for Flora to kick off her shoes, call for a cup of tea and drop into the lumpy old cook's chair beside the fire for a well-earned rest.

She hardly had time for a single sip of tea before she was interrupted. One of the Upstairs footmen arrived at the kitchen door with a request that she present herself in the dining room straight away.

It was what Flora had hoped for, but also what she feared. Mary found her a clean apron while she buttoned up her shoes again, tidied her hair and put in a few more hairpins to secure the curls that always managed to escape from beneath her cap when she was working. The reflection staring back at her from the kitchen mirror was as white as paper. She was too nervous for words.

If Upstairs had summoned her because they had liked the meal that was one thing. If they were displeased, that was quite another.

She accompanied the liveried footman up in the service lift. The rattling clank of gears and chains could hardly blot out the sound of her thumping heart. The footman was silent and unapproachable, so there was no reassurance from him.

When the lift jerked to a halt she followed the footman along a shadowy landing lined with bleak, anonymous doors and scornfully aristocratic family portraits. He paused before one of the highly polished doors. Flora took a steadying breath as the footman checked the fit of his gloves then opened the door to reveal a brightly lit dining room. The blaze of electric light was almost as wonderful as hearing the footman introduce her as 'Mrs Westbury, the cook'.

The impressive lighting revealed a worrying fact. The ladies had left, and Flora was confronted only by gentlemen. They were all seated around a long table decked with Mr Stacey's floral garlands. There must have been more than a dozen men, all in evening dress and smiling expansively with the effects of good spirits and an excellent meal.

The Duke of Alvoe was seated at the head of the table with his son Ralph beside him. All the other men seated around the long dining table, most of whom looked close to Ralph in age, were strangers to her.

With the exception of William Pritchard.

Flora first saw him without meaning to look. He was seated at the far end of the table, deep in conversation with an elderly gentleman wearing a clergyman's collar. The flash of light rippling across the medals pinned to William Pritchard's chest had caught her eye before she could discipline herself to look down at the thread-bare carpet. She wanted to make sure that Captain Pritchard's familiar, intimate expression could not ensnare her again.

The guests were laughing and joking over the Alvoe cognac, but her arrival eventually caused conversation to lapse. It was left to the Duke of Alvoe to take the initiative. He was florid with indulgence and smiling broadly.

'Come a bit closer, girl! We don't bite.'

At his words Ralph unexpectedly reached out and took hold of Flora's wrist, tugging her forward.

Laughter ran around the table at her obvious alarm. The smoky, intimate atmosphere and the uncomfortably damp grip on her wrist did nothing to calm Flora's nerves, but at least it was not the silence of disapproval. She moved forward as requested, firmly resisting the temptation to look along the table at Captain William Pritchard.

'I was delighted with the show you put on for us this evening, Mrs Westbury.' The Duke's voice was rich after the celebrations. He was in his late sixties, with thinning grey hair slicked around his scalp with plentiful dressing. 'Shooting lunches went well, too. Grand idea to have a bit of a change. Grand.'

Relief washed over Flora and she smiled at the Duke. He smiled back, but his brow soon puckered with the effort of remembering the other thing that he had to say to her.

'Only boring thing about it was the ham, Mrs Westbury. Nothing duller than plain ham, in my opinion.'

Agreement murmured around the other gentlemen.

'Old Mrs Wells would have had the guns live on it, I believe,' the Duke added with a touch of real regret.

Flora knew at once what must have happened. Ivy had defied her and put cold cuts into the shooting hampers after all. *That* was why the girl had been so quiet all day. Guilt.

To redeem the situation Flora knew that she would have to mix truth and diplomacy to keep peace both above and below stairs.

The Duke paid her wages, but when all was said and done she had to work with Ivy.

'If you please, your Grace, I gave orders that the ham was not to be included. One of the girls must have misheard. The remains won't be wasted.'

'I suppose you'll be expecting poor Ralph and his family to live on ham sandwiches at every meal for the next month?' William Pritchard interjected with maliciously playful intent.

He's determined to get me into trouble one way or another, Flora thought, with an icy shiver at her poor choice of thoughts.

'Certainly not, your Grace.' She ignored Captain Pritchard and spoke directly to the Duke. 'It will be made up into nourishment for the parish poor.'

Flora was rewarded with a beaming smile. Seeing his father's expression did at least cause Ralph to let go of her hand and Flora quickly withdrew it from his reach.

'Good! That suits me, playing the benefactor,' the Duke said with satisfaction. 'Specially when it involves no thought and less effort on my part. Getting rid of plain boiled ham at the same time makes it even better. What do you reckon, Standish? Does that redeem this old dissolute in your eyes, eh?'

The Duke was staring at William Pritchard's companion. Flora took care not to look in the same direction.

'I think it is fortunate that your lady wife is such an excellent judge of staff, your Grace,' the Reverend said diplomatically.

'Hmm.' The Duke refilled his glass with cognac and frowned before taking a large swig. 'Pity Isobel wasn't in good enough condition to enjoy the feast. Got any sovereign remedies in your armoury, Mrs Westbury?'

If the Duchess was unwell Flora wondered why a doctor had not been called. Beef tea and possets could only have a limited effect.

Before she could enquire further about the Duchess, William Pritchard answered for her.

'Oh, Mrs Westbury is sure to know all the cures, your Grace. She wouldn't want to miss a chance like that to increase her stock with you.'

Stung beyond all endurance at being talked about rather than to, Flora spoke to William Pritchard but did not look at him. 'It's to my advantage to do as well for the Duke and Duchess as I am able, Captain Pritchard.'

'Then let's hope that the Duke and Duchess can fulfil all your ambitions, Mrs Westbury.' William Pritchard answered with his usual ease but his friend Ralph was more outspoken.

'I would have thought it should be more a matter of *her* fulfilling *our* expectations,' he said, inciting another burst of laughter. This time it was not such a welcome sound.

Flora did not look up to see if William Pritchard had joined in the fun. At least her conscience was clear. As long as she worked hard and kept out of the way of devious scoundrels like him she knew she would do well.

'Don't tease the poor girl, gentlemen.' The Duke interrupted the laughter. 'I must say she looks awfully young to have put on such a splendid show. Still, age is no indication of ability. Mrs Wells kept us eating food even my father was sick of. Makes a change to have good food,' the Duke went on with satisfaction.

During the Duke's reminiscences Flora let her attention slip. It was drawn straight back to William Pritchard.

'Well, you know what you can do with Mrs Westbury if you're not satisfied, your Grace,' he said, catching her eye.

There was a scatter of satisfied amusement at his words and Ralph Morwyn was quick to cultivate it.

'I'm surprised at you, Will! What about little Cherie Barclay, waiting so patiently back at Woolwich?'

The amusement became open laughter, in which William Pritchard joined to damning effect.

I *knew* he was the sort to have a girl in every town, Flora told herself, and tried to take comfort in being proved right. She couldn't find any.

'You don't want to make her any more unhappy than you do at the moment, do you?' Ralph persisted, blowing a thick gale of dark cigar smoke across the ice-white tablecloth.

The Reverend gave a meaningful cough and William Pritchard looked first at him, then over to the Duke. With annoyance Flora saw that his expression was one of long-suffering amusement. The fact that someone so faithless could find it so funny only confirmed Flora's worst suspicions about him.

'I meant that Mrs Westbury could always be found another position. Even Mr and Mrs Fielding back in London would sound to be less exacting employers than your son, your Grace.'

'Reckon I'm hard on the staff, do you, Will? Here— I'll show you. Watch this!' Clamping his cigar between his teeth with a wicked grin, Ralph started to delve in the pocket of his waistcoat.

'Keep your money for betting on three-legged nags!' William Pritchard called across, but Ralph quickly took a small piece of folded paper from his pocket, pressed it into Flora's hand and winked at her before turning back to ask his father some question about racing.

Flora realised that her audience must have come to an end, but there was no formal dismissal. Like the Duke and his son, all the guests were engrossed in conversation again. They had turned their backs on the temporary entertainment, and were more interested now in their cognac and cigars.

The footman approached silently and touched a

gloved hand to her shoulder. With relief Flora realised she could make her escape.

She followed the footman to the door, afraid to even look at whatever token Ralph Morwyn had given her. Then she realised that she had not thanked him for his gift. She looked back, ready to smile her gratitude, but William Pritchard was the only one looking in her direction. Their eyes met, and the dark curve of his eyebrows rose in an expression of such deep amusement that Flora caught her breath.

Pushing Ralph's donation deep into her apron pocket, she forgot all thoughts of polite behaviour and hurried out of the room.

Flora was determined not to make too much of her audience in the dining room. However, the staff were delighted with her success and eager to hear what had happened. Ralph's gift stayed hidden deep in her pocket but to balance that Flora added to her account of what had happened up in the dining room. She told the kitchen staff that the Duke had sent thanks to all of them. This pleased them still more, and even Ivy thawed a little.

Flora was not one to bear grudges, and decided that Ivy would not suffer for long over her deceit with the ham. She had already decided that the girl could be set to work first thing in the morning to use up the wasted meat. It would teach her to obey in a more sensible manner than argument and ill feeling could.

Retrieving her cup of tea from the range where it had been keeping warm, Flora escaped to her room. Only when she had reached its sanctuary and closed the door behind her did she take out the fold of paper that Ralph Morwyn had given her.

It was a ten-shilling note.

Flora could hardly believe it. Nearly half a week's

wages handed out as a casual gesture. She stared at the note while the gaslight bathed it in a seductive glow. She went hot and cold at the thought of such extravagance, but her excitement was short-lived.

The look William Pritchard had given her as she'd left the dining room swam back into her mind. He must know by now what Ralph had handed over, and he looked and sounded like just the sort of man who would consider such a gesture some kind of payment in advance. Oh, why didn't I refuse it, or at least explain that I'm not that sort of girl? The thoughts crowded in on Flora with growing horror. What on earth would Captain Pritchard be thinking about her now?

The only thing a member of the gentry *could* think about a girl who accepted money so easily from a gentleman.

Flora's first thought was that she ought to go straight back to the dining room and return the money to Master Ralph, however embarrassed she might be. That way there could be no misunderstanding.

Then she reconsidered. No. To make a scene would be unforgivable, and would probably be a sacking offence. Her next idea was, on reflection, no better. To try and corner Master Ralph in secret with such a potentially indelicate matter would be even worse— like stepping into a lion's den.

She placed the ten-shilling note in the corner of her dressing-table mirror, thinking long and hard about what to do. As she washed and got ready for bed it reproached her silently. Eventually, when Flora was giving her hair its customary one hundred brush strokes before plaiting it for the night, she came to a decision.

On Monday, her day off, that ten-shilling note would be going straight into the post office. There it could stay. If Master Ralph once tried to capitalise on his 'investment' Flora would tell him that he could have his wretched money back again in full, together with any interest.

She stood in front of the fly-spotted looking-glass for a long time, brushing her hair. With luck he might even write the money off to experience, when faced with an honest woman.

She could dream.

The ten-shilling note had barely grown into the deposit on a little shop when a faint sound from the corridor outside interrupted her reverie. She paused, a curtain of hair drifting down from the brush as she listened.

Mary had told her that apart from the cook's room this part of the servants' wing was empty.

Perhaps it was a girl bringing a message from the kitchens. It might even be Ivy with an apology.

Or. . .Master Ralph Morwyn, looking to capitalise on his investment.

Flora turned up the gas and moved quickly to lock the door. To her horror she discovered that there was no key. Petrified, she flung all her weight against the door. Panic rose in her throat, pressing the breath out of her in small gasps of pain.

This was it. In a few seconds the door-latch would be raised and slowly, inexorably his brute force would ease the door open to reveal her helplessness. . .

She heard the footsteps pause—then they reached the creaking floorboard that ran directly under her own feet. He was right outside the door now. Her skin dewing with the cold perspiration of fear, Flora closed her eyes and waited for the end.

After an eternity three light taps struck the other side of the door, close to where Flora's face was pressed up against the wood. She hadn't thought it possible for her heart to beat any faster, but at that sound it found an extra burst of speed. The blood was singing in her ears with the effort.

Perhaps it wasn't him. She had to cling onto that hope, desperate to believe that some guardian angel was looking after her and wouldn't let her fall.

'Who—who is it?' Flora made herself say when the silent agony of not knowing became too unbearable.

'It's me,' Captain William Pritchard said in a low, confidential tone.

Flora's heart dropped like a stone. His voice had seemed threatening out in the park, in the reassuring light of day, light and teasing when heard in the company of others in the house. Now, when his mind must be full of the fact that she had accepted money from Master Ralph, it represented all the nameless terrors of night.

'William Pritchard,' the voice added eventually, causing Flora to start afresh.

'*Go away!*'

It was impossible to keep her eyes squeezed shut any longer. Now Flora stared at the door-latch with frozen horror, her mind supplying movement where there wasn't any.

The door would open and she would be lost. She knew it. Once a vile seducer had his eye on a girl nothing was allowed to stand in his way. She was only too well aware of that from her weekly visits to productions at the Palace Theatre in Gloucester.

'Don't be frightened,' the soft voice tried again. 'I only want to talk to you.'

He had still made no move to open the door. He hadn't even tried the latch.

'What about?'

The question gave him pause for thought.

'I don't know,' he said at last, but the usual smile had returned to his voice. 'What would *you* like to talk about, Mrs Westbury? Come on, open the door. I can't be expected to display my elegant wit and repartee to the blank face of a door, can I?'

He didn't *sound* like any of the vile seducers portrayed at the Palace.

Flora thought long and carefully, trying to recall every nuance of his voice. He had sounded. . .well, *nice*.

She thought of those sea-grey eyes, that mischievous smile. She felt indecisive in a way she would not have believed possible a few moments before.

'I don't want you in my room,' she said carefully. In the silence that followed Flora became frightened that he would leave—even more frightened than she had been at the thought of him besieging her.

'In which case I shall forget all intentions of inviting myself in, Mrs Westbury.'

Her reply was sudden, instinctive. 'Are you sure?'

'Sure I'm sure.'

Her brother David had told her how that had been a favourite saying of foreign Empire soldiers during the war. Flora found herself smiling, and it was no distance at all from that point to the lifting of the door-latch and the opening of the door.

Captain William Pritchard was even more good-looking than she remembered. The soft gaslight flickering out from her room danced over his medals, the burnished shine of his shoes. . .and the light of laughter in his eyes.

Flora immediately wedged herself against the door again but he had made no move to pounce. Instead, silent laughter rocked him a step or two back from her threshold.

Flora kept a good hold on the door-latch but stopped short of closing it completely.

'I know what you must have thought when I took that money from Master Ralph, sir, but *I* didn't think about it until it was too late to refuse—to tell you the truth I didn't even realise it *was* money to begin with,' she gabbled in a rush, but the watchful amusement of his expression made all explanations hopeless.

'One step out of line and I'll scream the house down, mind,' she finished with difficulty.

He was too worldly-wise to be put off by that threat.

'If you scream you will lose your job, Mrs Westbury. Employers don't like staff who make a fuss.'

'I'd rather lose my job than my honour.'

At that moment, it was true.

'I certainly wouldn't want to be the architect of your downfall, Mrs Westbury. I would, however, very much like to make your acquaintance.'

She waited for him to explain himself further. When he realised that she was not about to make conversation easy for him he cleared his throat and continued.

'I was on the adjoining landing earlier, and saw you through the door that leads to the servants' quarters. It was open,' he said unnecessarily, his hands making reassuring gestures as he saw her alarm.

'You must have missed your way! What on earth are you doing here, of all places?'

'I came here on purpose, Mrs Westbury.'

'Ah.' Flora tightened her grip on the door. 'I thought as much, Captain Pritchard.'

'No. . .you misunderstand. I only want to talk to you. Honestly.'

He gave the impression of being relaxed and completely at ease but every now and then his glance would flicker back and forth along the deserted landing at sounds the old house made as it settled for the night. It made Flora nervous, but when he looked at her directly that was even worse. His face was so animated with the delight of this adventure that it set a most disturbing sensation in motion within the deepest recesses of Flora's body.

Standing firm against those wicked grey eyes was taking a great deal of effort.

'That was a cracking spread you put on for us this evening, Mrs Westbury.'

'Thank you, Captain Pritchard.'

She was afraid to make it any easier for him.

'I don't know much about cooking,' he volunteered, clearly beginning to find the conversation hard work.

'You know more than most gentlemen do about custard, sir.'

'You remembered that?' The laughter that was never far away rose again behind his words.

'It was quite a surprise, Captain Pritchard. Young gentlemen don't usually make a habit of hanging around kitchens—leastways, not for any legitimate reason!'

They both laughed at that, and suddenly Flora bit her lip. Her fear had been a funny thing—so intense, so easily inflamed, but it had been so quickly eased by his words and his expression.

Especially his expression. The way that Captain William Pritchard was looking at her now would have pacified the most determined enemy.

Flora began to wonder about the girl from Woolwich—Cherie Barclay, that was what they had called her. What sort of a girl was she? What did she look like? Had she ever been treated to such an expression? Flora didn't want to know the answer to that. The look in William Pritchard's eyes was proving a difficult invitation to resist, and Flora had never felt such temptation before.

The dim light from her room highlighted the crisp white formality of his dress shirt and his impressive arrangement of medals. Flora was not to know that the same light was adding a similar allure to the rich chestnut depths of her hair, which was rippling around her shoulders like the first hint of autumn.

'If we've got nothing else to say to each other I really think you ought to go, Captain Pritchard.'

'Yes. Yes, perhaps I should. Goodnight, Mrs Westbury.' He took another step back, but regretfully this time. 'In fact, I'm *sure* I should go.'

Flora was not at all sure. She stood in the doorway, he hovered on the landing, and they both looked at each other in silent expectation.

Flora was the first to come to her senses. This is no good, she told herself crossly. He's on the verge of going, and I ought to make it final.

If I'm going to, a small voice whispered somewhere within her mind. It was immediately quashed by what she told herself was common decency.

'Goodnight, Captain Pritchard,' she said sharply.

He turned to leave, still smiling. Then he stopped. Someone was strolling toward them along the unlit passageway.

'Aha! You *dog*, Will Pritchard!'

A cloud of cigar smoke preceded Ralph Morwyn's good-natured rebuke. Reaching a point where he could take both of them in with one glance, the Marquis took the cigar from his mouth and grinned rapaciously.

'Looks like I'm too late. Ah, well. Better luck next time. It'll be open season with all these soldiers staying here. They'll be queuing up to dance attention on you, Cookie!'

William Pritchard cleared his throat and took a step forward.

'I missed my way in this great warren of a place of yours, Ralph. Mrs Westbury was attempting to put me on the right track.'

'I'll bet she was.'

Flora saw the covetous look on the Marquis face and wondered how anyone could ever consider him attractive. In the poor light his features were masked by an acquisitive shadow and his voice was as unsteady as his stance.

'It's just as well you came along, Ralph,' William was saying. 'Apparently Mrs Westbury is as good a navigator as I am. Neither of us knew what to do.'

He studiously avoided looking at Flora as he said these words. 'You can act the perfect host and escort me to the right landing, then I can play the perfect guest and see you to bed.' William laughed as he slung one arm companionably around Ralph's shoulders.

Ralph removed a shred of tobacco from the tip of his tongue. His eyes never left Flora despite her obvious discomfort.

'My pleasure, Will.'

'We all know what *your* pleasure is, Ralph,' his friend muttered, patting the unsteady Marquis on the arm and setting off down the passage. 'Come on. Goodnight again, Mrs Westbury.'

Flora did not wait to answer. She dived back into her room and shut the door. To reinforce the satisfying click of its latch she added the heavy bedside chair, wedging it against the woodwork.

The previous cook doesn't sound the type to have been worried by visitors after dark, Flora thought. If I'm to live here safely I'd better change my plans and

invest that ten-shilling note in a couple of good strong
bolts for the door.

In her hurry to take the note from the mirror and
put it away it fluttered from her fingers. There was a
moment of panic as she felt about for it on the shadowy
floor, then horror as the true reason for Ralph
Morwyn's generosity was revealed.

The money bore a message. On the reverse of the
note the simple message 'Your room—12 p.m.' had
been written in a careless scrawl.

As the clock on her mantelpiece struck midnight
Flora realised exactly what that message had meant.

Chapter Three

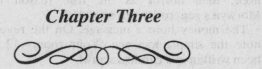

Flora finished plaiting her hair, humming to herself in a desperate attempt to shut out any unwelcome sounds from the hallway outside. She drank her tea, which by this time was stone-cold, and got into bed.

The feather mattress had been worn into a comfortable hollow by the previous occupant of the room. Despite their age, the bed and linen had a freshly aired feel, but the scent of lavender still hung heavily about them.

Flora turned down the gas, her exhaustion finally free to flood through her, but she did not sleep immediately. Normally, it would have been thoughts of the final preparations for Sunday's meals that kept her awake, but tonight the thoughts running through her head were far more disturbing.

Despite her best efforts, her mind was now centred solely on Captain William Pritchard.

Sleep eventually enveloped her, but it felt like only minutes later when she woke again. A gentle tapping at the door of her room had her groping for her dressing gown. Not knowing what to think, and not daring to hope, she dragged it around her shoulders and tried to push the confusion of sleep out of her voice.

'Who is it?'

'It's me, Mrs Westbury. Mary. With your tea and hot water.'

With a mixture of relief and exhaustion Flora put her hands to her face. It felt as though she hadn't managed more than five minutes' sleep all night.

'Oh, thanks, Mary. Come in.' She began unfastening her plaits, only remembering the trap she had set as Mary clattered the door against the obstruction. Leaping out of bed, Flora pulled back the chair and opened the door.

'You've been having trouble, then, Mrs Westbury?' Mary slid a crafty look at the pretty new cook as she put the breakfast tray down on the washstand. Flora decided that reticence was best.

'No. . . It's just that—being the first time that I've lived away from home. . .' Flora let her voice trail away, hoping that her unusually high colour as Mary turned up the gas would be taken for innocent embarrassment and not guilt.

'I didn't expect to get a tray!' She changed the subject quickly.

'We thought that you deserved it, miss. After you treated us all so well yesterday, and considering that you can't have had that many jobs in your time, and that Ivy must have got you into trouble over the picnic hampers—'

'She told you about that?'

'Expected a dressing-down about it, she did— especially when every scrap of ham came back untouched. Then when we heard about what had been said to you Upstairs. . . Ivy's in a real fix. She doesn't know what to do, there being so much of it.'

Flora began to feel uneasy. 'How much is there?'

'Best part of a whole hock, miss.'

'Oh, dear. I told his Grace that it could be used for the parish, but that was when I thought there would only be a few slices.'

Flora took the yellow and white china jug from Mary. It steamed with the cleanliness of hot water and Flora poured a good measure into the white china basin on her washstand. A small block of carbolic soap stood in a saucer beside the basin, giving Flora a good excuse not to use the special rose-scented soap that she had brought with her. Servants at Alvoe Court were evidently expected to smell like servants—clean and efficient. There was nothing like carbolic soap for seeing to that. The tang of it had already cleared Flora's mind for action.

'I know! We'll mince some of that ham and make it into rissoles for Upstairs breakfast. The bone can go for soup and the fat can be rendered down, once Ivy's scraped all the breadcrumbs off.'

Mary was incredulous. 'Leftovers? For Upstairs breakfast?'

'With plenty of mushroom ketchup, herbs and seasonings they'll never know. We can't let all that good meat go to waste. The parish will have its share, but the Alvoe accounts won't be the poorer for Ivy's extravagance.'

'Considering the money this family is sitting on I doubt if the cost of a ham will mean much to them.' Mary took a dry towel from the cupboard beneath the washstand and exchanged it for the damp one that Flora had used the evening before.

'I would have thought such a grand household would have had electricity in the servants' quarters by now,' Flora said with mild concern.

'Oh, there's electricity laid on for us, all right. Mrs Wells, the old cook, wouldn't have anything to do with it here in *her* room, though. She was adamant she didn't want electricity seeping out of the sockets unnoticed while she was asleep. Gas she could smell — electricity was a different kettle of fish.'

Mary folded the damp towel over her arm and prepared to leave. 'Mrs Wells always reckoned that electricity was bad for the eyes, too. She took to wearing a green eyeshade for her visits to her Grace to discuss the menus.'

Mary had watched Flora's reaction to these revelations carefully and was giggling now. 'I don't suppose you'll be wanting me to look it out for you if you have to visit her Grace today?'

Flora finished her first cup of tea of the day and handed the large white breakfast cup and saucer to Mary.

'Do you think I'm likely to get a summons, Mary?'

'Cook — I mean Mrs Wells — always used to. Cook's arrangements were special. She was paid on Sunday afternoons, before her day off on Mondays. It was always Ivy's turn to do the cooking on a Monday.' Mary grimaced, then laughed again. 'We used to reckon that Cook left it to Ivy on purpose. After a day of grey pastry and gravy that could be cut with a knife everyone was so pleased to see Cook back on Tuesday that they would forgive her anything!'

'I'm going home to Falgrave first thing on Monday morning,' Flora said thoughtfully as Mary opened the door to go back downstairs.

'Make sure you leave us plenty of soup and sandwiches, then!' the girl called back cheerfully.

'Oh, I think we can do a bit better than that between us.' Flora smiled to herself, adding as she closed the door behind Mary, 'Or at least I think Ivy will.'

* * *

Flora did not regard herself as being particularly religious, but she had always enjoyed her weekly trips to church at home. Sir Hubert and his family had always put on an impressive display in front of the villagers, and Alvoe family tradition was bound to outshine even that.

Unlike the self-appointed squire of Falgrave, his Grace the Duke of Alvoe had generations of forebears stored in chilly marble tombs around his ancient family chapel, all whiling away the time until Judgement Day by keeping silent vigil over their heirs. A memorial plaque still bright with newness laid out the latest chapter of the family history: dedicated to William Henry and Geoffrey John Alvoe, eldest and second sons of the current Duke and Duchess. William had been lost at Cambrai, Geoffrey at Passchendaele, Flora read. Stark facts, but for Flora the plaque was soaked with the images that she and her father had followed from the news reports. Barbed wire and mud.

A chill ran through her. Geoffrey Alvoe had been barely twenty-one years old—the same age her brother David had been when he had written that last letter home.

'Master Ralph's the only one they've got left now,' Mary whispered, nudging Flora back to reality as the last Alvoe son and heir took his place in the family pew.

His parents were slow to follow. They were finding it difficult to extract themselves from the conversational clutches of the vicar.

'Course, the Reverend's in their pay,' Mary muttered as the Duke and Duchess took their places. 'I bet he prays twice as hard for *them* as he does for us!'

Mary's discontent was stifled by the announcement of the first hymn. The congregation rattled to their feet and dutifully droned out the verses of 'All Things Bright and Beautiful'. Flora's position at the end of a row gave her a good view of the Alvoe family and their guests. She felt a little self-conscious about looking at them so openly, but then all the other servants were taking the opportunity of having a good look at the people they called their betters.

The Duke and Duchess of Alvoe stood in splendid isolation. Andrew Morwyn was dressed in an unexceptional dark suit, which if Flora had been inclined to be critical she might have noticed was wearing a little thin in places. In contrast his wife was a picture of thoroughly well-groomed elegance. Her dress of deepest mourning violet was complemented by a large, heavily veiled hat set upon a regal sweep of luxuriant brown hair. Everything about the Duchess spoke of wealth and privilege, but Flora thought she could see a distant, haunted look etched into the heavily veiled eyes.

If she's anything like my mother, she'd give up everything she owns for the chance to have her sons back, Flora thought wistfully.

She did not have long to think about the Duchess's unhappiness. The church was hung heavily with flowers, great swags of late lilies draped along each windowsill, tinted every colour of the rainbow by the early autumn sunlight filtering through the stained glass. Dust motes spiralled into the thick air of the stuffy little church as the bouquets of flowers dispensed their dying pollen into the air.

It soon proved too much for Flora. She tried to suppress the tickling at the back of her throat, the threatening sneeze, but knew the effort was hopeless. Fortunately her seat at the end of the pew meant she could slip out of the church almost unnoticed and she managed to get outside before sneezing. As she dabbed her eyes with her handkerchief the sound of running feet made her compose herself quickly.

It was Captain Pritchard. He grinned when he saw her and fell back into a fast walk, rapidly joining her at the church doors. She was impressed to see that although he had probably run all the way from the house he was barely out of breath. Immaculate in full uniform and medals, he immediately removed his hat, instinctively giving its already glistening badge a quick pass with his sleeve.

'Mrs Westbury! I suppose the service has already started?'

The faint drone of the first reading answered him. There was no question of them interrupting that solemnity. The only thing to do was to wait and slip in when the next hymn brought everyone to their feet.

To her shame Flora found that she was delighted by the prospect. Nothing could ever be allowed to come of such a meeting with the Captain—but it was nice as ninepence to dream.

'Didn't the staff wake you in time this morning, Captain Pritchard?' she said with a proper, servantly concern for his welfare, concentrating on pushing her handkerchief back into her handbag rather than looking at him.

He was laughing, which seemed to be his normal outlook on life.

'Hardly that! Some joker altered the clock in my room. I was awake at six—or rather seven, as it must have been—but I didn't like to be the first one down to breakfast. No wonder it was so quiet when I finally *did* go down.'

Flora's professional concern instantly became more personal.

'Did you manage to find anything left to eat, Captain Pritchard?'

'The gannets had eaten every scrap. They were kind enough to tell me how good it had all been, though. Especially the rissoles. . .' He frowned with a rare expression of annoyance, then brightened. 'But then I suppose you'll have a gargantuan and irresistible feast ready for our lunch, Mrs Westbury? I shall wait in happy anticipation of that.'

Flora had felt a blush threatening for some time and these words of his released the colour. She muttered something about the meal being ready for one o'clock, wishing that she could think of more to say.

It was already too late. The organ was wheezing into the introduction of the next hymn, Captain Pritchard had tucked his hat beneath his arm and was now preparing to enter the church.

'Perhaps we had better advance under cover of the distraction, Mrs Westbury.'

Flora stood aside to let him pass into the church first, but he put out his arm to her.

It's nothing but a joke to him, Flora told herself, seeing the twinkle in his eyes. She almost refused, then decided to call his bluff. After all, she had taken the arm of Mr Perry, the butler, for the walk across to church earlier that morning. That had been seen by Flora and all the rest of the staff as a proper gesture of formal Sunday manners.

She accepted Captain Pritchard's arm, smiling at his wordless surprise that she had taken the joke so well. All the same, as the dashing young Captain escorted her to her seat, then closed the pew door carefully behind her, worries about what the other servants might be thinking seeped into her mind.

Captain Pritchard treated her to a final smile, then went to take his place beside Ralph Morwyn.

Luckily, the hymn was a well-remembered one from Flora's Sunday-school days. She was so flustered that she could not find the place in her hymn book, then committed the awful sin of dropping the wretched book in the awkward silence between the end of the hymn and the racket of the congregation resuming their seats. Flora was thoroughly glad of the chance to hide her burning face in prayer, but Mary was not so reticent.

'Looks like it's not just the family you've been making a good impression on, miss!' she hissed before the butler cut her short with a meaningful cough. Flora bowed her head still further. Only when the prayer was ended did she risk an exploratory glance at the Morwyn family pew.

Captain William Pritchard was looking straight back at her. When their eyes met he smiled.

That was enough for Flora. When a member of the gentry not only got you talking but then kept smiling at you for no good reason it meant only one thing. Trouble. The *News of the World* was packed with tales of serving girls lured to their doom by men who were Only After One Thing.

And on a Sunday, of all days.

Flora fixed her eyes on the vicar and pursed her lips. She would have to forget all her silly fantasies about the handsome hero. Allowing his charms to work on her was a sure way to disaster.

She must have none of it—her mind was made up.

For the moment, at least.

There was no time for Flora to put her determination to the test after the service. The servants marched straight back to Alvoe Court, two by two, like the

animals into the ark. The Morwyn family and their
guests stood around in pleasant conversational groups,
with nothing better to do until luncheon than talk and
laugh and bask in the golden sunshine of a lazy autumn
morning.

The servants had no time for idling about. There was
luncheon for ten to be ready by one o'clock, and
provisions to be packed into the tin boxes belonging to
the Marquis of Dayle and his friends. The young
officers were off on a short training course to an army
camp in Dorset and as the perfect hostess the Duchess
of Alvoe had insisted on providing them with a little
something for the trip. It would cost her nothing, her
husband only money, but the kitchen staff a lot of time
and effort.

Five small tin boxes, each stencilled with a name,
rank and serial number in an extension of boarding
school traditions, stood in an orderly line on one of the
kitchen tables. Once the preparations for luncheon
were under control, Flora set about supervising the
filling of each box.

The Duchess had provided writing materials, bars of
Cadbury's chocolate and packets of cigarettes for inclu-
sion. Mr Stacey had sent up boxes of fresh fruit from
the kitchen garden and a large quantity of wood wool
for packing. For their part Flora and the girls had made
enough cakes to feed an entire army.

Flora cut good wedges of ginger cake, cherry cake
and rich fruit cake for each tin, wrapping the slices in
paper before packing them. Then a small selection of
notepaper and envelopes went into the appropriate
section of every box, together with the cigarettes.

'She's only giving them paper so they'll write back to
thank her,' Mary observed mutinously.

'Keep your mind on your job! Those early apples are

soft and easily bruised—there, look! You've made a hole in that one!' Flora took the small apple from Mary. It was prettily striped in red and yellow and despite the dent that the kitchen maid's finger had made it looked almost too good to eat.

Mary looked from Flora to the apple and back again, as though she had more sense than to ask the question that was on the tip of her tongue.

'I suppose Mrs Wells would have sent it to the pigs?' Flora put the apple on a side table and returned to the methodical slicing of cake.

'Yes.' Mary sighed with real longing. 'Mr Stacey only ever lets us eat the ones with maggot caves in. It's not the same.'

'How would you know, if you've never tasted a good one?' Flora was concentrating on cutting another neat slice from the slab of ginger cake and did not look up as she spoke. She was smiling. 'Go on—spirit that one away somewhere. Don't spoil your appetite by eating it before your dinner, mind!'

She laughed as Mary pounced on the little apple and stuffed it down into her apron pocket.

'And if you've got any sense you won't tell the others about my little lapse,' Flora added warningly. 'I don't want them to think I'm as soft as butter!'

'Oh, thanks, miss!' Mary went back to her task of addressing the return labels for each tin with new enthusiasm. 'There'll still be enough apples for the gentlemen, won't there?'

'Don't worry—there's plenty of everything. . .' Flora began to look quizzically at the amount of provisions still waiting to be packed up. 'In fact there looks to be far too much. Mr Stacey doesn't strike me as the sort of man to be over-generous with his produce, Mary. . .'

Mary pursed her lips in a silent whistle. 'You haven't

made *another* conquest, have you, miss? Old Mrs Wells always had a dickens of a job getting supplies out of the old misery. Don't say Old Stacey's trying to butter you up, too?'

Flora had no time for jokes. 'No. . .we look to be a box short. I thought there were six officers staying here—how many names have you got on the list, Mary?'

'Morwyn, Babbage, Davies, Teague and Wainwright. That's only five, miss.'

'But what about—?' Flora stopped, and busied herself in polishing imaginary fingermarks off the nearest tin with a tea-towel.

Mary leaned across the table confidentially. 'Why don't you go up and ask why there's no box for Captain Pritchard, miss?' she whispered with a giggle.

Flora almost considered it, but the delight in Mary's eyes made the whole idea impossible. A cook couldn't be seen to be the least bit interested in one of Them Upstairs. Especially not one who was as good-looking as Captain Pritchard. The only way around it was to ask Mr Perry, the butler, to relay the question, which he promised to do when serving the Upstairs drinks before luncheon.

He was away from the kitchens for a long time. The maids were already slipping dishes into hot water to warm them ready for serving the luncheon vegetables when he stalked back into the kitchen. Flora was informed that Captain Pritchard had eventually provided a reason for the missing tin. Apparently, the Captain's mother held the opinion that as soldiers were employed by the King then the King should be in charge of feeding them. Respectful of her opinions, Captain Pritchard never imposed on his hosts in that way and so he never provided a tin.

That was quite a confession. For Captain Pritchard to have been singled out by the butler's questioning as different from his fellows must have been horrible.

Flora looked around the busy kitchen. Everything was running according to plan If she was quick there would be time to make amends for the embarrassment she had accidentally caused him.

She ran up to her room and pulled out the small wicker suitcase that had brought her few possessions to Alvoe Court. Empty, it would make a suitable container for Captain Pritchard's share of the provisions.

It was a perfectly respectable thing to do. There could be no misunderstanding—a return label would be tied onto the suitcase so that it could be sent back to her—and Flora would tell the butler what she had done.

Her conscience would be salved, and there could be nothing in the gesture apart from simple good manners.

At least, that was what Flora told herself.

Flora barely had time to finish her dinner before a summons came from Upstairs. The Duchess wanted to discuss the menus for the following week.

There was little time to be nervous. After changing her apron she tidied her hair by pushing a few more pins into her still neat bun, pulled on a fresh starched cap and tucked her notebook and pencil into her apron pocket. Praying that her palms wouldn't become damp with nerves, Flora followed Mr Perry up into the hallowed residence of the family.

The upper hall was very quiet. Rows of doors, their patina and handles buffed to a dazzling shine by overworked housemaids, stood dumbly protective of whatever might be going on behind them. A beautiful arrangement of fresh flowers stood beneath one of the great vaulted windows, surrounded by a halo of golden afternoon light. Chrysanthemums and freesias vied with each other for attention, one flower a star of burnished copper and gold, its opponent heavy with fragrance. Flora remembered her unfortunate attack of sneezes in church that morning and hoped the same thing wouldn't overcome her during the interview with the Duchess.

'Mrs Westbury, the cook,' the butler intoned as he led Flora into the large, light room.

The Duchess of Alvoe was seated at a writing desk set beneath a tall, perfectly proportioned window. She took some time to acknowledge them, which gave Flora the chance to take a quick look around the room.

Like the rest of the family's territory it was heavy with the scent of beeswax polish and fresh flowers. An oriental rug, thick with expense, glowed in bright colours that had been picked up by the flower arrangements set around the room. Heavy velvet drapes sweeping to the floor at each side of the tall window echoed the rich reds of the rug and gave a feeling of opulence. Everything was new and beautiful and just like something out of a fairy story.

Flora liked this job better by the minute.

The Duchess finished her correspondence and laid down her pen before inclining her head toward the intrusion.

'Thank you, Perry. That will be all.'

The butler reversed out of the room, closing the door behind him. To Flora's great relief the Duchess's face immediately softened into a smile.

'We have been delighted with your work so far, Mrs Westbury. It is a pity that the agency we engaged when Mrs Wells passed away could not have provided us with someone of your calibre.'

'Thank you, your Grace.' Flora bobbed a curtsey to cover all eventualities. She might have added that some of the less scrupulous agencies were the refuge of idlers and time-servers, but she did not. It never paid to say any more than was strictly necessary to the gentry. Flora prided herself on knowing her place, and keeping her thoughts secret.

That was why it was so important to keep her distance from Captain William Pritchard.

'Have you enjoyed your first taste of working here, Mrs Westbury?'

'Oh, yes, madam,' Flora said with total honesty. 'It's a wonderful experience.'

'Good.' The Duchess studied Flora intently for a moment, then reached for a small brown envelope that was lying on her blotting pad. 'Good. Here are your wages, and it is to be hoped that you are as thrifty as you are talented—'

'Oh—but your Grace—'

'Yes?' The Duchess arched an elegant eyebrow in surprise at the interruption.

Flora had spoken without thinking, guilt loosening her tongue. Now she had no alternative but to go on. The Duchess was looking at her intently.

I—I was given some money by Master Ralph last night. I wouldn't want you to overpay me, your Grace. . .'

Flora's voice died away as Isobel Morwyn's slender white fingers tightened on the envelope. Her expression had hardened into granite. There was a horrible pause.

'My son has given you money?'

There was nothing for it but to make the explanation short and simple.

'I was summoned to the dining room after dinner

last night. His Grace the Duke thanked me, and Master Ralph gave me a ten-shilling note.'

'In view of everyone present?'

'Yes, your Grace.'

The Duchess subsided a little.

'Ah. I see. In which case I will claim the overpayment in your wages back from my son. Your honesty has served you well in this instance, Mrs Westbury. You may keep both the money that my son so unwisely gave you *and* the full amount contained in this envelope,' she said slowly. She placed a long, elegant finger against her lower lip, her brow contracting slightly as she gazed past Flora, lost in thought.

'I hope that you will always bear in mind during your career in service, Mrs Westbury, that there are frequent pitfalls for the unwary. Work hard, take a real pride in that work and above all lead a blameless life.'

'Yes, your Grace.'

'A clear conscience is a precious thing, Mrs Westbury.'

'Indeed, your Grace.'

The Duchess had sounded almost wistful. Her reverie was interrupted when the door opened and Mr Perry announced himself with a small cough.

'Master Ralph asked me to inform you that his party is preparing to leave, your Grace.'

The Duchess gave a gracious smile, although the expression did not reach her eyes. They remained pale and haunted. Flora could only wonder at what it must be like to watch your last remaining son continuing his career in the army when his brothers had both lost their lives in service.

'Thank you, Mr Perry. Assemble the staff in the courtyard, would you? I am sure that they would like to see Master Ralph and his friends being driven off.'

Turning back to Flora, the Duchess handed her the envelope.

'Run along and pay your respects with the others, Mrs Westbury. We shall discuss the week's menus on your return.'

The smile had more genuine warmth in it now, and Flora began to feel more relaxed in her employer's presence. She turned toward the door quite happily — then received a nasty shock. Mr Perry had already disappeared. The warren of staircases and landings were still a mystery to Flora and she wasn't sure how to get out of the house from the family's apartments.

The despair must have been obvious in her face, for the Duchess's smile widened.

'This great old house too much of a maze for you? It took me six months to find my way about. That's why I always summon the staff to my rooms. I've never quite worked out how to get down to the kitchens. Here —'

In a totally unexpected gesture the Duchess of Alvoe laid her hand lightly on Flora's arm and led her to the door.

'Go straight down the great staircase — that's the one in front of you — and out through the front door. Just this once!'

Flora felt her mouth drop open as she was pushed gently in the direction of an imposing marble staircase.

'Quickly, Mrs Westbury — before Perry sees you. You can follow the rest of the staff back to the kitchens after Master Ralph has left.'

Flora stammered her thanks. Hurrying down the stairs, she would have liked time to marvel over the spacious tiled hall, but she was afraid that the Duchess might still be watching her. Instead she slipped quietly through the great front doors and out into the open air.

Alvoe Court was surrounded by a sea of gravel.

Once upon a time this had been kept regularly weeded and levelled, raked several times a day by a fleet of garden boys under the military discipline of Mr Stacey. Now weeds flounced luxuriantly around its edges and a haze of seedlings greened the whole turning circle in front of the house. Footprints made by the shooting party the previous day still scored its surface.

Too many staff had left during the war to keep up the old standards. The remaining garden boys had more important tasks to do than weeding and raking gravel. New staff were almost impossible to recruit. Men who had returned from the war had new skills now and could name their price, and youngsters were enticed by better paid work available in the factories and cities.

Flora stood on the gravel apron of Alvoe Court and tried to look inconspicuous. The same war that had reduced the appearance of the great house had improved her own situation. 'Grand folk will always want feeding,' her mother had said.

Too young for war work, Flora had seized her chance when most of Sir Hubert's servants had left to work in munitions. Flora had made herself useful, washing up, scrubbing down and taking on any of the kitchen jobs that came up. She'd shown herself interested in every aspect of kitchen work and Sir Hubert's cook had been quick to encourage a willing and talented assistant. The shortage of good cooks had soon been illustrated by the Alvoes' staffing problems and had given her this chance of advancement.

'No—that's not mine. . .'

An all too familiar voice jerked Flora back to the present. Captain William Pritchard had been stopped by a footman as Ralph Morwyn and his friends made their escape from the house.

'It has your name upon it, Captain Pritchard,' the footman maintained firmly, used to the so-called jokes of Master Ralph and his associates.

'No, there must be some mistake. A trunk was sent here from the station, but I brought only one item of hand baggage,' the Captain persisted, looking at the small wicker suitcase the footman held out to him as though it might contain an unexploded bomb.

Flora cursed her impulsive action, but knew she had to speak up.

'If you please, Captain Pritchard, when there was no container provided for her Grace's gifts. . .'

He was looking at her with that direct, penetrating stare. Flora's heart was bouncing up and down, but she had gone too far to turn back now.

'. . .I took the liberty of providing one.'

He was smiling. *At her.* At that moment Flora could call to mind every single word he had ever said to her, and wished that she could not.

'Well, thank goodness you were on hand with the explanation, Mrs Westbury! It saved us having to open the basket out here in full view of everyone, anyway!'

He turned straight back to the footman, accepting the basket and thanking the man for his assistance.

Flora felt strangely let down. The arrival of the rest of the indoor staff trooping around the side of the house put paid to all chance of speaking with William—Captain Pritchard, she corrected herself swiftly—again.

The unspectacular little scene began to fuel her fantasies again. He *might* have spoken to her again. . . If he had been able to.

The indoor staff lined up, a dutiful edging to the gravel turning circle as the Alvoe cars swept around from the garage yard. Three of the soldiers piled into the back seat of the Albion while their hand luggage was stowed away for them. William Pritchard and another soldier were directed into the Rolls while Ralph said his goodbyes.

Flora noticed how all the young female staff blushed and giggled as they curtsied in turn to Master Ralph. It made her all the more determined to remain properly dignified. When he extended a smart gloved hand to her she looked him straight in the eye.

'Have a safe journey, Master Ralph.'

He grinned, leaning forward to whisper in her ear.

'Don't worry, Cookie. I know I'm not really the one you'd like to give a fond farewell.' He turned back toward the cars. 'Hey, Will! Over here a minute!'

Guests, family, indoor staff, outdoor staff—Flora felt every one of them turn to look at her with undisguised interest.

I shall die, she thought in agony. *I shall die. . .*

Captain William Pritchard unfolded his tall, athletic frame from the rear seat of the Rolls-Royce and strolled across the gravel turning circle toward his friend Ralph.

'Mrs Westbury couldn't bear the thought of you sloping off without saying goodbye, Will. What do you say to that?'

The almost irresistible force of Captain William Pritchard was within yards of her now. Flora squirmed inwardly as he increased the full power of those soft grey eyes with a lazily seductive smile.

'I'd say that any man would be a fool to pass up an opportunity like that,' he murmured.

He was within touching distance of her now and that was exactly what he did—reached out and touched her, raising her hand to his lips for the mock formality of a kiss.

Chapter Four

Captain Pritchard smiled, saluted, then swung away to take his place in the car. Flora felt like curling up and dying with embarrassment. How dared he make a fool of her in front of everyone? The whispering had already started, rippling along the neatly turned out line of staff despite the gimlet-eyed glare of the Duchess of Alvoe.

Ralph gave his mother a cheery wave as he climbed into the car, but it did nothing to soften her expression. The Duchess turned on her heel and stalked back into Alvoe Court before the powerful engines of the two cars had started to turn over.

I'm in trouble now, thought Flora, and suddenly the whispers and glances she was suffering from the rest of the staff seemed the least of her worries. The displeasure the Duchess had shown overshadowed everything.

Flora followed the file of indoor staff back to the kitchens. The younger girls were still giggling and nudging each other, but Flora knew how to deal with that. She set the girls to work on cleaning out the kitchen cupboards. There were dozens of them—packed and stacked with all the meat tins and baking trays and patty pans and fancy moulds gathered by several generations of Alvoe cooks. Flora knew that most of the utensils hadn't seen the light of day for years and would take a lot of cleaning. There would be no time for sniggering whispers while all that was going on.

She gave the girls their instructions in a tone that left no room for complaints. Expecting a summons from the Duchess at any moment, she needed some peace and quiet to work out what she was going to say when the time came. She would have to explain why Captain Pritchard had made such an exhibition of her, and she was hoping she didn't know the answer to *that* puzzle.

Eventually, Flora decided to say that Captain Pritchard must have been trying to impress Master Ralph, and hope the explanation was accepted.

She waited all afternoon for a summons from the Duchess, her nerves tightening with every passing minute. The call never came. When evening came with still no word from Upstairs, apart from a curt note about the week's dining arrangements, Flora's anxiety eased a little.

She had her Monday off, and by Tuesday morning, she was congratulating herself on a very narrow escape. The Duchess must have forgotten all about Captain Pritchard's indiscretion by now, she thought, vowing never to have anything to do with men again. Not even the wickedly handsome Captain Pritchard, with his laughing grey eyes. And his tall, dignified bearing. And the cool, firm touch of his lips against her hand. . .

Flora found herself sighing every time she thought of him, although she tried not to think of him at all. There had been nothing but low mischief about his actions, and nothing good came of that sort of association between staff and gentry.

* * *

Later that week Flora was summoned unexpectedly to the Duchess's salon. Expecting some sudden change in the family's eating arrangements, Flora took her note-book and pencil and hurried upstairs.

The way that the butler was immediately dismissed from the room told Flora that something was very wrong. The Duchess stood at the tall window, omin-ously dark in silhouette against the brightness. She was looking down over the park, and continued to do so for some considerable time after she and Flora had been left alone in the room.

'Sit down, Mrs Westbury.'

The words rapped out like bullets from a Mills gun.

Flora sat down.

'You have received a letter, Mrs Westbury.'

The Duchess turned her head to intensify all the proper feelings of guilt and grovelling remorse that a wayward young servant should show.

Unfortunately Flora didn't realise that she had any-thing to be guilty about. Who on earth would be writing a letter to her at this address? All her friends back at Falgrave would be well aware that any letters with an Alvoe Court address would be delivered directly to the family. Only someone who didn't know that would write a letter to her at Alvoe Court.

Suddenly Flora went cold all over.

Only someone who wasn't in the habit of corre-sponding with servants would make that sort of mistake.

The Duchess moved to her writing table with the predatory grace of a leopard.

'Here.'

She took a slim cream envelope from the letter basket beside her blotter and thrust it imperiously at Flora. Flora put out her hand, taking the envelope between finger and thumb as though it might be red-hot.

Let it be a mistake, she prayed fervently. Let it be for somebody else, from somebody else — *anything*. . .

There was no mistake. The beautiful copperplate handwriting of the address was only too clear.

'For the attention of Mrs F. Westbury,' it read in bold black ink, then, in paler, carefully blotted ink, 'C/o The Kitchens, Alvoe Court, Alvoe, Gloucestershire.' To his credit he must have stopped and thought for a while before completing the address, giving her name time to dry naturally.

'Well? Aren't you going to open it, Mrs Westbury?'

Flora turned the envelope over in her hands. The Duchess would have opened and read any such letter addressed to a lesser member of staff, but cooks were different. Any cook of the old school would have stuffed the letter deep into her pocket and stamped off, refusing to be intimidated. Flora hadn't had time to gain enough confidence in her position. Instead she stared down at the back of the envelope in hopeless and growing desolation.

Not only had she received a letter, but the writer had been careless enough to inscribe his name and temporary address on the back. That denied her the chance of inventing a long-lost friend who didn't know the rules about writing to servants.

All she could do was make a clean breast of things, and hope for the best. She began to work the envelope open with her fingers. With a click of her tongue the Duchess picked up the paper-knife from her writing desk and handed it to her.

With a wan smile Flora accepted the paper-knife and slit the envelope open. It held two sheets of notepaper. Flora recognised them as the type that she had packed into the wicker suitcase for him. Fingers trembling, she unfolded the knife-edged creases and began to scan the words.

'Well?' the Duchess said pointedly.

Flora looked up in bewilderment.

'I mistrust any gentleman who takes too great an interest in my staff.' The Duchess had a face like thunder, and a tone to match. 'You have a choice, Mrs Westbury. You may read the letter aloud to me or let me read it for myself.'

There is another option, Flora thought bleakly. I could refuse.

It wasn't worth considering. Flora liked her work and she liked Alvoe Court and despite the fact that there would be plenty of opportunities elsewhere for a good cook a lack of glowing references would be bound to narrow the choice.

She cleared her throat.

'"Dear Mrs Westbury,"' she began, thankful that he hadn't used her Christian name. '"Thank you so much for your kind action in preparing a box of provisions for me. It was a kind thought and much appreciated. The food here is pretty rough stuff—not a patch on your cooking—so it's a good job that you've given us all plenty to remember Alvoe Court by.

'"They're keeping us exceptionally busy here so I'm afraid I don't have time to write much—"' Flora thanked her lucky stars for that '"—but I must tell you how beautiful the countryside is around here. It's all very parched with the drought, of course, as things are at Alvoe, but the heathland is alive with all manner of creatures. Robins have started singing again after their summer break, and it's not so bad getting up in the half-dark if one can do it to the sound of birdsong. I suppose you know all about getting up early!

'"We are off on some gruesome map-reading exercises in a moment—they abandon us miles from anywhere and we have to get back before nightfall if we don't want to be locked out of camp—so I must close now. I will bring your case back in person when I return to Alvoe Court, when I am looking forward to making your acquaintance again. Until then, best wishes, Captain W. Pritchard."'

'I *don't* think Captain Pritchard will be making your acquaintance again. Do you, Mrs Westbury?'

'No, your Grace.'

'A servant who does not know her place is one thing. A gentleman who pesters staff is another thing altogether. Not to be trusted *in any way*.' The Duchess spoke through clenched teeth, her powdered beauty hardened into the chill of ivory. 'I should not like to think that my son cannot invite whom he likes to this house. In view of Captain Pritchard's singular home life I should imagine he finds friends of quality hard to come by. It would be a shame if he had to sacrifice the friendship of a Marquess for the sake of a momentary lapse, would it not, Mrs Westbury?'

'Of course, your Grace.' Flora's mind was racing, already wondering what a 'singular home life' could possibly be. 'The only thing is—well, I shouldn't like you to think that I had been encouraging Captain Pritchard in any way, your Grace. I haven't. Not at all—'

'Not taking his arm in church? Lending him a hamper? Fooling about with him in front of this very house, in full view of all the other staff?'

Stung into silence by this outburst, Flora stared at the letter. Any affection for William Pritchard that might have been rekindled by his letter died within her. All he deserved was to be cursed from the bottom of her heart for making such a fool of her, whatever troubles he might have at home.

'Shall I reply, telling him not to contact me again, your Grace?' Flora desperately tried to placate the Duchess, but her words only made her employer even more angry.

'Certainly not! *I* will deal with that. Go back to your work, Mrs Westbury. That will be all.' The Duchess dropped her glittering gaze to a pile of papers on her desk. The audience was over, and Flora rose to leave.

The Duchess had one final barb ready as Flora reached the door.

'I am particularly strict when it comes to the matter of my staff knowing their place, Mrs Westbury. It is one of my particular crusades.'

She levelled a final glare at Flora, who knew when she was beaten.

Any dreams she might once have had about Captain William Pritchard coming back to sweep her away from all this had been extinguished in an instant.

She went back to the kitchens, reminding herself that it was her proper position in life. There was one thought, though, that Flora could not leave alone. Dreams of the dashing Captain Pritchard might have crumbled, but her curiosity hadn't been satisfied. She wanted to know more about him, and if there was one class of person guaranteed to be able to find out anything and everything about anybody it was a kitchen maid.

Flora had a whole platoon of them at her command.

She left the matter for a little while, then sidled up to it casually as she checked the kitchen accounts with Mary.

'That Captain Pritchard who stayed here—' she began airily, but Mary interrupted her.

'You mean *your* Captain Pritchard?'

'He's nothing to do with me,' Flora said shortly, 'and I'm certainly going to have nothing to do with him in the future. Remember, Mary, it's down the road with no references for any member of staff caught trying to mix with any of Them Upstairs. The Duchess won't stand for staff getting above themselves.'

To her astonishment Mary laughed out loud.

'Well, if that isn't a joke coming from somebody the Duke picked up at a stage door!'

Flora put down the accounts book and looked at Mary sternly.

'It's true!' the girl asserted. 'Her Grace used to be on the halls before she took up with the Duke. I thought everybody knew that!'

'I didn't,' Flora murmured thoughtfully.

'Not that anyone is allowed to mention it,' Mary went on. 'Her Grace must have dropped all her old friends like hot potatoes when she met up with the Duke. We never see anyone but gentry here, that's for sure. The Duchess is one of those that pulled them-selves up by the boot-straps then cut the leather to stop anyone else doing the same,' she finished darkly.

'*Mary!*' Flora narrowed her eyes in a warning. 'There's no call for that. I'm only telling you what the Duchess told me to tell all of you down here. We must all keep ourselves to ourselves, and keep the proper distance between us and the family.'

'Is it true that Captain Pritchard keeps a woman locked away?' Ivy chipped in from the next table, where she stood whipping egg whites for the afternoon meringues.

Flora's heart lurched, and she gripped the kitchen account book convulsively. Mary gasped, but Flora was quick to regain her self-control at the thought of learning more about Captain Pritchard.

'What do you mean, Ivy?'

Ivy had been looking for any excuse to stop the joint-jarring job of whisking the egg whites and paused for effect before continuing.

'I was talking to one of the Upstairs maids the other day and *she'd* overheard two of the young gentlemen talking about one of the others, saying he had a mad wife locked up in the attic, and *that* was why he never invited any of them back to his own home. . .'

The Duchess must pity him, Flora thought. A mad wife. . .no wonder he turned to the staff for comfort.

Flora remembered how trapped she had felt in the few days that she had lived as Alfred's wife. How much worse it must be to be imprisoned in a marriage with absolutely no hope of escape. . .

She kept her thoughts to herself and quickly changed the subject to the arrangements for dinner that evening. Her mind was filled with thoughts of Captain Pritchard. There could be no excuse at all for his over-familiarity, Flora told herself sternly, but when she thought of what his home life might be like there was a pang of understanding. The last thing Captain William Pritchard needed was to be banned from Alvoe Court, where he could at least mix with decent company and fill up on good food. The army might provide him with company in the normal way of things, but according to his letter the food was sadly lacking.

Flora could at least give him some comfort there when he visited Alvoe Court, even if all other contact with him was to be denied to her.

It wasn't long before Flora's good intentions were put to the test again. Before the following week was out she was to be risking her job and her reputation in a way she would never have thought possible.

The heatwave showed no sign of easing, and by the time lunch was despatched upstairs each day the kitchen was as hot as a tropical bakehouse. Flora, who never had much of an appetite at midday, had fallen into the daily habit of taking some fruit and a cup of tea out into the walled kitchen garden. With the family at lunch and the garden staff doing service as forestry workers deep in the woods during the hottest part of the day she could be sure of snatching a few minutes' peace and quiet. No member of staff other than Cook would dare trespass in Mr Stacey's kitchen garden.

A summer house stood in one corner of the walled garden, offering a good view of the neatly laid out vegetable beds. These were stitched about with rows of bright flowers, grown to supply the arrangements that graced each room at Alvoe Court. Today Flora walked quickly through the garden, her boots crunching on the only well-kept gravel on the estate.

Opening the glazed summer-house doors, she smelled again the fragrance of warm air and the expensive if faded upholstery of the seats inside. It was always a real treat to sit on soft feather cushions and rest her feet for a few minutes.

She ate her makeshift dinner, then took out the kitchen notebook that went everywhere with her. She had noticed that the grapes in the fruit range were looking particularly good, and wanted to make a note to ask Mr Stacey when they would be ready.

That was when she heard the garden door ride back on its hinges.

Someone was coming.

Flora was on forbidden ground, and there was

nowhere to hide. With a gasp she grabbed at her notebook and started to rise, but it was too late.

Captain William Pritchard strode into view. Spotting her immediately, he called out, 'Mrs Westbury? Hang on a minute!'

He reached the summer house in a few strides, quick enough to stop Flora darting past him to safety.

'*I'll lose my job!*' Frantic and flustered, she tried to dodge past him but he put out a hand to stop her flight.

'Mrs Westbury? Aren't you glad to see me back?'

His voice was as incredulous as her expression at the question. Flora stopped dead. Of all the things he might have said this was the most unexpected. No man — much less a gentleman — had ever asked her what she felt or thought before.

'I. . .I— The Duchess has warned me never to contact you again, Captain Pritchard,' she said in a rush, looking up at him guiltily. Her hands clenched on her kitchen notebook even tighter when she saw the all too obvious disappointment in his eyes.

'Oh. Then I'm sorry about that. Although. . .everyone else is at lunch at the moment. I know for a fact that the kitchen gardens are the last place any of them would visit anyway.' The serious tone in his voice slipped away. 'They might see someone working, and that would be *far* too much of a shock for their systems!'

'That's why I come here at dinner — *lunch*time,' Flora corrected herself, and they both grinned.

That did it. They were fellow conspirators now, bound together in a plot to evade the family and their guests.

'I hope there was nothing wrong with your lunch, Captain Pritchard?'.

'I had something earlier, on the way here. I wanted

some peace and quiet to write a letter, and this is the ideal spot. As you must appreciate, Flora. It *is* Flora, isn't it?'

She nodded wordlessly, wondering how he had found out.

'Why don't you sit here with me for a bit? I can tell you how we got on down in Dorset. Did you get my letter?'

'The Duchess got your letter,' Flora said with a sigh.

He raised his brows and exhaled with a whistle at her expression.

'Oh, dear. Did it make things too awful?'

'I got away with it,' Flora said cautiously. 'Although I won't manage it again. That's why I really must go. . .' She started to move away from him once more, but reluctantly this time.

'In any case, Captain Pritchard, I have to get back for half past one—'

Quick as a flash he pulled a pocket watch from his waistcoat.

'You've got ten minutes,' he whispered archly, then saw the way that Flora was looking at his watch. He turned the beautiful gold timepiece over in his hand to give her a better view. 'Grand, isn't it? It was a twenty-first birthday present.'

'Goodness! I won't be getting anything half as expensive for *my* twenty-first!' Flora said without thinking, then shrank back as his face relaxed into its usual knowing smile. He had seen a chance, and he seized it.

'And when will that be?'

'On Thursday, sir.'

'Oh, come on, Flora. You don't have to call me that. I've got too many people at work forced to give me a title. It would make a change to be William once in a while.'

Flora was not at all happy with that. The Duchess
had been adamant that there should be no contact
between her and the Captain, and that was law as far
as Flora was concerned. Besides, there was something
else. That wife, mad or otherwise.

'I'm sorry, sir. I'd love to, but I can't. The Duchess
has warned me about being over-familiar with the
guests.'

'Do any of the others speak to you as I do, then?'
He looked at her quizzically, head on one side.

Flora lowered her lashes. When he looked at her as
he was doing now, those clear grey eyes full of laughter,
it would be the easiest thing in the world to surrender
to his charm.

'Oh, no, sir. You're the only gentleman to do so.'
Speaking the word 'gentleman' reminded Flora of the
habits of gentlemen, the twist of disappointment she
had felt, and it strengthened her resolve a little.
'Besides, sir, I'm sure you want to get on with your
letter to your wife.'

'Wife?'

He was watching her carefully, a contraction of those
dark brows narrowing his eyes.

'Your wife. . .I understand she is indisposed. . .' Flora
could no longer meet his gaze and she looked down,
squirming inwardly. His silence continued, forcing her
to say more than any amount of questioning could have
done. 'They say she's locked away, sir. . .'

He started to laugh, and the hand that he had put
out to stop her running away fell to his side.

'Not me. They must be thinking of my friend Mr
Rochester. Now *he* keeps a mad wife. Locked up in the
attic!'

Flora realised that Captain Pritchard was trying to

have some fun, but she wasn't going to let it be at her expense.

'I wouldn't have thought a soldier would have been caught reading *Jane Eyre*,' she countered, meeting his amusement with a challenging smile.

'I make sure that I never get caught,' he replied with a mischievous arch of his brows. 'Except by mad wives, apparently. Tell me—how on earth did you get hold of that tale?'

'It was nothing but silly gossip, sir,' Flora said before wishing that she hadn't. It must be horrible to find out that people were talking about you behind your back. 'One of the girls overheard two of Master Ralph's friends saying that was why one of their party never entertained at home.'

'That's me all right.' Realisation made the smile melt from his face and the grey eyes were serious again. 'It's my mother. She never entertains, so when it's my turn to host an "at home" I entertain everyone in an hotel.'

Flora's eyes widened at the thought. 'That must be fearfully expensive!' she burst out without thinking.

The Captain looked haunted. 'It is. That's why I don't do it very often. To tell you the truth, Flora, the company I keep is as much a liability as a pleasure. Even when I get the chance of a free holiday in a wonderful place like this I can't escape them. The family are very welcoming, of course, but I work with the chaps all the time. I would like to see a bit of life beyond their shadows.'

Flora wondered what sort of life he had in mind. She knew she should be wary, but one small corner of her mind dared her to find out.

'Do you ever get any chance to escape from them?' she said slowly.

True to her idea of a predatory gentleman, he pounced.

'I could put them off the scent for a few hours. I could take you to the cinema, Flora.'

Flora gasped, but her blushes wouldn't let her look up at him.

'Oh, go on!' he teased her. 'It'd be such fun, escaping from all these eagle eyes for a few hours of reckless enjoyment. Say you'll come. Just this once? I still have to give you back your suitcase—we could always use that as an excuse if we get caught—'

'Oh, we *mustn't* get caught!' Flora was panicking again.

'Then you'll come?'

Flora's head jerked up at this and she saw what he had been doing while her head had been lowered in embarrassment. He was gazing at her ankles with undisguised relish.

Flora knew what a look like that meant. For all his good looks and easy charm Captain William Pritchard would soon take advantage of his position as her superior and the secrecy that any situation would need.

He would use her as Alfred had done.

Flora felt faint, a sick feeling rising with the memories until it robbed her of all thoughts but that of escape.

'No! I won't ruin myself for a little bit of pleasure!' She pushed the Captain aside although he had offered no resistance. 'I must go. . .'

His voice followed her, calling her name, but Flora was gone. Long black skirts fluttering and unintentionally displaying a froth of lacy petticoats, she ran back to the safety of her kitchen, her work, and the painless certainties of everyday life.

* * *

For the rest of Tuesday, Flora divided her time strictly between the kitchens and her room. She never ventured out into the grounds at all in case she should meet *him*. However, although she could hardly bear the thought of his casually treacherous intentions, Flora found herself listening to every scrap of kitchen maid's gossip, while carefully pretending not to.

It did her no good. Captain William Pritchard's name never featured in the stories of late-night excess and practical jokes. The girls never mentioned him in their coquettish complaints about the young gentlemen and their wandering hands, either. Then again, Flora thought crossly, he's just the sort of plausible rogue whose attentions the girls would keep to themselves.

The Marquis of Dayle's party must be egging each other on, Flora thought as the giggling complaints reached epidemic proportions. There would be serious trouble if the high spirits weren't nipped in the bud, so she decided to lodge a formal complaint with the Duchess. The difficulty lay in making a trip Upstairs without running into Captain William Pritchard. Luckily an opportunity presented itself early the next morning when the Duchess summoned Flora unexpectedly to the drawing room.

She's bound to make sure that Captain Pritchard is well out of my way, Flora thought with relief as she followed the butler up to the Apricot drawing room. As they walked the long gallery with its great windows overlooking the park, Flora heard a commotion from below then saw one of the Alvoe cars speeding away along the drive. Any relief she might have felt at the thought of being denied an accidental meeting with William Pritchard was soon tinged with a strange element of disappointment.

The butler ushered her into the grand Apricot drawing room. Flora didn't have much time to take in the beauty of her surroundings other than to realise that, rather than the room being full of apricot bushes as the kitchen maids imagined, it was the deep pinkish russet of the portrait-hung walls that gave the room its name. A faint mutter of conversation filtered through the half-open door that led on into a further salon, but it was the Duchess who seized all Flora's attention.

'Ah, Mrs Westbury!' she gasped, falling on Flora as though she was the answer to all her prayers. 'And you should stay and hear this too, Perry. The young gentlemen have decided to go up to town tomorrow, so I have decided to host a bridge tea in their absence. The invitations have already been despatched, including one to Vallets House. It is my intention that Lady Molly Berkhamstead should attend. . .'

The Duchess looked more alive than Flora had ever seen her. In the space of a few weeks the Morwyn family had advanced from eating meat paste and margarine to giving fancy tea parties. Better still, the Duchess was confident enough to invite the best hostess in the county. Flora knew all about Lady Molly Berkhamstead. She was so famous that her social events were reported in the *Citizen*—and Gloucestershire had no higher honour.

Flora shot a sideways glance at the butler and caught him stifling a smirk. The Duchess obviously had a rare talent for pushing herself forward which hadn't stopped at getting herself out of the music halls and into Alvoe Court.

'Everything—the staff, the arrangements, refreshments—will all be a credit to me. Will they not?' the Duchess announced, her stiffly corseted hourglass figure swelling with pride like a prize pouter pigeon.

Flora and Mr Perry agreed dutifully, then the full

consequences of the arrangements suddenly struck Flora.

'Oh, but that's my—' she burst out, then stopped as the gimlet gaze of the Duchess fixed on her.

Staff weren't supposed to have a life of their own. The Duchess wouldn't welcome being reminded of such an insignificant thing as her cook's twenty-first birthday, but she was waiting in grim silence now for some sort of explanation.

'I'm sorry, your Grace,' Flora faltered at last. 'I was about to remind you that I had arranged to work next Monday so that I could have tomorrow off instead.'

Taking her cue from the Duchess's warning glare, Flora added quickly, 'But of course that is out of the question now.'

'Indeed.' The Duchess looked at Flora hard, trying to spot any signs of resentment, but she was well practised in hiding such things. Something had to be said, though, and as the murmur of conversation in the adjoining room died into silence Flora took a deep breath.

'If I might ask you to send a message to my father, your Grace, to let him know that I won't be home tomorrow?'

The Duchess was looking forward to a social triumph and decided to be generous.

'Take the rest of the day off, Mrs Westbury. Visit your father now, then you can be back here in time to organise all the kitchen work for tomorrow.'

Flora frowned. 'There won't be any carriers to Falgrave this afternoon, your Grace, and the omnibus only runs once a week. I shan't be able to get home today.'

The Duchess was too busy thinking about her grand

guest list to worry about Flora's domestic arrangements.

'Then you will simply have to take your day off another time, Mrs Westbury. Spend your time today considering what you will be preparing for us tomorrow—'

A rattling crash from the adjoining room silenced her. Flora saw a small object skitter across the floor towards the folds of the Duchess's gown. Isobel Morwyn started and gave a little cry.

'I'm most dreadfully sorry, your Grace—'

William Pritchard walked through from the adjoining room, an apple in his hand. If he noticed Flora at all he gave no indication of it. 'You see, I was showing the Duke how to juggle—'

'*What?*' the Duchess hissed furiously, before remembering that there were staff present. Trapped into watching the scene unfold, Flora saw the Captain stoop and retrieve a second apple as the Duchess flicked the train of her gown aside to reveal it.

'Captain Pritchard—I am in the midst of addressing my staff,' the Duchess said in a whisper that was clearly forced out between clenched teeth.

'Sorry. . .' He began to back away.

Flora knew she should have been glad that his glance lingered no longer on her than it did on Mr Perry the butler. As the Captain retreated under the withering stare of the Duchess he brightened suddenly. 'Well, while I'm here—perhaps I might ask a favour, your Grace. May I borrow the Rolls today? While the chaps are out I thought I might take a trip down to Bristol—'

'By all means, Captain Pritchard.' The Duchess dismissed him icily, then thought of something. She wanted everything just right for her bridge party and a fretful cook would do nothing for the smooth running of her household.

'Although, if it would not inconvenience you too much, could you ask the driver to drop our cook off at Falgrave along the way?' The regal gaze fastened onto Flora again. 'She would sit quietly in the front next to James and would not distract him from his driving.'

Captain Pritchard was already strolling back to rejoin the Duke.

'I think it's a mile or two out of my way,' he muttered doubtfully, clicking his tongue. 'But if it's all in the cause of domestic harmony I suppose I *could* put up with it. . .'

Flora was fuming silently and refused to look at him. She was being made to feel like an unwanted parcel and would have refused to go at all if it had not been at the Duchess's suggestion.

'I shall be ready to go within the hour, if you could tell your girl to be down in the car by then,' he concluded before closing the interconnecting door behind him.

Flora's eyes widened with indignation. He hadn't even bothered to give her a name. 'Your girl' indeed!

She had stamped halfway back to the kitchens before her fury had subsided enough for her to remember that she had forgotten to mention the behaviour of Master Ralph's guests.

Never mind. That could wait.

The staff were whipped into a whirlwind of enthusiasm by the news of Lady Molly's visit, dashing about to clean and polish everything. Flora didn't bother arguing that her ladyship was about as likely to visit the kitchens as their own Duke and Duchess were.

As soon as she had started the girls working on a

chicken casserole for Upstairs dinner, Flora ran to her room to wash and change for the journey to Falgrave.

At least she wouldn't have to endure Captain Pritchard's close company all the way home.

'Your girl'. That was what he had called her.

The phrase still rankled. And to think that the Duchess had been imagining there was some sort of understanding, Flora raged silently as she stabbed hatpins into her best hat, fastening it so securely to her hair that a hurricane would not have dislodged it.

To think that *I* thought he had designs on me, she added to her stern reflection in the looking-glass. He obviously doesn't even think of me at all. If he did, he would have given me a name.

Preparations complete, she stood back and looked her reflection up and down critically. Navy blue jacket with matching three-quarter-length skirt, crisp white blouse with lots of latticework tucks and a straw hat with blue ribbons and a battery of silvery hatpins. Flora allowed herself a small smile. Smart as threepence, she had to admit, pulling on her gloves and looping her handbag over her arm. At least Captain Pritchard won't be able to see my ankles when I'm sitting in the front of the car.

She hesitated, then picked up a hand mirror from the dressing table. Standing with her back to the full-length mirror, she checked the view that a rear-seat passenger in the Alvoe Rolls would have. Swallow-tailed blue ribbons fell from the neat little hat while the rich luxuriance of her auburn hair was coiled in a smooth roll at the nape of her neck. The collar of her white blouse with its lacy trim lay neatly on the spotless collar of her jacket and it all looked smart and tidy. That was as much as Captain Pritchard would be seeing.

In a way Flora was glad that he wouldn't be seeing the full-length version. If the glimpse of her ankles given by her old-fashioned working dress had set him staring, goodness only knew what he might do at the sight of six inches of calf.

She hurried down to the stable yard and got there in good time, hoping to hide herself and her calves decently in the front seat of the car before Captain Pritchard arrived.

She was lucky. James, the chauffeur, was alone in the yard, fussing over the thrumming engine of the Rolls as though it were a highly strung hunter. He grinned as Flora picked her way across the cobbles. Closing the lid of the Rolls, he went round to open the front passenger door for her as though she were a real lady.

He didn't act the dutiful servant for long. To get into the car Flora first had to step onto its high running board. This would have been no problem in her full-skirted working dress, but this smart new skirt was cut much more narrowly.

'You'll have to wriggle it up a bit.' The chauffeur smirked with the air of a man who had enjoyed such sights before. He had the reputation of being a bit of a ladies' man, and Flora began to feel uncomfortable. The thought of being trapped in the front seat of a motor car with James and speeding along country lanes at twenty miles an hour suddenly lost all its appeal.

While James leered at her meaningfully she tried to step up into the car, but in the end she was forced to lift her skirt almost to her knees before she could manage the high step.

'Good morning, James.'

The familiar low voice of William Pritchard catapulted Flora into the car. Trust him to arrive just as

I'm showing everything I've got, she thought furiously, trying to arrange her clothes and settle herself in her seat rather than look at him.

She was so busy ignoring the Captain that she took no notice of the conversation going on between her tormentor and the chauffeur. Only when James strolled away across the stable yard, pulling off his driving gauntlets, did she stop to wonder what was going on.

Then Captain William Pritchard threw open the driver's door and swung himself into the car.

'That was easy!' he laughed, clapping both hands to the steering wheel. 'Now then, Flora—where shall we go for your birthday treat?'

Chapter Five

'I'll lose my job!'

Breathless with terror, Flora scrabbled at the door-catch but could not open it.

'*I'll lose my job!*'

Looking back at him in one last, helpless entreaty had no effect. In an instant he had turned the Rolls in a graceful arc and they were gliding past the front of Alvoe Court, past the reproachful windows and down the long, lime-lined drive.

'Leave the door, Flora. After the trouble I've gone to, I don't want you falling out!'

They had almost reached the main gates and as the car slowed he risked looking across at her.

'Cheer up! We're off to enjoy ourselves!'

'You don't understand—I have to get out—I must get back—I mustn't be seen with you like this. . .' Sobbing with fear, Flora finally managed to wrench the car door open.

'No, Flora!'

Conditioned by years of unthinking obedience, Flora froze.

'There's no one here to do the gates at the moment. I checked. There's no one around to see that James isn't driving the car. *Sit still and behave!*'

He brought the car to a halt, got out and pegged back the black wrought-iron gates. After fastening Flora's door he got back into the driver's seat, moved the car out onto the road then went back to close the gates again.

When he resumed his seat he trapped Flora with a penetrating stare.

'That was a *very* dangerous thing to do, Flora. If you had fallen out you would have been hurt.'

Not half as hurt as I'll be by staying, Flora thought, staring back at him like a rabbit caught in a beam of light.

'You will *not* lose your job,' he continued gravely. 'Everyone in the house is far too busy getting ready for the Duchess's bridge party to be looking out for us. A keen mechanic like James thought it the most natural thing in the world that I should want to have a go at driving the Rolls, and in any case the price of a few pints will have bought his loyalty.'

Flora's eyes opened still wider. This combination of innocence and beauty caused her kidnapper to reach out a hand as though to touch her cheek, but she shrank back instinctively.

'You're right, Flora. Not this close to home. First stop Falgrave?'

Flora could not answer. She spent the whole journey in a state of terror, trying to tuck her feet in close to the passenger seat and hide every visible part of her legs with her skirt and her handbag.

The countryside outside was reeling past at an incredible speed.

'I love driving,' William said with real relish as they reached the part of the road known as The Straight Miles. 'Let's see how fast she can go, shall we?'

Flora gasped as the powerful car leapt forward, the purr of its engine rising to a low thunder of power.

'Good, isn't it?' He laughed, grey eyes mischievous and his whole body animated with daring. Flora gave a little cry and clapped her hands to her face, but all he did was laugh.

'My word, Flora, you're a regular corker out of uniform. I do hope it's true what they say about taking a girl for a ride in a fast car!'

The car slowed down at last, but it was some time before Flora could bear to take her hands from her face. When she did it was to find that her best white gloves were dusted with face powder—and it was no wonder that she had covered her eyes. They had travelled two miles in less time than it took to boil an egg.

'How are you feeling, Flora?'

'Not very well.'

'Really?' His surprise was tinged with disappointment. 'That isn't how it's supposed to work at all. Oh...I'm sorry about that.'

He was, too. Flora could see it in his face. The car slowed down still further and they swept through the next two villages at a far more sensible pace. Flora began to feel a little easier. By the time Falgrave's church tower came into view she was almost enjoying herself.

'Is that better?' he asked softly at last. This time Flora was able to turn and look at him directly.

'Much better, sir. Thank you.'

His brow furrowed immediately. 'Great Scot, Flora! I've told you before. None of that "sir" business. I'm on leave, for goodness' sake!'

'No, sir—' The habit was very hard to break, but made easier by his smile. 'No, Captain Pritchard.'

'William.'

When she did not reply he shot her a mischievous wink.

'William, then,' she said, and found it quite easy. Especially when he looked so well, dressed in a light tweed jacket, grey flannels and another colourful jumper.

'Just for today, mind. It had better be back to "sir" in front of the others.'

'Yes, William,' she replied meekly. It was getting easier every time.

'That's better. Now—to business. What time shall I pick you up from your father's house? The matinée starts at two, but if you wanted more time at home—'

'Matinée?' Flora gazed at him, confused.

'The picture theatre runs a programme starting at two o'clock,' he explained patiently. 'It's called a matinée.'

'You want to go to the pictures?'

'Yes. Don't you?'

'You want to go to the pictures *with me*?'

'*Yes!*' Incredulous at how long it was taking to get a simple answer to a simple question, William brought the car to a halt beside Falgrave's memorial drinking fountain.

'*Why?*'

Flora said the word slowly, giving it plenty of meaning.

'Why do you think? I've given the chaps the slip, which gives me one whole day off in which to find myself some grown-up entertainment for a change. I fancy going to the cinema, it's your birthday tomorrow and you're going to have to work it, so you'd better get a bit of excitement in now, and besides. . .' He had been counting off the reasons against his fingers but now he half turned in the driving seat, giving her the full benefit of that knowing, enticing smile of his again. 'You're a *very* pretty girl, Flora.'

'Oh!'

In her embarrassment at the compliment Flora barely noticed that he had got out of the car and walked around to open the passenger door for her.

'A very pretty girl with very pretty legs,' he murmured softly, revelling in the further panic that this brought. 'Here, let me help. . .'

Torn between keeping her skirt down and trying to hide her legs behind her handbag, Flora floundered.

Still laughing, William reached into the car and lifted her out. Those strong brown hands encircled her waist and held her with a firm insistence that would not be denied. When he set her down on her feet his hands lingered, keeping her close to the warm male scent of him, shaving soap and polish all mixed up with a more elusive, animal fragrance.

'My dad will be at work—he won't be expecting me home today,' she gabbled in a mixture of shyness and an urge to fill the sudden silence between them. 'He might call in for his break at eleven o'clock, though, if he's working near—'

'I wasn't really expecting you to invite me in.' William's hands fell from her waist and for the first time he sounded uncertain, then brightened. 'It's a pleasant surprise, though.'

This put Flora in a difficult situation. If William considered himself invited then she could hardly refuse him. On the other hand, the neighbours were sure to start gossiping.

Especially her mother-in-law.

Flora thought of all the times her mother-in-law had poured scorn on her. Not only during the days that she had lived under old Mrs Westbury's roof as Alfred's wife, but even when Flora had wanted to go back to work in service, long after Alfred's death.

Perhaps it was time the old woman had something else to moan about.

The decision was made. Flora showed William the way to her home, trying to ignore the twitching curtains that marked their progress through the village.

'Was your husband a local man?' William asked as they reached the neatly hedged gardens of the estate cottages. He had spoken in such an unusual tone that Flora glanced up at him sharply. He was looking decidedly hot and uncomfortable, and for the first time did not look her in the eye.

Something about their relationship had changed subtly and Flora was quick to sense that, for the time being at least, she had the upper hand.

'Alfred lived in the cottage next door to ours— Oh, no! Look, there's his mother watching us now!'

To her alarm William raised one hand in greeting to Alfred's mother as she pretended to rearrange her curtains.

'Now she's seen us!' Flora hissed furiously.

'She'd seen us before,' William corrected her. 'If we act as though we have a perfect right to be going into your father's house together she'll think nothing more of it. You must still have a lot to learn when it comes to the art of deception, Flora!'

For a moment he had regained most of his usual easy manner, but it soon left him again. He started to hang back a little. Flora went down the garden path and brought out the front-door key from beneath the mat.

'I'm afraid I can only offer you tea,' Flora began, opening the door and letting all the familiar, well-loved scents of home envelop her. 'Although Dad—my father—might have a bottle of beer put by some-where—'

'Tea will be fine,' William said abruptly, following her into the tiny kitchen. Flora filled a kettle, then stoked up the slumbering fire before settling the kettle on it to boil.

'Sit down, William. I always do a bit of baking when I visit. To fill Dad's cake tins. . .'

She busied about the kitchen getting out scales and weights from beneath the sink and a flour crock from the cupboard. William drew out one of the hard old kitchen chairs and lowered himself down onto it carefully.

'Do you have a regular, Flora?'

'A follower, you mean? Goodness, no. When would I get the time for that?'

She crossed the kitchen again to fetch butter and cheese from the perforated zinc meat safe beside the big white china sink.

'You must be very keen by now, then. . .' He said, but again did not meet her eyes when she looked at him. Instead he concentrated on getting out a cigarette and matches from his pocket. At the rustle and rattle of packets landing on the kitchen table Flora hesitated and looked across at what he was doing. Drawing out one cigarette and lighting it seemed to take all his concentration. Then he looked around for an ashtray. Flora brought out a clean, empty cocoa tin from her store of useful containers and put it on the table beside him.

'Oh, I'm sorry, Flora. I should have asked—'

'Don't worry. Just because I don't like the habit doesn't mean you have to spare my feelings,' she said lightly.

He was obviously very uneasy. Flora didn't think it

could be the surroundings. The cottage kitchen was as clean and neat as the kitchens at Alvoe Court and he'd never looked so uncomfortable there.

'What is it, William?' Flora said solicitously, playing her advantage of home ground as she made the tea then poured him a cup.

'Nothing. Nothing. . .' he said absently, taking great trouble over adding sugar to his tea and stirring it into a whirlpool. 'It's just that. . .well, I hoped but never expected things to go this far, this fast, Flora.'

Flora was busy unpinning her hat and lodging the pins safely on the mantelpiece.

'Well, you're a strange one and no mistake!' she teased him gently, tying on an apron before washing her hands at the sink. 'You think nothing of whisking a decent girl off in a fast car and putting her in fear of losing her job, but you come over all remorseful when it comes to taking tea in a respectable home!'

She dried her hands at the roller towel fixed on a rod behind the back door, then returned to the kitchen table to weigh out fat and flour.

'That's all you're offering?' He looked at her expectantly.

Flora thought hard. 'There will be cheese scones within a quarter of an hour, and I could go and have a look in case Dad has been saving a bottle of beer for a special occasion—we don't get many visitors, so you might as well have it—'

His exhalation cut her short. 'I thought that with no regular, and after having been married—'

Flora was looking at him quizzically, and he faltered.

'I thought you'd be mad keen to—'

Faced with her quiet curiosity, the words kept dying on his lips. It was clear she didn't have the first idea what he was talking about.

'Mad keen to have a man about the place again,' he finished lamely.

Flora frowned and went back to her baking.

'Alfred was never going to be any good about the house, as far as I could see,' she said wearily. 'And I think that Dad keeps this place up together pretty well, don't you?'

'Yes—yes, of course. Sorry, Flora. I wasn't thinking straight.' He took a good long drink of tea then set the cup down with a sigh. 'Just what I needed,' he muttered.

The strained atmosphere that had stretched between them began to ease. Soon they were talking, if not like old friends, then with some of the casual companionship that stemmed from both staying at Alvoe Court and knowing some of the other residents.

By the time Flora took a batch of cheese scones from the oven, William felt sufficiently at home to steal one straight from the baking sheet. He had to bounce it from hand to hand to stop it burning his fingers.

'Serves you right,' Flora chided gently as she slid a sponge cake into the hot oven.

'You shouldn't be such a good cook.' He stubbed out his cigarette then broke open the feather-light scone with his fingers. A puff of steam escaped into the air while a scatter of crumbs landed on the table.

'What are the bridge party going to get tomorrow?' he asked as Flora slid a plate beneath his hands and offered him the salt cellar.

Flora pursed her lips thoughtfully.

'That rather depends on what Mr Stacey feels like providing. I sent a list out to the kitchen gardens before I left, but he likes to get the fruit and veg lists first thing in the morning, and at no other time. I was taking my life in my hands sending a list out of hours.'

'The Duchess has only just decided on the bally party! It's hardly your fault, is it?'

'No, but Mr Stacey would want me to wait until tomorrow morning to submit an order, as usual. He doesn't seem to realise that I like to get as much ready in advance as I can. I can't do that if he's going to turn around tomorrow morning and say I can't have half the things I've planned for, can I?'

'Do you want me to have a word with him for you, Flora?' The look on her face answered his question. 'No, perhaps not. What are you planning?'

He finished his first scone and watched pointedly as Flora transferred the rest, brown and irresistible with bubbled cheese, to a cooling rack.

'Well—' Flora dealt him another scone before he could steal one '—a cold collation as the centrepiece, of course, served with finger rolls and green salad, then there will be hot fish ramekins, cheese aigrettes, individual fruit salads, a *gâteau de millefeuille* and a choice of little cakes and pastries, just to keep their strength up.'

'I wonder if I'll be able to wangle an invite?'

'You think it sounds all right, then?'

'Yes. . .' He considered for a moment. 'Except for the fruit salads.'

Flora stopped. This was serious.

'*What about my fruit salads?*'

'Nothing. . .nothing. . .' William was so keen to placate her that he even put down his cheese scone. 'Fruit salad just sounds a bit. . .well, ordinary. . .'

He was rewarded with a smile of triumph.

'There will be nothing ordinary about *these* fruit salads. Alvoe Court melons took first prize at some big flower show up in London last week. Mr Stacey prides himself on being able to produce grapes a good fortnight before anyone else, and I happen to know that he's got some alpine strawberries ready.'

'Strawberries? But I haven't seen any of them in the shops for months!'

'Every entertainment needs its novelty. The Duchess provides something special at one of her parties, and it raises her stock mightily among her guests. They all go home and demand that their gardeners produce the same.' Flora gave him a wicked smile. 'But that's not my department. I just have to keep thinking up more and more outlandish ways of serving up Mr Stacey's latest triumphs.'

'Poor old bird. No wonder he dreads your little billets-doux.' Despite his pretended concern for Mr Stacey, William was visibly impressed. 'You're all there, aren't you?'

'When it comes to my work, I like to think so.'

He regarded her quick, economical movements for a long time as she finished setting out the scones, took the sponge cake from the oven then began making a buttercream filling for it.

'You don't look as though you should have anything to worry about tomorrow,' he said at last, but Flora giggled.

'To tell you the truth I'm petrified! It matters so much to the Duchess that her party is a success.'

'You'll be all right,' he said with genuine sincerity. 'With that battalion of staff behind you it's sure to be spectacular. I know—' He dropped his voice to a whisper and leaned forward. 'I'll contrive to leave one of my books in the room so that I can overhear what this sainted Lady Molly has to say about the quality of the catering when I go in to retrieve it. I'll tell you everything.'

'Are you making fun of me?' Flora levelled a meaningful gaze at him as she turned the sponge out onto another cooling rack.

'No, Never.' His grey eyes were soft and thoughtful.

Flora decided that he meant what he said—a rare quality when the newspapers were full of tales of likeable rogues.

She smiled, and was rewarded with an open smile in return.

With the oven cooling down again Flora made up a casserole of potato, onion, turnip and carrot to bake slowly in the bottom oven ready for her father's supper and slipped a dish of rice pudding in beside it. She thought William would busy himself with the cheese scones while she went to try and find her father, but he insisted on going with her.

'Can't have your mother-in-law telling tales about strangers being left alone in your house, can we?' he said lightly, taking her arm as they left the house. Flora turned pink with a mixture of pride and embarrassment at such a distinguished escort. She refused to look back as she walked up the front path arm in arm with the gallant Captain Pritchard. There was no need to. She could feel old Mrs Westbury's furious stare burning into the back of her neck.

Her father was equally curious about Flora's handsome new friend. But at least he tried to hide his interest when the couple met up with him in the byre at Manor Farm. Flora told her father that her birthday celebrations would have to be put off until the following Monday. George Collinton was as disappointed as Flora that they wouldn't be together for her twenty-first, but as a loyal estate worker he knew that there was no alternative. As usual, Flora had to promise to remember every bit of Downstairs gossip that she heard.

'He'll have great fun re-telling it all to the crowd down at the Porter Stores,' Flora laughed as she wandered back to the Rolls-Royce with William. He had let go of her arm before they had met up with her father, but Flora was very glad to find that he took it again as soon as they had left the byre.

'It'll be your greatest triumph yet, Flora. You'll see,' he said as they drew level with the estate cottages.

Flora hesitated, wondering if he would want to come into the house again or if they would have to part here. He cleared his throat then looked at her a little uncertainly.

'Are you game for this trip into town, then? To the pictures?'

Flora almost smiled, but at the last moment had to bite her lip. There were such awful stories going around about those picture theatres. If only he could have suggested something else. . .

'If you don't fancy the pictures, the Reverend, Mr Standish, says there's a grand new bookshop opened up in Park Street—'

'Oh, yes! I'd like that much better!'

'It's agreed, then,' he said with satisfaction, and opened the car door for her. 'I'd like to pick up something to keep me occupied during the voyage back to India, so we can kill two birds with one stone.'

'You're going back to India?' Flora struggled to keep the disappointment out of her voice.

'Not for a while, but I might not get another chance to go into Bristol before we leave. Leastways, not in the company of a pretty girl,' he finished as Flora hopped up into the passenger seat, forgetting for a moment the shortness of her skirt.

'Captain Pritchard!' Flora warned, trying to hide her

calves behind her handbag again. 'I shan't come if you're going to be forward.'

Her expression and words said one thing but her heart was thundering with daring. A ride in a motor car all the way to Bristol—and with a dashing young officer for company. Flora could hardly breathe at the thought.

'I shall be the last word in restraint.' He smiled kindly and closed the car door with a reassuring click.

The journey to Bristol was a delight. They laughed at every jolt from the uneven road surface and marvelled at the parched countryside that lay on either side of their route. From the thin grey line of the Severn in the west to the slopes of the Cotswolds in the east the farmland of the Berkeley Vale shimmered and suffered in the heat.

'No wonder the Americans call this sort of weather an Indian summer,' William said as Flora pointed out a herd of russet and white cattle sheltering in the shadow pool cast by a group of ash trees.

'Is it really as hot as this in India?' Flora wondered.

'Much hotter.'

'Isn't it *awful*?'

He shrugged. 'You get used to it. It's not the heat that is the worst thing. It's the dust—or rather mud, in the rainy season.'

Flora studied the dozing cattle. Productions at the Palace Theatre always made India and the East sound so exotic and mysterious. Not hot and dusty, or muddy. There was quite enough of all that at home in season, thank you.

Bristol was chock-a-block with carts and bicycles, as Flora had expected. What she hadn't imagined was the number of motor cars that would be bowling along the already busy streets. She hadn't been to Bristol since before the war, and the single motor they had seen on that occasion had been an unimagined wonder at the time. Now motor cars were everywhere.

'Are they really safer than horses?' Flora wondered aloud as William brought the car to a halt at the side of the road, causing urchins to scatter from the steaming Rolls with its smell of hot metal and fuel.

'They're more fun. And you don't have to worry about feeding and watering them when they're left. Although the crowds can be a bit of a problem,' he said as the children edged toward the Rolls, eyes wide with curiosity. Reaching into his jacket pocket, William retrieved a rather soggy bar of Nestlé's chocolate and held it out to the urchins.

'*No one* is to touch this car,' he said forcefully as the clamouring children fell on the rare treat.

The bookshop was cool and welcoming after the brilliant sunlit heat of the street. They stepped down into the small book-lined room with its counter and shelves of highly polished wood. The scent of beeswax was almost as strong as it was in the Alvoe family rooms, but the fragrance of Alvoe Court was usually mixed with the smell of old things—old paintings, old rugs and old dust hidden in forgotten corners. Here the beeswax mingled with the scents of new paint and turpentine.

At first William and Flora scoured the bookshelves together, but gradually Flora ventured further afield. The bookshop was a quiet luxury for her. While William went off with the shopkeeper to find a book he wanted, she wandered past shelves packed with brand-new books.

Here were titles she had experienced only at second hand through the little vicarage lending scheme at home. *Pride and Prejudice*, *Vanity Fair* and *Jane Eyre* were all there, leather bindings tooled in gold. Flora decided then and there that she would save up and treat herself to one of these beautiful books for Christmas. Master Ralph's contribution would help there.

She lost track of time, running her finger along the leather-spined lines of books. She was lost in a volume by Thomas Hardy when she became aware of a presence close behind her. Turning, she looked up into William's face and found that he was looking at her with as much pleasure as she was beginning to feel herself.

'What have you got there, Flora?'

She held the book out to him. '*The Woodlanders*. It's by Thomas Hardy. *Far from the Madding Crowd* is my favourite book, but our library can never get hold of any of the others.'

He took the book from her but instead of scanning the words casually as she had expected showed every sign of studying them with great care.

'Would you like it?' he said at last.

Flora looked at the leather-bound, gold-tooled volume stiff with expense.

'Call it an early birthday present,' he continued. 'Or a good luck charm for all that party catering tomorrow.'

'Oh. . .I couldn't. . .' she murmured, but knew that she could, given just a little bit of persuasion.

'Go on—you'll never have another twenty-first birthday. And to have to prepare a party for other people. . . You might as well treat yourself. Or at least let me treat you!'

Flora took the book again and let the bible-thin pages flicker through her fingers. The words danced invitingly before her.

' :houldn't really accept. . .' She looked up at him. All the time her heart was telling her that acceptance would only be the beginning, not the end of the matter. 'You've been so kind already, William, taking me to Falgrave, bringing me here—'

'This is something different,' he murmured, taking the book from her gently. 'A simple present for a special occasion. Nothing more threatening than that. Now, are you going to let me treat you?'

Flora pursed her lips. If old Mrs Westbury ever got to hear about this. . .

She made up her mind. Taking a deep breath, she smiled and nodded. 'It's a lovely present, William. Thank you. I would be very happy to accept.'

He placed her book together with the one he had chosen for himself then took her arm again.

Flora realised that, for good or ill, there could be no going back now.

As a once respectable war widow now fallen far enough to accept presents from a gentleman, Flora expected withering scorn from the shopkeeper. He must surely guess at her recklessness. Instead he merely made the usual cheerful comments about the weather, wrapped their purchases and accepted William's money.

When the polite goodbyes were over, William took Flora's arm again to lead her out into the street. Her relief led her into an indiscretion.

'Well? What did you buy for yourself, William?'

He looked evasive and pushed his packet into his pocket.

'Oh, nothing much.'

At once Flora thought the worst and cursed her curiosity. After all, on a long voyage thoughts were bound to turn to all manner of things.

'Oh, my goodness — how embarrassing! I'm sorry. . .'

'Here.' With a rueful smile he pulled out the package and handed it to her. 'Have a look. I shouldn't like a respectable widowed lady to imagine I'd picked up the latest by Mrs Stopes.'

Flora unfolded the brown paper bag. Its sharp creases still smelled of the expense and luxury of the small book it contained.

'*The Aeneid*,' she managed with a little prompting. 'Marcus Tullius Vergilus. I've never heard of it. What is it about?'

'Love, death and the Roman Mission.' William grinned as she flicked through the pages, frowning. 'If a bit of translation is going to be light relief, you can guess what the trip will be like.'

It was all in a foreign language. Latin, Flora guessed from his mention of Rome. Despite her love of books she could see no sense in having to puzzle through a foreign one.

'Having to work at your reading must take away all the excitement.'

'In my job there's usually more than enough excitement to go round. If there's a chance of spending long hours travelling and hanging about you aren't eager for excitement, I can tell you.'

The way William spoke of the army was quite different from Ralph Morwyn's eager exhibitions of his uniform and experiences. The more Flora thought of the difference between Ralph and William, the more she wondered about the friendship between the two men.

'Do you like being in the army?' she said as they strolled along the dusty pavement.

'Of course.' The reply was immediate, but he did not

look at her. 'It's a job, after all. Thousands don't have that much.'

'Is that what Master Ralph thinks, too?'

'I think he prefers the uniform.'

He spoke lightly, and Flora was tempted to continue.

'I'm surprised that you two are friends. You aren't a bit alike.'

'I think that's the attraction I have for him,' William said thoughtfully. 'He was pretty miserable when we first met. That was at school. Outshone by his older brothers at home and by just about everybody else at school, he needed a bit of encouragement. He got that from me at school but now he is his family's last hope he looks to be getting more at home.'

'You don't sound very sure, William.'

He considered this as they walked.

'I'm not, if the encouragement comes from the fast set that has tried to attach itself to him since his brothers were killed.' He looked down at her with a hint of Ralph's mischief in the steady grey eyes. 'Not a word of this to anyone, mind. I shouldn't have said anything disloyal.'

'That's quite all right.' Flora remembered their first meeting, and her indiscretion about Alfred. Something had come over her then and made her open up to William. Now it looked as though the magic could work both ways.

William squeezed her arm. 'Look—there's a picture house sign. Are you sure you don't feel like giving it a try?'

Flora remembered the dens of danger that such places were supposed to be, and hesitated. He was quick to apologise.

'No. Of course not. You must have a thousand things

to get ready for tomorrow. It was unthinking of me. I'll
take you straight back to Alvoe Court—'

'Not at all,' Flora said quickly, fired by the thought
of spending more time with him. 'I'd be glad of
something to take my mind off worrying about
tomorrow, to be honest. Actually, I was wondering if
picture houses are really safe. . .'

He sighed, giving her a look of disgust. 'It's *perfectly*
safe. I can see you've got no sense of adventure.'

Flora felt her hands dampen and hoped to goodness
that wet marks weren't adding to the powder already
on her gloves. Despite her worries, she could not bring
herself to let go of William's arm. He must have
thought her wet for not wanting him to drive fast, and
now this.

'I should love to go. If you say it is all right then I
trust your judgement, William.'

He looked down at her narrowly. 'I'd always
expected you to be a bit of a woman suffragist, being a
working girl. *That* didn't sound like a woman suffragist
speaking!' He looked away. 'Anybody would think that
you were afraid of being alone with me.'

'Oh, no. Not at all. I mean—well, we've had a good
time so far, haven't we?'

They had almost reached the picture theatre and
William stopped.

'I know—you can keep your hand on my arm
throughout the performance if you like, Flora.'

Flora would have been scandalised if anyone else
had suggested such a thing, but coming from William it
seemed the most natural thing in the world. It was all
she could do to keep a proper sense of decorum.

'All right,' she said, looking down at her shoes. She
was relieved to find only the slightest traces of street

dust. 'As long as you understand that I never usually carry on like this.'

She had expected him to hurry her on toward the queue of people shuffling into the dark depths of the picture theatre, but he did not.

'Does that mean you still think I'm being too forward, Flora?'

It was nice to be asked. Flora almost forgot the horrible memories of Alfred's liberties, and smiled.

'That depends. I'm a decent girl, and if you treat me decently then we'll have no arguments, will we?'

He put his hand over hers and squeezed it. Flora realised something then that had never struck her when she had been with Alfred. Men could have feelings, too. For a fleeting instant she saw that William had been as desperate to conform to the rules as she had been.

Chapter Six

There was a tiny bow-fronted confectioners in the rank of shops, and Flora saw a way of distracting herself from looking into William's eyes for too long.

'Look—a sweet shop. I can replace the bar of chocolate you gave to the boys.'

He laughed again. 'You don't have to worry about that!'

'I do. Although perhaps chocolate isn't such a good idea. If the picture theatre goes up in flames it will melt, after all!'

'And I thought that I would be the one teasing you,' he said with amusement as they stepped down into the shop.

Flora bought some sweets as well as another bar of Nestlé's chocolate for William. As they went into the picture theatre he joked that perhaps they had better sit near one of the fire buckets for safety's sake as well as the sake of the chocolate, but Flora took his teasing in good part. She could imagine that his friend Ralph's humour would be of a very different sort.

They sat together in the flickering darkness, the projector shafting scenes through a haze of blue-grey cigarette smoke. The first film was a comedy. Two men painting a house spent five minutes stepping into buckets, being hit by swinging ladders and generally falling over each other, to the noisy delight of the audience.

Then a reverent hush descended over the ranks of viewers. Mr Thomas Payne, long-distance champion pedestrian and first-class violinist, showed in an advertisement how Phosferine, the world's greatest medicine, had saved him from premature decay.

Advertisements for coming attractions were not so well received. The coal-black eyes of a heroine clasped to the hero's manly bosom brought only howls of derision from the hordes of little boys packed into the cheap seats.

'It seems that some chaps don't appreciate the charms of a pretty girl,' William whispered, shifting slightly in his seat. He had removed his hat in deference to the viewers behind and Flora supposed that, being tall, he had to edge down in his seat for the same reason. She turned to reply, but saw that he was looking unusually withdrawn.

'Would you like a toffee?' she said, uncomfortable that he was watching her so intently.

To her delight the smile returned to his face.

'Wonderful. It saves on cigarettes, after all,' he added. 'Less of a fire risk, too.'

When they emerged, blinking, from the picture theatre the afternoon was almost gone. The light was flat and grey, as though exhausted from drawing the evening along in its wake.

'Are you hungry yet?' William asked as he took her arm once more.

'Not really,' Flora replied. She would have loved a cup of tea, but had only small change in her purse. The sort of places where a gentleman was likely to take refreshments would be far out of her price range.

'I could murder a pint.' William straightened his back in a discreet stretching movement. 'Come on. Let's find a pub.'

His hand slipped to hers and Flora found herself pulled into the narrow back streets of Bristol. The warren of streets around Broad Quay held any number of public houses, but to Flora's relief William stopped at only the cleanest and most respectable-looking ones. After a swift glance into several interiors he finally found one that satisfied him. Flora stared at the floor as she was led in, feeling that this must surely be the end of her good reputation.

The public house was a surprise. Its floor was uncarpeted, but the boards were scrubbed as clean and fresh as any private house. The bitter-sweet smell of beer was not unpleasant, and the place was quiet, which really surprised Flora. Even if it was a place where strong drink was served, there was no raging here.

Flora risked looking up. The bar itself was highly polished, with a little old lady dressed in rusty black bombazine busily polishing a glass. Anywhere that took such care over its glassware could not be all bad, Flora reasoned. She smiled at the old lady, who smiled back. Surprised again, Flora looked down at her feet once more. She had expected a bawdy house full of semi-naked girls and huddles of villains straight out of the pages of Dickens. This was a revelation and no mistake. It was light, warm, and welcoming.

William installed her at a corner table, sheltered from any possibility of a draught by a screen of dark wood and etched glass.

'What would you like, Flora?'

'What do they have?'

He looked confused, then saw her darting quick glances around the room.

'Haven't you ever been into a public house before?'

'No fear. The Porter Stores at home don't even let women over the threshold.'

William laughed and went off to the bar, jingling change in his pocket as he went. Flora clutched her handbag and kept her eyes on him, counting the seconds until he returned. He brought a pint of beer for himself and a glass of cold, cloudy liquid for Flora.

'Lemonade. Home-made by the innocent little old lady behind the bar. A harmless taste of dissolute living.'

Flora waited until he had sat down beside her before risking a sip of her lemonade. It certainly tasted like the real thing. She glanced at the little old lady still polishing glasses behind the bar. *She* certainly looked the type who would take the trouble to make real lemonade, and the proof was in the drinking. Flora began to relax.

William straightened his jacket then took a long pull at his glass of beer. Sitting back with a satisfied smile, he sighed.

'Lovely. A real taste of home. I shall be back on the India Pale Ale all too soon.'

'You're not looking forward to going, are you?'

He took another drink, studying the glass for a long time before replying. Then his face cleared, as though he had admitted something to himself at last.

'Not really, no. I don't want to go back to India. I'd rather stay here in England. I don't want to go halfway around the world to face heat and flies, dust and Mr Gandhi's non-cooperation tactics. Not with curried goat and India Pale Ale my only consolations.'

'Isn't there any consolation in your work?'

'The ability to identify one thousand and one varieties of insulated cable at twenty paces must have held an appeal at some time, I suppose.'

William had a way about him that refused to be dampened by any passing regret. He wasn't going to take himself too seriously, and Flora found herself laughing again.

'Is that what you were doing in the East? Laying cables?'

'Laying it, fraying it, splicing it and dicing it. The message must get through,' he said with mock gravity.

'I remember when men came to lay electricity on at Falgrave Manor,' Flora said after another sip of lemonade. 'The mess and noise went on for weeks. Men down holes and men up ladders everywhere you looked. Is your job like that?'

He thought for a minute, taking the opportunity to savour another mouthful of his beer.

'Our job,' he said at last, 'is like ringing pheasants during a shoot. On one side you've got the beaters advancing, on the other there are the guns, and in the thick of it we're trying to work while the pheasants are running round in circles, taking off, landing, crowing their heads off and generally getting in our way, and their own way.'

Flora frowned and pursed her lips 'Oh. I thought laying a few cables would be really simple.'

'*Nothing* in war is simple. It's a breeding ground for horror and confusion.'

'But we aren't at war now, are we? Your job must have been a lot easier since the Armistice was signed.'

He laughed, showing his good, even teeth. They looked very white when contrasted with the pale gold of his skin. 'There's always someone spoiling for a fight somewhere in the Empire. Show me a man with ambition and I'll show you a war in the making.'

Flora drank her lemonade and wondered how to take his mind off India. She tried changing the subject.

'Well, you've seen Falgrave now, for what it's worth. I expect you come from somewhere much grander.'

'Just London.' He looked a little evasive and took another drink.

'*London!* Oh, that must be *wonderful!*'

At her delight the faint trace of concern left his face and he laughed, starting to tell her about his trips to the moving pictures, walks in the royal parks and visits to Buckingham Palace.

'Only to look through the gates,' he said quickly, delighted by her excitement. Not even this admission could disappoint her. William's stories of the noise and bustle of London and its grand stores painted a picture almost as exotic as talk of India.

Flora realised that it must be William's natural modesty that stopped him from talking about his home. All she managed to get out of him was that he came from a part called Kilburn. He was very reluctant to go into details, so Flora let him change the subject. The house in Kilburn must be very grand indeed for him to be so modest about it.

Flora was halfway through her second glass of lemonade when she remembered the tales of 'spiked' drinks in low drinking places. A quick look around the bar soon reassured her. Another customer had wandered in and stood at the bar while the old lady cut him a slice of bread. This she put on a plate with a chunk of cheese carved from the wedge standing beneath a spotless glass dome on the bar. The customer was smartly dressed, and studying the sporting pages of his evening paper with as much care as her father always did. This was the sign of a true and honest Englishman, and Flora relaxed again.

She was almost sorry when the time came to leave the pub. Again William took her arm for their walk through the streets. It seemed the most natural thing to do, but Flora was not so relaxed that she could accept William's offer of his jacket when she shivered in the early evening chill.

'That's a pretty outfit,' he said as he helped her up into the Rolls. Flora did let him tuck one of the travelling blankets over her lap, but waited until he had started the car and was settled in the driving seat before replying.

'My mum would have had a fit if she thought I'd gone out in public in such a short skirt. She used to reckon that even girls who showed their ankles were no better than they should be.'

William lit a cigarette with one hand, smiling at her in the temporary illumination.

'Oh, that's an admission, Flora! Does it mean that I shall have to look out when I'm with you?'

Flora dissolved in a flurry of embarrassment.

'No...that isn't what I meant at all, Master William—'

'You can cut that out again for a start,' he said cheerfully, easing the large car through the still busy streets.

'We're on our way back now, sir. It's too late for familiarities.' Flora looked into the distance, narrowing her eyes against the draughts and the growing dark to try and see where they were. 'I still don't know how I'm going to explain arriving back at Alvoe in this car. Unless you could drop me along the way and I'll cut through the park—'

'With everything around Alvoe so deathly quiet?

The gatekeeper would hear and get suspicious, for a start. Not to mention the gamekeeper. Any man worth his salt would sit up and take notice at the sight of your pretty little figure flitting about alone. No. You sit tight. If anything needs to be explained I'll do the talking. Don't go looking for trouble before it arrives.'

Flora was anxious, but William laughed off all her worries. He was so persuasive that in the end she began to think that they really might get away with it. If they were lucky.

As it grew darker William started to look around at the countryside. Eventually the Rolls slowed and he turned it into a green lane. Cart ruts baked by the summer stopped him from risking the car too much, so they stopped barely ten yards from the main highway.

Flora suddenly remembered all her fears again. She kicked off her shoes for a quick escape and found the door-handle before William had even managed to turn off the engine.

'Sorry—I didn't mean to alarm you.' His voice was soft and gentle. At once Flora regretted thinking that her life was in danger.

Now it was only her honour that she had to worry about.

'I need to take a break for a minute. I didn't think you'd like to sit about waiting on the roadside.'

His light-hearted apology had such a ring of truth about it that Flora slipped her shoes back on as he opened the car door. She was already feeling silly for suspecting him.

He left quietly, absorbed by the overhanging shadows of the lane. Alone in the gathering darkness, Flora watched bats flicker through the elms like dreams. The countryside at night held no terrors for her. Instead she relished the last few minutes in the luxury of the elegantly upholstered Rolls-Royce.

When William returned she was glad that he did not disturb the silence too much with his arrival.

'Isn't it peaceful?' he whispered.

Flora murmured a reply then they both fell into reflective silence again. An owl quavered across the shadowy valley in front of them, to be answered by another close at hand.

'Look! A bat!' William leaned forward, looking intently into the gloom.

'Yes, I know. I think they're coming out of that old elm.'

'Aren't you afraid?'

'Why?'

'Well. . .aren't you afraid that they'll get caught in your hair, or something?'

Flora laughed. 'Of course not! When I was little, my brother David and I used to swing the clothes pole around our heads to try and catch one.'

There was an awkward silence.

'Did you catch any?' William said at last.

'What?'

'Bats.'

'No. Never.' Flora fumbled for something to say that would either revive the conversation or stir him into starting the car up again. 'We did find an owl once, though. It had fallen out of its nest. Mum nearly had a fit when we brought it home. She reckoned that it was a bird of ill omen, and told Dad to kill it. He took it away, but only back to its nest hole.'

'Flora. . .' William had moved a little closer to whisper into the darkness.

'Yes?'

'Can I put my arm around you?'

'Yes.'

The exchange had been rapid but for a moment neither moved. Flora had enough time to think better of it, but she was too stunned by such an unlooked-for miracle to change her mind. William continued to stare straight ahead for some time, out into the fluttering dusk. Finally he slid his arm along the smooth leather of the car seat. Flora felt the warmth of his hand through her jacket and shivered.

'Are you all right?' he whispered.

'Yes. Just a bit of a chill.'

With his other hand he pulled the car blanket further up over her lap. His movements were perfumed with the scent of soap and peppermints.

'It really doesn't matter about the blanket,' Flora whispered. She was trying to convince herself, but also secretly worried that he might let go of her if he decided to use both hands on the blanket. She was desperate to keep his arm about her, despite knowing what it might lead to. Afraid of having him near, she was also afraid of losing him. The confusion of feelings kept her silent, unable to reconcile the thought of William, his laughter and his thoughtful, easy manner with her memories of Alfred.

The moment enveloped them like the dusk.

'I wanted to do this in the cinema, Flora.'

Flora was shocked, but sensed from his reticence that she was in no danger. Yet.

'That might not have been a very good idea with all those people about.'

His fingers were working over her shoulder now in small, tense movements.

'Ralph says that all domestics are at it like rabbits.'

The spell was broken.

'*What?*' Flora jerked away from him. 'Not *this* domestic!' Her hands started scrabbling for the handle of the car door again, but William had already sat back in his seat.

'Don't, Flora,' he said quietly, but made no move to stop her. 'I didn't mean to upset you.'

Another surprise. Flora had been fired by moral indignation, but now she began to feel strangely cheated. Staff were supposed to have the morals; gentlemen had none. It was a well-known fact.

Now William was doing his best to set all that on its head.

She stopped trying to escape from the car. Willing him not to abuse a second chance, she settled back down in her seat, hands neatly folded in her lap.

'All right. But if you don't behave, Captain Pritchard, I shall get out of this car right now.'

A reminder of his rank might nail his morals into place even more firmly. Flora heard him exhale softly and saw a faint trail of condensation shine against the dark. It was almost as though he was relieved. Still, she added, 'An arm around the shoulder is as far as it's decent to go.'

She leaned forward a little way and was rewarded with his arm slipping back around her. His hand lay relaxed on her shoulder this time, instead of making those tense and furtive movements.

'I thought that as a married woman you might expect—that is, you might want...' he began awkwardly.

Flora cleared her throat meaningfully and took a tight hold of her handbag.

'Ralph says that once a woman has—'

'Captain Pritchard, I'm surprised at you! I don't want to know!'

Flora felt him relax and immediately became more uncomfortable herself.

'I've told you before. I'm a decent girl.'

'Yes. Yes, I know that now.'

There was a warmth in William's voice now, so unlike Alfred's attempts at coercion that Flora wondered what was going to happen next. With Alfred she had always known. This was more uncertain. Far more worrying. She tried to think of something to distract him—if only slightly.

'What about your Cherie Barclay?' she whispered as the rim of the moon rose above the horizon.

If the question unsettled him he did not show it.

'Cherie? She's just one of the nursing staff attached to my regiment. Her father is colour sergeant.'

'And?'

'Why don't we change the subject?' he said sharply. 'You can tell me all about your husband and your doubtless delightful marriage. That sounded like an interesting topic of conversation when we touched on it the other day.'

'My marriage was in the past. That doesn't matter.'

'No. Quite. And neither does Miss Barclay.'

There was a quiet triumph in this final statement that Flora almost resented. Only his arm about her shoulder made her reconsider a sharp retort. His touch was so undemanding—at the moment. Warm, steady and reassuring rather than a threat of things to come.

'I was only going by what Master Ralph was saying on the evening I was called up to the dining room,' she said slowly.

'Ralph says too much—' William's voice softened in the growing moonlight '—but he's a good friend. He can overdo the noise and bluster now and again, but that's for the benefit of others more than himself. His parents in particular. He's much more clever than they've ever given him credit for.

'His only fault was to be born a third son. He was quite happy with the overgrown sports and social club they call the army, where he could forget all about Alvoe and be left to his own devices. The trouble began when his brothers were lost. Ralph was catapulted into his father's favour. Both of them resented it, I think. Making the best of a bad job is the phrase that springs instantly to mind.'

He suddenly remembered himself. 'Not a word of this to anyone else, of course?'

'Of course not.' Flora let herself relax into his encircling arm, surprising herself. 'This is nice.'

'You could still take my jacket.' He moved to slip his other arm out of his jacket, but Flora stopped him.

'Then you would get cold instead.'

More sure of him now, Flora had stayed his movement with her hand. As he subsided back into his seat her touch lingered a little longer than was strictly necessary, until she remembered herself.

Then the moon was splintered into shards by a wrack of cloud. Instead of obscuring his good looks, the half-light made William all the more hauntingly handsome. Flora had originally been ready with a smart rebuff for any more over-familiarity, but now she found herself almost wishing that he would try to go further. Yet she knew that if he did it was certain to be the ruin of her. She could not face what she had gone through with Alfred again.

'Tell me more about your home,' Flora managed, trying to put off the moment of her downfall.

'There's nothing much to tell, although in a round-about way it's part of the reason why I became so friendly with Ralph. Mother came from this area but left here before I was born, and got away to London.'

'Pritchard.' Flora racked her brains, but could come up with only one family of that name. 'There's a Pritchard family that live over Westing way. Led by a man called Gully—a chap of short temper and long memory. They call him over to help with the farm work or on the roads sometimes. I don't think anybody in their right minds would fancy claiming kin with him!' She giggled at the thought of it.

'I hope this doesn't mean that you're laughing at my relatives.' William put on an injured tone but the arm about her shoulders squeezed her reassuringly.

'Only if you're related to an old prize fighter who catches rats with his bare hands!'

'A likely story!'

'It's true—I've seen him do it. Mind you, I'm not sure about the other things they say about him.'

William squeezed her again, but playfully this time.

'Out with it. You can't leave a good story hanging in mid-air like that!'

'Well, they do say. . .' Flora dropped her voice to a conspiratorial whisper '. . .that he once ate a live rat for a bet.'

'What's the matter with that? Sheer luxury. We only get to eat dead ones in the army.'

Flora looked at him quickly, remembering what her brother David had said about life on the front line in France. In the silence William worked a cautious caress over her shoulder again.

'It was a joke, Flora.'

'Not a very funny one. My brother was on the Somme.'

His fingers lay still. 'Oh, Flora. . . I'm so sorry. . . Did he survive? I know your husband didn't.'

'David did—only to be killed a week before the Armistice.'

William took her words to heart, turning aside with a muttered oath. Flora realised that however hard her personal loss might have been it did at least have the shroud of ignorance about it. She had not been there to witness David's death. William must have seen men die. The horror of that would have been much worse, even if he had not known the victims personally.

'I lost five men from my unit during the time that we were in Mesopotamia. They say you get used to it, but I never have. I shouldn't have tried to make light of it, Flora.'

He was still looking away, out into the evening. On impulse Flora put her hand on his knee and patted it reassuringly.

'Things might go better for you in India after this break.'

'I'd almost managed to forget the wretched place until you said that.' The look he gave her tempered the words. 'I've had a wonderful time today, Flora.'

'So have I.'

She smiled, and in a sudden, shared response they kissed.

His mouth was cool and firm, delicate suggestions of peppermint and hops adding to Flora's intoxication.

'You didn't mind?'

Flora's hand went up to his face and she shook her head.

'Although I suppose I ought to say, yes, I do mind and don't do it again, Captain Pritchard.'

'What happened to William?'

'I think perhaps one of us ought to keep half a mind on the proprieties,' Flora said, but he guessed that her heart was not in it.

'May I kiss you again?'

'I don't know.'

'Didn't you like it?'

Flora could not tell him how much. It was a new experience for her and she did not want to spoil it. William sat back in his seat again, but she took heart from his gentle expression.

'Things would be different if there was any chance of us reaching an understanding, Captain Pritchard.'

He levelled his gaze at her and she was relieved to see that he had taken the gentle rebuff with good humour.

'If you were any other girl, Mrs Westbury, I should certainly sweep you off your feet with an immediate proposal of marriage, but—'

'But?' Flora was too quick with her alarmed question and the interruption made him pause for thought.

'But you have your career at Alvoe Court to consider. You left me in no doubt what that means to you on our first meeting, Mrs Westbury.'

He was still looking at her. Flora had to take the chance.

'That was only our first meeting, William. I wasn't sure I wanted to encourage you then.'

'What about now?'

Flora looked down at her hands. In the evening shadows the new white gloves appeared as dark as her memories. When she did not speak he continued.

'You called me William again. You let that much slip,' he probed gently, trying to look around into her face. Flora squeezed her fingers together and would not look at him.

'I think we ought to be getting back, William. Dinner will be served at eight o'clock. You'll need time to dress, and I've got to get everything ready for the party tomorrow.'

William sat perfectly still for two heartbeats. Then he opened his door.

'I'll start the car up.'

As he began to get out Flora put her hand on his arm.

'William. . . I am sorry. . .'

He shrugged and did not look back.

'That's all right.'

The door slammed behind him, shutting out all Flora's hopes. William took his time walking around to the front of the car, and paused to check his watch in the moonlight before starting up the engine. It was a long time before he returned to the driving seat, and it felt like an eternity to Flora. His kiss had been gentle and she had wanted more, but in her heart she knew how things would end. It would be the same old ritual, tears and recriminations.

'I'm sorry.'

'I am, too,' he said, with a hint of bitterness in his voice. 'What did I do wrong?'

The question was so unexpected that Flora forgot her own pain.

'Nothing. Nothing. . .and that's the trouble.'

'Flora? What is it? Don't cry.'

'I'm not,' she sobbed. 'I must have got a smut in my eye from this beastly engine.'

'Here.' He drew an immaculately pressed white handkerchief from his pocket and gave it to Flora. 'Are you going to tell me what's gone wrong, or am I going to be sentenced to wondering for ever what I did to upset you?'

'It's not you. Well, unless you count the fact that

you'll be off across the world soon and I shall never see you again.'

'Would you want to?' he said gently, but Flora was too wrapped up in her own worries to notice his concern. He put his arm around her shoulders again but this time her nerves were taut and she did not relax against his support.

'I don't like it.' She twisted the handkerchief between her fingers, watching the tear-stains soak into the fine fabric.

William took his arm away.

'No—no, not you. . .I liked that. It's just that—I'm not very good at it. Kissing. . .and things.'

'You felt very good at it just now.'

'That's the trouble. I didn't want it to go any further. But then in a way I did— Oh, I don't know.'

'I do.' He adjusted the note of the engine to a distant thunder. 'I know exactly what you mean, Flora. You liked the kissing, but you were worried about what might happen next.'

'Yes.' She stopped crying and looked at him in surprise. 'That's exactly it. How did you guess?'

'A gentleman *should* know about these things.' He relieved her of the damp and dishevelled handkerchief, touching it to her lashes one last time before pushing it back into his inside pocket. 'What's more, I can show you exactly what *would* have happened.'

He kissed her again, even more gently than before. Flora closed her eyes as a warm exhaustion began to flow through her body. When the kiss ended this time there could be no mistaking the feeling it left behind, despite its novelty.

'There.' William touched one of her curls back from her brow. 'That's all. Nothing more. And now we shall

go back to Alvoe Court. Nothing more hideous than
that.'

He looked pleased with himself. Flora was pleased
with him, too. If only they could have spent more time
like this. If only he wasn't going away. . .

'Oh, dear,' William said as he tried to turn the car
around in the narrow confines of the green lane and
caught sight of more tears. 'What is it now?'

Flora swallowed hard, choking back the tears that
were threatening to engulf her again.

'I wish we could have today all over again,' she
managed as the car rolled up onto the offside bank and
edged round in a circle.

'I wish we could have met before.' William sighed as
he brought the car to a standstill pointing toward the
main road. 'It won't be long before I'm off on my
travels.'

'It's all right for you. Once you get back to your
work—' and Cherie Barclay, Flora added silently to
herself '—you'll forget all about me.' She could hardly
bear to form the words.

'Flora, I've had more fun in these past few hours
than I've had on all my other home leaves put
together.' William moved as though to kiss her again,
but stopped short. 'I don't want to come across as over-
familiar. Although I should like to ask if I may write to
you?'

'Of course you can.' Flora knew he would be unlikely
to remember the request, but she had to hope. 'But for
heaven's sake don't send it to me at work. Address it
to Falgrave. Two, Estate Cottages.'

He repeated the address carefully, and Flora wondered how many other girls he had promised to corre-
spond with. The fine features and the winning smile
had certainly worked their charm on her. Doubtless

Cherie Barclay was not their only other victim. Flora knew that another of his kisses would have her on the point of surrender. How much more irresistible must he be to a girl like Miss Barclay, who saw him all the time?

'I hope the writing won't interfere with your work. You've got your job to consider. And I've got mine,' Flora said firmly, trying to sound sensible. 'I ought to get back and see about keeping it.'

'Yes, it's gone seven,' William said with real regret. 'Shall I see you again before I leave?'

'I shouldn't think so. What with the Duchess keeping an eye on us both, and with me working, and you—'

'Idling about?' he laughed. 'Yes, that's all there is to do as a guest around here. All those hours, and no possibility of filling them.'

'You've got Master Ralph.' Flora reached across to touch his hand as it held the steering wheel.

'I shall be blessed with his company for the next few years. I'd rather—' He stopped.

'Go on. I know—you'd much rather stay at home with me!' Flora teased him gently.

'Yes.'

'Get away with you! You're the same as every other soldier I've met. A girl in every billet!'

'You've been out with other soldiers, then?' His voice was curious but Flora could reassure him on that point.

'I've been approached by plenty, but walked out with none,' she said firmly. 'Until now, that is.'

'Why am I so different?'

Flora did not have to think about that. 'You're a proper gentleman. Not insistent.'

'Not even when I do this?' He took one hand from the steering wheel and stroked her cheek. Flora's enjoyment was spoiled by her fear that the car might run away. Laughing, he took his other hand from the wheel to show her that the car was held quite securely by the brake.

'I don't suppose there's any way that we could meet again before I leave?'

'Not a chance.' Flora took hold of his hand and squeezed it.

'I've still got your case to return. I'm sure I could get to your room again—'

'William!' Flora's eyes were wide open with shock but he was almost equally horrified.

'I didn't mean for *that*.' He looked as uncomfortable as Flora felt. 'I thought we could talk. I've got some playing cards, and a tinned fruit cake that Mrs Fielding sent me.'

Suddenly Flora knew exactly what he meant. She realised that she was not the only one subject to human failings.

'You're lonely, aren't you?'

The question struck him like a blow.

'Not especially,' he said defensively. 'Like you said— I've always got Ralph.'

'There's no shame in it, William. You don't strike me as the type of chap whose idea of a good time is a lot of noisy rough and tumble.' Flora thought of her brother's friends. 'But that doesn't mean that you can't appreciate company now and again.'

He had taken hold of her hand and looked at the neat little white glove.

'That's it. I've never minded being alone, but now I've found you, Flora, I've got a feeling that I shall be finding out what it means to be lonely. Are you sure I can't come and visit you later?'

'I only wish you could.' Flora sensed that he would

behave decently, but she was almost reaching the point where she did not want him to. 'We have to be sensible, William. You'll just have to leave my case with Mr Perry. We can't risk meeting again, for any reason. Your reputation and my job would be at stake.'

'What about *your* reputation?'

'That's quite safe. Especially since I'm not going to let you come calling.'

'Then this is probably the last time that we will be together,' he said flatly.

Flora was already beginning to believe that he meant what he said about corresponding.

'We must get home, William. Before we both say more than we intend.'

He drove the car onto the road, but stopped to hold her again once more before moving off. Flora responded, putting her arms around him. She had the terrible feeling that this was her one and only chance of happiness, and it was about to slip through her fingers.

Chapter Seven

William drove back to Alvoe Court carefully, despite only having one hand on the steering wheel. The other was holding Flora's hand. Only when they slowed down to approach the gatehouse of Alvoe Court did he let go in preparation to meet the gatekeeper.

After passing through the gates he reached for her hand again, which was hidden beneath the folds of the travelling rug. The curving drive through the park had never seemed so short. All too soon the car was throwing long shadows across the well-lit stable yard as it drove toward the garage.

Stopping the engine, William leapt down and went around to help Flora from her seat. As he did so he spoke, keeping his voice low in case anyone should overhear.

'It will be at least a year, probably much longer, before I can get any more home leave. I can't ask you to wait for me, Flora—not all that time—but will you think of me sometimes?'

'Every time I get a letter.'

Flora was still not convinced that he really would write. It would be asking a lot, and she decided then and there not to build up her hopes, although the disappointment would still be hard to endure.

The sound of feet pounding down the stairway from the stable flat flung them apart. James, the chauffeur, burst through the door and into the yard, his collarless shirt unbuttoned and a towel around his neck.

'Sorry, sir. Thought I'd have a quick swill while no one was about— Oh, hello again, Mrs Westbury!'

'Cook here was trying to walk back from town.' William searched for a cigarette and lit it with an ostentatious movement. 'Taking a bit of a risk, weren't you, Cook?'

'Yes, sir,' Flora said meekly, remembering to let William do all the talking.

'You never know who's about these days. You might have come across any rapscallion on the way. Make sure you don't give any man the chance to take advantage of you in future, won't you?'

'Yes, sir.'

'And mind you give that untrustworthy carter who was supposed to drive you back a piece of your mind next time you see him.' He flicked aside a spent match and strolled out of the stable yard. Without looking back he went around the corner of Alvoe Court to present himself at the front door of the great house.

Flora felt completely let down. The end, when it had come, had been so quick.

'It's all right for them,' the chauffeur said grumpily. 'What sort of notice is any carter going to take of the likes of us?'

'Not enough,' Flora said quietly.

'What *is* the matter with you?' Ralph Morwyn nudged his friend. The Duke and his son had both heaved a sigh of relief when the Duchess had risen and left the dining room. Now the men could enjoy their port and cigars free from female company.

'You've been grinning like a Cheshire cat all evening, Will!'

'There's thoughts of a girl behind a look like that, if I'm any judge.' The Duke narrowed his eyes against a gale of cigar smoke.

'At *last*.' Ralph took a healthy draught of port and immediately topped up his glass. 'I was beginning to think he'd spent too much time in the desert.'

'Duty comes before pleasure.' The Duke looked at his only surviving son meaningfully.

'I agree, your Grace, but everyone needs a little light relief now and again, don't you think?'

Ralph looked at William with undisguised astonishment.

'I don't believe you just said that, Will! You're not sickening for something, are you?'

'Good luck to you.' The Duke examined his cigar with satisfaction. 'Although you will spare a thought for the Duchess, won't you? We all know these things go on, but for a guest to get up to anything and get found out—well, it upsets the servants.'

'I understand, your Grace.'

'And be careful. You'll have quite enough to put up with in India without receiving tearful letters from home.'

'Yes, your Grace.'

'Never mind the helpful warnings, Pa. Let's get down to the really important stuff. Who is she, Will?'

'Oh, you wouldn't know her, Ralph.'

'I'll have you know I'm on excellent terms with all the young ladies within a twenty-mile point,' Ralph said with a relish that brought a wistful smile to his father's lips. 'I know! It'll be Lucy. Lucy Page-Smith. She's had her eye on you ever since you arrived, Will. Hooked you at last, has she? You've left it a bit late, that's all I can say. Mind you, she'll make up for lost time. She's always been a fast worker. They don't call her Lucy Lastic for nothing.'

William took a sip of his brandy, but the Duke was not so discreet.

'Ralph? Does that mean that you and she—?'

'I'll say.' He laughed craftily. 'Oh, I could tell you some tales—'

'From what I've seen, Pritchard's too much of a gentleman to be interested in stories like that, Ralph,' the Duke interrupted his son, before turning a wicked grin toward William. 'Pretty, is she?'

'A regular bobby dazzler, your Grace.'

'Blonde or brunette?'

'Auburn.'

'Redhead, eh?' Ralph filled his glass again. 'Like that corker of a little cook of ours!'

'No. Not at all,' William said quickly, noticing a sudden change in the Duke's expression. 'They're not a bit alike.'

Ralph had even more interest in the conversation now.

'Talking of Cookie, why don't we call her up here again now? We can thank her for the. . .for the—whatever concoction it was we've just had.'

'Shouldn't think she'd be down there. It's her afternoon off. William ran her home before lunch, didn't you?' the Duke said, causing William to study the swirling depths of his brandy as he muttered a reply.

'Wouldn't mind giving her a trial run myself,' Ralph mused acquisitively. 'Got a lot of the Lillian Gish about her, that one.'

The Duke tapped his finger on the table in admonition. 'Now you *know* what your mother thinks about you playing about with the staff, Ralph. You can always stoop and pick up nothing. Or something far more unpleasant, eh?' he finished with a throaty chuckle.

'Lucy Page-Smith *is* something unpleasant. Though I can't say I've ever noticed anything particularly red about her hair,' Ralph said thoughtfully.

The Marquis of Dayle was overflowing with good humour by the time he and William left the Duke some time later.

'Listen, Will.' He touched one finger to the side of his nose with some difficulty. 'Not a word to a soul, but I'm off out later. Coming?'

William looked at him. 'It's already past eleven. Where on earth can you be going at this time of night?'

'I met a pretty little girl at the races today, but her father put a block on it. You know what these boot-strap industrialists are like. We've been forced into a secret moonlight assignation.'

The glint in Ralph's eyes left William in no doubt of what sort of an assignation it was to be.

'Listen—your Lucy is a bit of a girl. Why don't we pick her up on the way and make it a game of mixed doubles?'

'Actually, I was thinking of having a relatively early night, Ralph.'

Ralph surveyed his friend wickedly. 'Can't stand the pace, eh?' Suddenly an uncomfortable thought struck him. 'Hey, you're not going to get too fond of old Luce, are you, Will? I'm being serious for once. She's not that sort of a girl. Don't go expecting her to wait for you, old scout. It's not in her nature. A generous girl, is our Miss Page-Smith. Not a loyal little pigeon like your Cherie.'

'For the last time, Ralph! Trying to pair me off isn't

funny any more!' William snapped irritably, in danger of losing his good humour as he supported his friend.

'Oh, come on! Everybody talks about the way she strips you down with her eyes!'

'Look, Ralph, will you shut up about Cherie Barclay?'

'Only if you tell me who your new light o' love is.'

'I'm not going to tell you because it wouldn't be fair on any of us. You know very well you can't keep secrets and when the word got out you'd end up having made her life a misery, and mine, and you'd be mortified.'

'Wouldn't!' Cackling with laughter, Ralph caught hold of William's arm, leading him away from the grand staircase. 'You can tell me. I'm the very heart and soul of discretion. Let's thrash it out over a bite to eat. I'm still hungry. Didn't think much of the amounts we got for dinner tonight.'

Still grumbling, he led the way into the shadowy depths of the kitchen corridor. William felt the first twinges of uncertainty.

'Do you think this is wise, Ralph? Wouldn't it be better to ring for something from your room?'

'The servants will all be in bed by now. Come on!'

William was still reticent and hung back. Ralph had already reached the kitchen door and shoved it open, blinking in the blinding light beyond.

'See? It's all right. There's nobody here, Will.'

With relief William went forward but Ralph had not finished speaking.

'Nobody except Mrs Westbury, that is.'

It was too late. William and Flora were facing each other across the brightly lit room before there was time for excuses.

Ralph was more interested in Flora than he was in

his friend's dismay. He crossed the kitchen to where
Flora, in slippers and dressing gown, was heating a
kettle at the stove.

'Good God, Mrs Westbury. We do keep you hard at
work. What's this? The night shift?' He grinned back
at William, but his friend was taking evasive action
around the outer edge of the kitchen.

'Where's the larder, Ralph? Tell me what you want
and I'll load up a tray.'

A lacquered papier mâché tray laid ready for the
morning stood on one of the side tables. William picked
it up and with a clatter of thick china removed the
crockery. Flora could not bear to look at him directly,
much less call out, but neither could she stand by,
knowing what he was doing. Pulling the kettle from the
range, she kept one eye on Ralph while hurrying across
the kitchen.

'No, sir. There are proper trays for use above stairs.'

She went to the silver cupboard, thankful that she
always kept her keys with her. Taking out a tea-tray,
she soon found napery and cutlery to go with it.

'Seems a lot of trouble to go to for a bit of ham and
egg pie,' Ralph said truculently.

'It's what I'm paid for, Master Ralph.'

As she laid the tray with the speed and accuracy
born of a careful apprenticeship, Ralph thought of
some fun. Perching on the edge of the table, he slid his
hand beneath her chin. Flora recoiled in horror, but his
grip tightened.

'You're not paid to be frightened of me.' He looked
into her eyes searchingly. 'Just checking. It looks as
though you're off the hook, Mrs Westbury. Master
William here has gone and got himself a red-headed
lady friend, but the only other information I've been
able to terrier out of him is that her eyes are blue, not

green. I reckon he was out with her this afternoon, but he's being damned secretive about the whole business. Did you pick up any hints about the affair when he swept you off in the Rolls?'

'No, sir. What would I be doing talking to a gentleman like Captain Pritchard?'

'I can't begin to imagine.' Picking up the silver tray with one hand, Ralph rolled from the table and sauntered off toward the game pantry. Flora followed him, waiting after she had unlocked the larder door to see the room safely lit. When William reached her side she was staring resolutely at Ralph's receding figure.

'I had to put him off the scent, Flora. He suspected, and nearly guessed. That's why I had to lie about the colour of your eyes.'

'Yes, sir.'

'There isn't anyone else.'

'No, sir.'

This wall of silence, thrown into relief by Ralph's discordant humming, was more than William could bear.

'It wasn't such a terrible thing to do, was it?'

'Of course not, sir.'

He was becoming exasperated.

'Then why are you being so distant?'

Flora checked that Ralph was busy before turning to William, eyes bright with shame and fury.

'Because I wouldn't have had you see me dressed like this and messing about with hot Bovril *for anything in the world*. I couldn't sleep for going over in my mind what happened this afternoon, and wondering if I looked all right. I gave up trying to sleep and came down here, and who should I meet but you, when I'm looking like *this*!'

'You look all right to me.'

Unthinkingly he had hurt her, and now he knew it.

'Oh, Flora—it doesn't matter.' He looked at her, expecting to be stuck for words but they came easily. 'Having your hair plaited suits you. You look. . .softer. Even more natural.'

'I look half-dressed.' Flora pulled her dressing gown closed at her throat, but her flush was prettier now.

'Can I see you again properly, then? Dressed up?'

'When? It's hopeless. I've used up all my free time for this week.'

'Tomorrow. At breakfast time. I'll miss the meal and meet you. At the pavilion. You'll have some time to spare then, won't you? Can I borrow that book you offered me? *Far from the Madding Crowd*? That can be the excuse.'

Ralph finished his inspection of the shelves and stood back to make sure that he had not missed anything.

'It'll have to be quick, William,' Flora whispered. 'Hello and goodbye.'

'It'll be worth every moment.'

His hand slid into hers, but they were on borrowed time. Ralph turned and began to bring his loaded tray back toward the door. William gave Flora's hand a squeeze before releasing it at the last minute.

'No chance of a bottle to go with this, I suppose?' Ralph looked at Flora over the tray that had once been laid out so neatly. The previously spotless cloth was now speckled with crumbs of pastry from the hefty chunks of game pie and the apple turnovers that were piled high on the plate. Flora looked into the thickness of Ralph's gaze and decided upon diplomacy.

'Mr Perry always keeps the keys to the cellar, Master Ralph.'

'Oh, never mind. I can snaffle a bottle from the library on the way up. Come on, Will. You can tell me all about the debauchery of your wild afternoon in the comfort of my dressing room,' he said in a crafty aside. 'Next stop the library for that bottle. . .'

Flora dutifully held the kitchen door open for them.

'Nine o'clock at the pavilion,' William murmured as he passed close by her.

'I'll try,' Flora said, without knowing how she would manage it.

The deceit next morning was easier than Flora had imagined. Once Upstairs breakfast had been despatched she refused her usual reviving cup of tea.

'I'm feeling the heat a bit, Mary. Make a start on reducing Wednesday's bread to crumbs for stuffing and I'll have a quick turn around the grounds to cool down.'

'If you keep over toward the lake there won't be any chance of them seeing you from the morning room, miss,' Mary said helpfully as Flora made her escape.

She reached the pavilion in record time. Luckily there was no one about, but that didn't stop Flora feeling sick with nerves. She had not had any appetite for breakfast and her empty stomach was now regretting that, too. Scanning the deserted park, she willed William to appear, although she could hardly bring herself to believe that he really would. It was too much to hope for.

An eternity passed, then she saw a movement among the trees. Relief soon turned to disappointment, then dread. It was Ralph Morwyn. He was strolling through the park in full evening dress, hands in his pockets and whistling tunelessly. Flora looked about for the quickest place to hide.

There was nowhere.

'Hello there! Hailing Mrs Westbury!'

Ralph's voice bounced through the woodland, startling a moorhen into noisy flight. His gait was deceptive, and before Flora could make her excuses he had joined her on the veranda of the pavilion.

'Can't say that I reckon much to this early morning walking business,' he said with his usual affability. 'What about you, Mrs Westbury? Lack of sleep catching up with you? Come out here to wake up, have you?'

He nudged her, but Flora could smell that his play-fulness owed a lot to strong spirits. She smiled politely, but took a step away from him.

'Oh, come on! Don't be shy!' Ralph flung his arm about her shoulders. 'I told you last night that you're not paid to be afraid of me. We should all be friends together.' He squeezed her companionably.

'Yes, sir.' Flora tried to free herself from his loose-limbed embrace. The pavilion faced away from the house. If William was on his way he would have no warning of Ralph's unscheduled presence. Flora would have to coax the Marquis out into the open where he could be seen.

'No—don't go. Here.' Reaching out, he grasped Flora's arm and swung her back into the shadow of the pavilion. 'I've got a proposition to put to you, Mrs Westbury.'

Flora backed toward the locked doors of the pavilion, but Ralph kept smiling.

'It's my friend. My very good friend William. He reckons he's got this girl, and for the life of me I can't work out who it is. Now, I saw him admiring your ankles the other evening. If you were to use a few of your feminine wiles on him—'

'I'm quite sure I don't know what you mean, Master Ralph.'

He was very close to her now, leaning against the

pavilion door. Flora could see the open pores on his coarsened skin and the thread-like red veins clouding his eyes.

'Don't give me that. A pretty girl like you? One look at those curls and dimples and I'd tell you anything. Actually, I'm not convinced that Will really has got a girl.' He hauled himself upright again. 'I reckon he's just got tired of my teasing. He's trying to put me off the scent. There's one way to find out, though. If I got the two of you together, and you made a bit of a play for him —'

'No, Master Ralph.'

'I'd pay you. What d'you reckon? A pound?'

'Master Ralph! I wouldn't stoop so low!'

'Oh, all right. A fiver, but that's my final offer. I'm not a charity.'

'But I *am* a good girl, Master Ralph.'

He grinned. 'I'll bet.'

Flora saw the look in his eyes, and was uneasy.

'I really must be going, Master Ralph. There's Upstairs luncheon to start —'

'Forget Upstairs luncheon.'

He kissed her, expertly and with an insistence that William had never shown. When the tip of his tongue pushed between her lips Flora was alarmed. Not even Alfred had taken a liberty like that.

She pushed him away, trying to keep her voice level.

'No, Master Ralph. I've told you. I'm not that sort of girl.'

'You are,' he murmured, taking a firmer hold of her. 'I know you are. I can feel it.' He kissed her again, and this time the insistence was unmasked. Forced back against the doors of the pavilion, Flora tried to lever him off but with no success. He was engulfing her, pawing at her now with hard, relentless fingers. Then he found bare skin.

Flora could not cry out. Her throat had constricted, choking off all but a pitiful mewing that sounded as though it was coming from a long way off.

Suddenly the thundering in Flora's ears was not the only sound.

'Sorry, I'm—'

Flora opened her eyes at the sound of William's voice, but he was lost in a blur of movement. He was on the veranda and Ralph was tumbling backwards off it in the same instant.

'Flora! Flora, are you all right? No, of course you aren't. Stupid question. . .' he said in a rush. With barely a glance at Ralph's prone and groaning body William went to her. He made a tentative attempt to rearrange her clothing, but could not help. Flora was frozen in time, reliving the instant that had expanded to fill her whole consciousness. The weight of him. The look in his eyes before she had shut out the sight. The awful, horrible sound of him—

'I'll take you up to the house.' William put out his hand and touched Flora's arm.

'I can't. . .'

'Yes, you can.'

Her legs would not move. He's ruined me, Flora thought. This is the vengeance. I'm paralysed for life.

Her eyes filled with tears.

'Flora.' William moved in close to her, working his hand between the pavilion door and the small of her back. 'It's over. Let me take you back to the house.'

A hollow moan rose from the ornamental grasses beyond the smashed surround of the pavilion's veranda. Flora shrank back still more as the stems began to shudder, disturbed by the movements of Ralph's painful recovery. Tears had started to trickle down her face, but she could not cry.

'I'll come back and sort him out properly in a minute.'

William's soft words to Flora were a stark contrast to those he spat at Ralph. 'Stay there until I come back, you swine.'

Flora tried to take a step forward but stumbled, and would have fallen if William had not been there to lift her into his arms.

He won't want me now, Flora thought in despair.

'Lean your head against me.'

It was an order. Flora obeyed, shutting her eyes to avoid the sight of William's grim disappointment.

It did nothing to shut out the awful memory of Ralph Morwyn. As they reached the house Flora found the strength to sob and suddenly could not stop.

'I'm sorry—' she cried, but if William understood he did not reply. Instead he barged straight through the back door of Alvoe Court and into the kitchen.

'Mrs Westbury has been overcome. Send for a doctor and see about some tea while I take her to her room.'

Flora neither knew nor cared what the reaction of the kitchen staff had been. It was only later that she realised how suspicious it must have looked when William did not need to wait for directions to her room.

Once upstairs he laid her on her bed. Sitting down on the edge, he took both of her hands in his.

'Flora, listen. If news of this gets out, it won't be Ralph who suffers.'

Flora had opened her eyes as he had started to speak and now looked at him in disbelief.

'You want me to keep quiet?'

'Yes.'

'You would put his feelings before mine?'

'Not Ralph's. Those of his mother and father. And your reputation.'

That's long gone now, Flora thought. How can he sit there so calmly asking me to deny everything?

'You want me to lie to the doctor when he comes? You want me to say that I just fainted?'

'Yes! but—'

'I won't! I'm ruined. I've got nothing left to lose now, thanks to your "friend". I'm *damned* if I'll lie to save Ralph Morwyn's skin!'

Her language shocked William almost as much as it shocked her. For once Flora did not care. If she didn't speak out, other girls would suffer at Ralph's hands in the future.

'Listen to me, Flora.' William's voice was dark and threatening. 'If you tell, it won't be Ralph that suffers. Men like him are supposed to act like goats with the staff. It's almost expected of them.'

'But it's not right!'

'I know it's not right!' He silenced her protest quickly. 'But you have to face facts. If you reveal any of this it will be you, and the Duke and Duchess, who will suffer. The Morwyn family have had troubles enough without their last remaining son bringing shame upon them.'

'If he gets away with it this time, he'll do the same thing again.'

William leaned forward and placed a kiss on her brow.

'Ralph Alvoe is not going to get away with anything,' he said firmly, patting her hand. 'I'm going to make quite sure of that. Right now.'

When he had gone, Flora hauled herself to the edge of her bed. Her legs still felt lifeless, but she made them work. There was only cold water left in the jug on her washstand, but she welcomed its numbing sting as she washed and washed herself, over and over again. Mary arrived with a cup of tea, but as soon as she had gone Flora went back to the basin. She felt sick.

Her working dress lay on the floor at her feet. She had to bring out a clean one, unable to handle the dress that Ralph Morwyn had defiled. Mary would have to collect it up with the rest of the washing.

Flora had pulled on her clean dress by the time the doctor arrived. He was a plump young man, taut with nerves. To conquer them he took off his spectacles from time to time and polished them on the merino jersey that was as colourless as his complexion. Despite these failings, his good humour and neat appearance almost betrayed Flora into confiding in him. She struggled with her conscience and William's warning as the doctor took her pulse and temperature. He questioned her professionally about her health in general, the weather in particular, then bit his lip.

'I am afraid that the time has come to be a trifle indelicate, Mrs Westbury. Is there any possibility that you might be—?' He stopped, clearly hoping that she would supply the information voluntarily.

Flora did not have the faintest idea what he was talking about. The doctor pressed on.

'Have you—? That is, Mrs Westbury—fainting fits can be an indication of—'

She saw him swallow hard. His indoor pallor was flushed with pink.

'A sign of pregnancy, Mrs Westbury.'

The bottom fell out of Flora's world for the second time in less than an hour. She had been so busy worrying about her present state that she had given no thought for the future. One look at her face and the hapless young doctor felt duty bound to carry on.

'Very well.' He looked away and swallowed hard again, relying on professionalism to see him through. 'If you aren't sure then perhaps I should examine you. If you could remove your skirt—'

He would guess. He would *know*.

'No,' Flora stated firmly, to the doctor's evident relief.

'I really ought to make sure if there's any doubt, Mrs Westbury,' he persisted, but nervously. 'Although I suppose I could manage like this. . .'

He palpated her abdomen gently but thoroughly through the thin fabric of her summer-weight uniform.

'No. I don't think so,' he said thankfully.

Overwhelming relief flooded through Flora.

'How on earth can you tell like that, Doctor?' she asked, relief making her talkative as she started to get up off the bed.

'Oh, it only actually works after you've had the suspicion for a bit,' he said, pleased that anyone should sound so in awe of his abilities.

'How long?'

'Well, if I could not detect anything and you've had no other symptoms apart from the fainting, then you are quite safe, Mrs Westbury. To the great relief of us both, I fancy. Although I cannot speak for Mr Westbury, of course.'

'He's dead,' Flora announced.

The young doctor was polishing his spectacles again but stopped to regard her closely at that revelation.

'In which case I am sorry for being indiscreet, Mrs Westbury. I did not intend to cause you any distress.'

'It was a long time ago. The event I thought might have got me into trouble was only very recent,' Flora murmured, hurriedly tying on a clean apron.

'Ah,' the doctor said thoughtfully. 'How recently would that be?'

Flora struggled with the truth. The doctor was already beginning to sound stern. She realised that William had been right. She would be the one to be judged and found wanting.

'Within the last day or so,' Flora muttered, staring at the floor in shame.

'In which case I can't let you off the hook so easily, Mrs Westbury,' the doctor snapped, suddenly efficient. 'Not until you have failed to see a course for at *least* six weeks.'

Flora felt as though she had been kicked in the stomach.

Luckily the sound of running footsteps outside and a rattling knock at the door saved her from having to try and think up any excuses. The doctor opened the door while she turned away to try and make sense of what he had said. She could not take it in. Six weeks of worry before she would know if her life was over. How on earth would she survive?

Her fingers went through the actions of pinning on her cap without her mind being there at all. Then Mary was breathless on the threshold, wringing her hands and hopping from foot to foot.

'If you please, Dr Pinkney, Master Ralph's in a bad way. Captain Pritchard found his car out on the road—there's been an accident. Seems like Master Ralph managed to crawl as far as the lake before passing out,' she added for Flora's benefit.

'Have you finished that stuffing?' Flora said sharply. Mary had expected her to be interested in the latest gossip, and was taken aback. The way Flora strode to the open door showed the doctor that he had outstayed his welcome too. He followed Mary out into the passage.

'I'll be down directly, Mary,' Flora called after her assistant, trying to soften the earlier blow with a gentler tone. 'And I must thank you too, Doctor. How much do I owe you?'

He backed away, shaking his head. 'Nothing, Mrs Westbury. The Duchess settles such matters. Just make sure that you don't become overheated again. The weather this year has been exceptionally bad for this sort of thing!'

The words were cheerful for Mary's benefit, but he wasn't smiling. Flora closed the door to give herself a couple of minutes' respite before she went back down to work. Mary would see the doctor safely through the house to the family's quarters. Her own faint would be explained away as a 'touch of the sun'. If only the truth were that simple.

Flora put her hands to her face, trying to scrub away Ralph's image. She had to compose herself and get back to work. There was nothing else for it. Work was the best cure for every problem. While she still/had a job, and hadn't been thrown out onto the streets. That was all she would be able to look forward to if her worst fears came true.

Flora looked around the neat little room that she had occupied for such a short time. There was one thing that work could not restore, and that was her peace of mind. If she had fallen for a child because of Master Ralph's stupidity all this would be snatched away from her. William had been right. She would be the one to suffer, not Ralph. It would mean instant dismissal.

No amount of good work could compensate an unlucky servant.

Chapter Eight

Less than twenty minutes later, Flora was back at work. The first pheasants had been hanging in the game larder for long enough, and luncheon marked their appearance on the menu. There would be plenty of time later in the season for fricassees and casseroles. These first birds of the season would be showing themselves to their best advantage, simply roasted. Young, tender and complemented by a savoury force-meat, they would be served with plenty of potato ribbons and served on a bed of fresh watercress. The tail feathers that had been carefully put to one side would be reinserted as decoration.

When they were finished, the birds looked a treat. Flora usually felt a tinge of envy along with pride at creating such a dish but today she felt nothing. She should have been hungry, having missed breakfast to get to the pavilion on time, but it felt as though she would never be able to face food again.

Flora was about to send the main course Upstairs when there was a commotion outside at the service lift. It was hot in the kitchen so the door had been left open, giving Flora a good view.

William was emerging from the service lift. While

one of the footmen unloaded trunks and baggage from the lift he advanced and knocked at the kitchen door.

The staff fell silent. Everyone immediately touched their caps and uniforms, instinctively checking their appearance. William did not look at Flora, but went straight to Mr Perry, the butler. After exchanging a few words with him William then looked directly at her, and Mr Perry stood aside to let him pass into the kitchen.

It wasn't only the sight of William in full uniform that had silenced the staff. The angry red swelling that was closing his right eye was also giving them pause for thought.

Flora did more than pause. She stared at him with growing horror. As he approached the kitchen table he brushed the back of his hand against his nose in a movement she had seen Alfred make so often.

'It's not bleeding,' she said faintly.

'I wondered. From the way you were looking at me.' His voice was insubstantial too, but gained strength as he saw the interest in Mary's eyes at the exchange. 'I came to see if you had recovered, Mrs Westbury.'

There was perfect poise in the perfect manners, but Flora could see the hurt in his eyes.

'Thank you, sir.'

Her glance slipped momentarily to the footman ferrying luggage out into the hall. There must have been a scene and William had been asked to leave. In the busy kitchen she could not ask, only wonder.

'I'm moving out,' he said with forced nonchalance. 'I'm off to stay with Mr Standish for a while. Until it's time for me to go off to India.' His voice had dropped, almost to a whisper.

Flora moved around to his side of the table, giving

the girls an abrupt signal for the salvers to be carried away to the service lift.

'Your face. . .'

'Walked into a door. You know how it is.'

Flora had done that the day after her marriage, and still remembered how it felt.

'Thank you again, Captain Pritchard,' she said with as much warmth as circumstances allowed.

'Regimental boxing champion three years running. You would have thought the door would have had more sense.' He smiled, and Flora felt herself die inside all over again.

He roused himself with a grimace. 'Well, I must be going. I have to make my excuses to the Duke and Duchess. And I've got a book to read.' His hand went to his pocket and he withdrew Flora's well-loved volume a little way. He must have rescued it from the pavilion. 'Got to get it back to a friend.'

Flora struggled to smile again, knowing that she would be unlikely to see either the book or Captain William Pritchard ever again.

He thanked all the staff for their care and attention, and then he was gone.

Desperate to blot out Ralph's attack, Flora worked. She kept to the kitchens, filling her days with industry and doing everything possible not to cross Ralph Morwyn's path. No task was too small to escape her attention. Stocktaking, clearing out all the cupboards again, consulting with Mr Stacey about table decorations or Mr Perry about suitable wines filled all the time she did not spend in cooking.

By Monday Flora was so tired that the journey home to Falgrave for her day off jogged her away into an uncomfortable sleep. Fortunately the carter woke her gently when they reached the Falgrave memorial fountain.

It was still early enough to be half-dark. A grey wash of morning threatened to submerge the cottages clustering around the village green, but here and there lamps glowed behind the tightly drawn curtains, beacons to a weary traveller. Flora took a few deep breaths of the cold, clear air then walked smartly up the road to Estate Cottages.

George Collinton already had the kettle boiling as she walked into the house. While she took off her hat and coat he took a clean cup and saucer from the dresser. After giving the tea a good swirl in the pot he poured out a cup for her.

'Want a bit of sugar in it, girl? Looks as though you're wasting away. Aren't they feeding you?'

'Not as well as I'm feeding them,' Flora replied dully.

'Well, here's something that might cheer you up. Came for you last week.'

He picked up a letter from the mantelpiece and handed it to Flora. 'Perhaps Lady Molly Berkhamstead wants you to go and work at Vallets after that big spread you put on for her!'

'Nobody writes to me,' Flora began until she realised what her father was handing to her.

It was another one of those tell-tale cream envelopes. The words 'By hand' had been printed above the address in handwriting that Flora recognised immediately. It was the same writing on the well-read letter that travelled everywhere with her, tucked safely into a corner of her handbag.

'Did you see who brought this?' She stared at the envelope as though opening it would destroy all her dreams.

'No. It was on the mat when I got home late one night.'

Her father tried not to look interested, but his curiosity soon got the better of him.

'Who's it from?'

'The vicar, I expect,' Flora said, thinking fast.

Her father laughed. 'Somebody else who's heard that you're a soft touch for good works? I suppose he'll want you to help out at some money-making do.'

'I expect so.' Flora flushed, but tried to sound offhand. She knew that there would be little work done around her father's house before she had read it, but reading it was going to take a lot of courage. 'Now, you ought to be getting off to work, Dad. You don't want to be late. I'll see you at eleven.'

'Right. But hadn't you better open your letter? It might be something important, and, like I say, it's been here a few days already.'

Evidently Flora was not going to be allowed to get away with reading William's curt dismissal in private. Trying to make sure that her face hid her feelings, she picked up a clean knife from the table and slit the letter open carefully.

There were two sheets of paper inside. That was a surprise. A snub, however polite, would only have taken a couple of lines.

The letter itself was even more of a shock.

Dear Flora,

I am so sorry for what happened. How can I apologise sufficiently? Ralph's behaviour was inexcusable, but I was thoughtless in suggesting such an isolated meeting place, and then being so late for our meeting. I had seen Ralph's car smashed into the estate wall and feared the worst. If I hadn't stopped to look for him, I might have found him sooner.

I wish we could have said goodbye properly. In fact I wish we did not have to say goodbye at all. May I see you again? The Reverend will ask your father to forward this letter to you, so if you would like us to meet again, please reply as soon as possible direct to the vicarage at Branxmere. If I have not heard from you by next Monday I shall take it that you don't want to see me again. After what has happened I shall quite understand, but I should like to try and make amends.

'Long letter,' her father said, strolling to Flora's side and trying to see what it said.

Flora edged away, concealing her prize. She was savouring the 'Yours sincerely' and still had the luxury of a postscript to enjoy:

P.S. Whatever your decision I shall return your book as soon as I have finished reading it. It may also put your mind at rest if I tell you that Ralph did not suspect that you were waiting for me, so your job at least would seem to be safe.

For how long? Flora wondered. The doctor's words had been haunting her every waking moment. What if Ralph had got her into trouble? There were still weeks of worry to go before she could be certain that she was safe. She folded the letter up again and put it back into its envelope, pushing both deep into her pocket.

'Aren't you going to tell me what's in it?' Her father looked at the unusual brightness of her eyes and wondered.

'No time.' Flora was already pulling her coat and hat from the pegs behind the door. 'The Reverend wants me over at Branxmere vicarage first thing this morning. To discuss the harvest festival,' she added artlessly.

'We've already had one in Falgrave. Don't different churches all have it at the same time, girl, like Christmas?'

Be sure your sins will find you out, Flora thought bitterly.

'It doesn't sound like it. Mr Standish wants the Branxmere festival to be the best yet, and he wants to talk about the work I did here in Falgrave.'

'That sounds a bit like poaching to me,' her father said, curious with concern.

I shall never go to heaven, Flora thought as she kissed her father then hurried out of the house. She could only wonder at her capacity for falsehood.

Breakfast was not going down well at the vicarage. William was persevering with the compulsory kipper. He was not helped by remembering Ralph's old jibe that the things had more bones than a corset.

'...then I thought that we might try out that pool below Beck's Bridge,' the vicar was saying enthusiastically. 'I've seen a quite magnificent old trout hanging over a shelf there. He eluded my hook all summer. If you visit in season next time, William, we could try for him, or one of his offspring. Then we could present Mrs McSweeney with a trout for our tea!'

Not more fish, William groaned inwardly.

'Topping idea, Vicar.'

'It's a very good spot for swimming,' the vicar went on. 'I find that a bout of hard physical exercise helps to put things into perspective. The cold is a wonderful cure for—well, it does help to take one's mind off the occasional pressing problem, shall we say.'

He had been watching William intently, and now

patted his visitor's wrist. Grateful of a chance to stop pretending to enjoy the kipper, William put down his knife and fork.

'There was nothing in the post for me this morning, Vicar?'

Standish leaned forward with a smile.

'Young men these days spend far too much time chasing after any pretty little thing in a skirt! Far too much time.' He returned to his breakfast cheerfully. 'There are other things in life, you know.'

'Yes,' William sighed, 'but all of a sudden it feels as though I've been spending far too much of my life absorbed in all those "other things" lately.'

There was a knock at the door, and Mrs McSweeney entered.

William had been prepared to make another valiant effort on the kipper, but he was too late. Mrs McSweeney swept the plate from beneath his knife and fork. In a second pass she then relieved him of his cutlery as well.

'You had better come down to the kitchen and find yourself something else to eat,' she said crisply. '*I'm* certainly not cooking you anything else this morning.'

'That's quite all right, Mrs McSweeney,' William said with hungry relief. 'I'll wait for the Reverend to finish his breakfast, and then we'll be off out.'

'You'll come to the kitchen for a good breakfast. Nobody leaves this house without one.'

The housekeeper stalked back to the door, her tray full of the remains of his meal. William was quick to see the vicar's expression and leapt up to open the door for her.

'The good lady is right, William.' Mr Standish winked at him. 'The McSweeney family have been keeping the chill out of the clans for centuries, haven't they? With the aid of nothing more formidable than a good English breakfast.'

The taunt was not lost on Mrs McSweeney, who stared at the vicar stonily.

'You'd better shift yourself, young man,' she addressed William as she swept past him. 'This isn't a come-when-you-like restaurant, you know!'

William took his leave of the vicar and followed Mrs McSweeney out into the hall. As soon as the dining-room door was shut she underwent a remarkable transformation.

'Quickly, then! Your young lady is waiting!'

'Flora?'

'She's in the kitchen. Don't let *him* know.' The housekeeper jerked her head back toward the door. 'He's sure to get on his high horse.'

The kitchen was on the other side of the house, well away from the dining room. William carried the tray, wishing that Mrs McSweeney would walk faster. Only when they reached the kitchen door did he hang back.

'After you, Mrs McSweeney.'

'Coward.' She bridled at his manners with a twinkle. Pushing the kitchen door open wide, she announced him with all the solemnity of Mr Perry at Alvoe Court.

'Captain William Pritchard, Mrs Westbury.'

'Flora!'

William went to the table and put down the tray while Flora looked nervously toward Mrs McSweeney. The housekeeper cleared the tray, and went to scrape the kipper remains into some newspaper.

'I shall be in the scullery washing the dishes.' She spoke sternly although there was a smile in her eyes.

William's first impulse was to take Flora in his arms, but her appearance had a new fragility about it. She was pale—'all eyes', as Mrs Fielding might have said.

'When I didn't get any reply to my letter I thought that you must have given up on me, Flora.'

She shook her head. 'I didn't see the letter until I got home this morning.'

'The vicar never gave your father the message to forward it,' William decided with a tight-lipped glance at the kitchen door. 'That doesn't surprise me.'

'Bacon and eggs?' Mrs McSweeney returned to the kitchen carrying a fat-blackened frying-pan. 'For two?'

William accepted on Flora's behalf. 'You look as though you need building up,' he said softly. When her wan smile did not reassure him he pressed on. 'Will you be free for supper this evening?'

'As free as she's been for breakfast this morning by the look of her,' Mrs McSweeney said over the chuckle of frying bacon.

'Oh, yes.' Flora's reply was eager enough but her gaze was restless.

'I'd like to see how you intend getting *that* past the vicar,' Mrs McSweeney said.

'I don't intend to. This isn't going to be some hole-and-corner affair.' William looked at Flora quickly, sensing that it had been a poor choice of words. She looked away.

'I'm so glad you've come, Flora. If you like I could gain us some extra time together, rather than just dinner tonight. I shouldn't like to impose on the time that you want to spend with your father, but—'

'I see him every week,' Flora said quickly. 'This might be the last time you and I will be together.' She coloured at such an admission, but William was smiling.

'Keep our guest entertained, Mrs McSweeney. I'll go and fetch your book, Flora, and sort something out with the vicar.'

He strode out of the room, leaving the door to swing shut behind him.

'I hope you don't take advantage of every poor young man you meet, Mrs Westbury,' the housekeeper said after some minutes of silence in the kitchen.

'Oh, no, madam.' Flora's genuine shock at such a thought was proof enough for Mrs McSweeney, but she had a harsh reputation to uphold.

'I suppose that means you don't know how he came about that black eye, then?' The housekeeper broke an egg into her pan and continued without waiting for Flora to reply. 'Still, it won't be the first time one of the vicar's waifs has turned up here the worse for wear. My only surprise is that one of them should have passed muster in a big house for so long.'

Flora had to leap to William's defence.

'You can hardly call Captain Pritchard a waif, Mrs McSweeney.'

'One of the vicar's lame ducks, then.' The housekeeper took a plate from the warming drawer and dealt Flora a helping of crisp brown bacon topped with a perfectly cooked egg. Putting the plate down before Flora, she handed out cutlery from the kitchen drawer then started to carve slices of bread to accompany the meal.

Flora picked up her knife and fork but looked at Mrs McSweeney in confusion.

'What sort of a lame duck?'

'You don't know?' The housekeeper concentrated on cutting the loaf of bread, then realised that she had said too much to avoid at least a partial explanation. 'Master William—' here she mouthed the words almost silently '—*doesn't have a father*!'

'I see,' Flora said darkly, trying to look as though she

was a woman of the world and interested only in her unwanted breakfast.

'That's not his fault,' Mrs McSweeney said quickly, then realised that Flora did not look as though she blamed him in the slightest. 'He's a good chap. One of the few to come back and thank the vicar. Part of the Reverend's salary goes to a home for fallen women in the London parish where he started his ministry. The Mission.'

'In Kilburn,' Flora said as realisation dawned.

Mrs McSweeney looked relieved. 'Then Master William has told you all about that?'

'No. He said he came from Kilburn, that was all.'

'In which case perhaps least said, soonest mended. Although I'll tell you this—I've seen a few of the vicar's waifs come and go in my time, but Master William— he's the best so far.'

A distant echo of the dining-room door closing started Mrs McSweeney buttering the slices of bread more furiously.

'Yet to think some poor girl might have been forced to let him die in a ditch when he was born. Doesn't bear thinking about, does it?' she murmured as William's insistent tread drew nearer.

'No.'

The bacon and egg had turned to ashes in Flora's mouth.

'I hope you're a good girl.' Mrs McSweeney paused in her buttering. Flora put another forkful of food into her mouth. The housekeeper wouldn't expect a reply if her mouth was full.

'Although I'm sure Master William will have learnt a lesson from his own lack of a father.'

'Bound to have,' Flora murmured. It was not William

that she was worried about in that direction. It was Master Ralph.

William knocked at the kitchen door before entering.

'That's settled. The day is my own, but the Reverend isn't very happy.'

'I can imagine,' Mrs McSweeney said, but Flora missed the look that passed between them.

He handed Flora her book, which she put carefully into her handbag with his two letters. Then he sat down at the kitchen table, smiling as usual as the housekeeper went to fetch his breakfast.

'Let's not waste a minute of it, Flora. What would you like to do?'

After the tantalisation of the kipper William wasted no time in demolishing bacon and eggs. He did not notice the unusual quality of Flora's silence for some time. When he did look up, his smile was undimmed.

'Flora?'

'Dad can fend for himself this morning, but I must get his dinner ready for one o'clock, so I shall have to go home first.' Past ditches and drains, she thought with growing dread.

'That isn't a problem. We could take a walk to Falgrave across the fields. You could show me the sights, then while you get the dinner ready I can go and have a drink. In the Porter Stores, isn't it?'

'You remembered that?' Flora was surprised.

'I'm a quick learner.'

William smiled at her across the table and Flora felt her heart break. He must know better than most what disgrace there was in a girl's ruination. If there *was* a baby and he got to hear about it, any letters there might have been would stop.

She would be dropped like a hot potato.

William laid his knife and fork neatly on his empty

plate, looking across to the meal that Flora had barely touched.

'Flora? Are you all right?'

'Yes. I'm feeling the heat a bit. That's all.'

'Come on. Let's escape.' He stood up, reaching across the table for her hand.

'Wait, can't you? The lassie's hardly touched her food!'

'Ah, but I've eaten all mine, Mrs McSweeney. That's usually your only concern.' He was teasing the housekeeper gently.

'Go on. Clear out of my kitchen, the pair of you! It's a good job I haven't had my own breakfast yet. It'll save on the waste,' she said with good-natured annoyance.

William took Flora through the house toward the front door of the vicarage. He was dressed in the same clothes he had worn for their outing to the pictures—a colourful jumper and lightweight trousers. At the coatstand he picked up his jacket, but paused before putting on his hat.

'I think perhaps we ought to put in an appearance at the lion's den before leaving. Do you feel up to an introduction?'

Flora nodded.

'You do seem terribly pale, Flora. Are you sure you've had enough to eat?'

His hand was already on the handle of the immaculately polished dining-room door.

'Yes.'

After knocking on the door William took her hand, and they entered together. Flora was overwhelmed by the number and variety of books lining the shelves and spilling onto chair seats, the table and every other horizontal surface. She was so busy looking about her

that the Reverend only caught her attention when he
stood up to acknowledge her.

'This is Mrs Flora Westbury, sir.'

William stood back and Flora wondered what she
was supposed to do. The Reverend peered over his
spectacles at her, his expression inscrutable. Flora
stepped forward and bobbed a brief curtsey.

'We're going for a walk,' William said cheerfully.
The vicar gave a small cough and picked up a neatly
folded newspaper from the nearest pile of paperwork.

'Tell Mrs McSweeney if you intend to take your
meals elsewhere,' the vicar said, shaking out the folds
of the newspaper then glancing at William over the top
of his spectacles. 'And *don't* do anything you could not
tell your mother about.'

'No, sir.'

William took Flora's hand and led her back to the
door. The Reverend rustled his newspaper irritably,
and Flora looked back to see that he was glaring at
their clasped hands.

'William?'

'Yes, sir?'

'Remember what I have said.'

William let go of Flora's hand, offering his arm
instead. Only when they had left the house and passed
out of sight of the windows did he take her hand again.

'You wouldn't think I was a grown man, would you?'
He laughed. 'Although the Reverend is a good old
bird. He's been very good to my mother, and there's
no doubt that he is an excellent host. It's the least I can
do to humour him.'

'It's good that there's someone to take care of you
while you're so far from home.'

'I'll be even further away from home soon. Who will
care for me then?'

Cherie Barclay, Flora thought bitterly.

'You'll find someone. I shall be the one left without anybody.'

They had reached the vicarage gate and William opened it for her. Stepping out onto the lane, he put his hand over hers as it lay on his arm.

'Will you miss me, Flora?'

His voice had the same haunting quality as his eyes.

'Of course I shall.'

'I can't ask you to wait for me—it's too long. It wouldn't be fair. But I really should like you to write to me until the time comes that you find a regular. Let me know as soon as someone else comes along with a claim on you. I shouldn't like to keep writing after you've tired of the correspondence.'

'You must promise to do the same.'

Her words were hollow—a formality. Flora knew that there would be no other young man for her. William was the only one that she wanted, and she would have to let him go if she had fallen for Ralph's baby.

She shook herself sharply. There would be no question of letting him go—any man disappeared as soon as he heard about that sort of calamity. She had seen it happen to girls in service before.

William's words broke into the grim silence of her thoughts.

'Flora, I'm worried about you. What is it? Are you ill?'

'No.'

He stopped, and by putting his hands onto her shoulders brought her round to face him.

'If you didn't really want to come out with me today you should have said. I would have understood.'

The secret was lodged inside her like a stone, pressing against her ribs and throat. If only she could tell him how worried she was. It would release him, and ease her awful pain.

'I'm not looking forward to seeing you go off to India, William. That's what it is.'

He did not reply. Flora looked across the short turf of the fields that edged the lane.

'Mushrooms,' she said faintly, trying to deflect the piercing stare that she knew he was directing at her. 'I noticed a late crop on the way here. Could we stop while I pick some for Dad's dinner?'

'Of course. You could have asked Mrs McSweeney for a basket.'

He took a fresh white handkerchief from his pocket.

'We can put them in this. There can't be a pastime more English than gathering mushrooms. I'll take the memory with me.'

There was a stile in the hedge and he went to it, helping Flora over before following her toward a large patch of mushrooms. Crouching down, he began to pick the largest, soon making a good pile of them in the centre of his large handkerchief.

When Flora made no move to help he looked around at her.

She was in tears, silent sobs shaking her body so that William left the mushrooms and dashed to her side.

'Cheer up, Flora. It's not the end of the world. Just the other side of it!'

His attempt at humour only made her tears flow faster. He started to say something else, but Flora could bear the burden no longer.

'I think I'm going to have a baby. . .'

William made a sound as though all the breath had been knocked out of him. Flora could not look up.

Consumed by her own guilt and fear, she did not want the sight of his horror to add to her own.

After a long time, when the initial outburst of her grief had ebbed, she felt a tentative hand on her shoulder.

'I don't know what question to ask first, Flora.'

'Neither do I.'

He sighed. Laying one hand on her hair, he pulled her into an embrace. It was the last thing that Flora had expected and the simple charity of the gesture released more tears. He held her lightly, stroking her hair and murmuring things that in her distress Flora could not bring herself to hear. Finally, when her tears had drained away, Flora rested exhausted against his chest, feeling the rapid but steady beat of his heart.

'Don't worry,' he said at last. 'I know exactly what to do. We'll get married. As soon as possible. Come on — let's go and find your father.'

Chapter Nine

Flora looked up at him in horror. 'Dad'll *kill* me!'

'Not if we're quick.'

'But *marry*? You and me?' Her tearful desperation had given way to complete confusion.

William was already leading her over to where the heap of mushrooms lay. 'Of course. It's not uncommon. Some of the men in the ranks have done it. There's a special arrangement available, I believe.'

He sounded casually confident, as though this sort of thing happened every day. What he didn't say was how such marriages of convenience turned out. For a man to get shackled to a girl he hardly knew was bad enough, but when the baby wouldn't even be his. . .

'We'll find out the details from the Reverend,' William continued, 'and then—'

'No.'

'No?' William's expression changed abruptly, but he managed to make his next words more controlled and considered. 'You don't want me.'

Flora shook her head.

'I can't let you marry me, William. You'll ruin your career, and people will talk—'

'Do you think I care about *that*?' For once, he had

snapped. Flora flinched, remembering Alfred's volatile temper. William saw the fear and put one hand to his eyes.

'I—I'm sorry, Flora. It's just that. . .well, my mother found herself in a similar position. I wouldn't wish my fate on any child.'

The truth was emerging, and the price was high. In the face of his inner torment at the admission Flora pushed her own worries to the back of her mind. She reached out and touched him gently. When he made no movement Flora moved a little closer to him, slipping her arm around his shoulders.

'You don't have to marry me,' she said evenly, although terrified of what would happen if he didn't. 'You can't. You mustn't. Think of all your grand friends, and your family—'

'My mother was only an ordinary country girl who made one mistake too many. I don't have any rights to those "grand friends", as you call them. Mother always warned me not to try and rise above my station. It looks as though she was right all along.'

'I knew I should never have told you.' Flora shook her head, screwing his handkerchief into a damp ball between her nervous fingers.

'You did the right thing,' he murmured. 'And now I intend to do likewise. You and I are getting married.' He stated this so firmly that Flora knew there could be no arguing about it. She couldn't begin to understand why he was acting in this way, but confusion was giving way to relief. It had to. Marriage would be her only chance of escaping lifelong shame.

'But—we couldn't possibly. . .' she began faintly, but afraid that he might see sense and agree.

'What's the matter?' he asked gruffly. 'Don't you like me?'

'Of course I do!' Flora was quick to reassure him. 'It's just that. . .well, I'm so worried that I'm not even thinking straight any more. I don't even know for certain yet whether. . .'

Her voice trailed away, but William's voice was brisk and efficient with relief.

'That was one of the questions that I didn't know how to ask you, Flora.'

Of all the things to happen. Flora would never have thought that she could be so stupid. To have let herself get into a situation where Ralph Morwyn of all people could take advantage. . .

William gathered up the mushrooms then led her back to the stile. Then he sat her down with her back to the deserted lane. While Flora searched for her own handkerchief he stared into the hedge bottom, one foot on the bottom rail of the stile.

'You don't have to go into details yet if you don't want to,' he said gently, 'but was it that business with Ralph? Was I too late?'

Flora nodded, pleating the hem of her handkerchief into creases.

William gave another long exhalation.

'I'll *kill* him. A few cracked ribs are as *nothing* to what I'll do to him now.'

'No, William, you mustn't. It was my fault, waiting around there in the open.'

'It comes to something when a girl can't stand alone in safety.'

William took out a cigarette and lit it, but without much enthusiasm for the act.

'Was that the only time?'

'Yes!' Flora started up indignantly but William calmed her.

'You might be lucky yet, then, if you're still not

certain. Ralph's said in the past that a chap doesn't have to be careful every single time. Mind you, I wouldn't trust anything that rat said now. When will you know for certain?'

'The doctor said about six weeks, William.'

He raised his eyebrows.

'Why so long?'

'Well. . .you know. . .'

'No? What?'

He was not making things any easier. Flora dug her toes into the dew-damp grass and muttered something about signs. Still perplexed at the delay, William took a pull on his cigarette and grimaced.

'I shall be halfway to India by then.' Grinding his unwanted cigarette into the nearest fencepost, he took a seat beside Flora on the stile.

'Listen, Flora. The best thing we can do is to get married before I go. Then you can leave here as my wife and no one will be any the wiser.'

'William, we hardly know each other!'

'What is the alternative? Think about it. A home for unmarried mothers, then nothing. You'd be unlikely to be able to keep the baby even if you wanted to. And you'd have to start your career all over again. With no references. Come away with me. It's the only way.'

Flora thought of the months and years of loneliness that would follow if she lost the man she already imagined that she loved so much, but common sense told her to shake her head.

'No. It wouldn't be fair on you, William. What about your girl, Cherie?'

He pulled a face. 'For heaven's sake! You're as bad as Ralph. Can't you forget about her?'

'You'd have more in common with her than you've got with me.'

'I'm not asking Cherie Barclay to marry me. I'm asking you,' William said, dangerously close to losing his temper. 'If you're not keen enough on me, then there's only one alternative. You'll simply have to move to London and have it there.'

'London?' Flora was aghast. It might have been as distant as India.

'Then you can have it adopted easily.'

Flora had no thought for children, much less any unborn baby of her own, but she had to speak out at that.

'Give a baby away? Oh, I couldn't!'

'You'd have to, Flora. If you don't marry me. The poor little thing would be handicapped for ever if you tried to bring it up on your own. Only an exceptionally lucky child can surmount the obstacle of illegitimacy. I know,' he finished quietly, looking down. His discarded cigarette butt showed very white in the dusty detritus of the hedge bottom.

Flora wondered what to say. Her own troubles, still only hinted at as yet, were nothing compared with the real disaster that William had managed to escape from.

'My mother got into trouble when she lived around here. Fortunately Mr Standish had only recently moved to Branxmere from a parish in London. He knew who to contact and what to do. He sent Mum to the Mission in Kilburn where she's stayed ever since.'

'You don't have much of a city accent,' Flora said, trying to take her mind off her own troubles.

'I had that thrashed out of me during the first term at boarding school. A scholarship boy with an East End accent—the bullies thought it was Christmas. Until I taught myself to fight back.' For the first time there was a hint of pride in his voice.

Flora hesitated, then reminded herself that this was

the man who had had offered to stand by her. She put her arm around him.

'Have you ever found out who your father was?'

'The vicar was dead set against it, so I didn't pursue the matter. You said that there's a nasty piece of work called Pritchard in the area. I don't think I need look any further, do you?'

'Oh, Will, but he must be old enough to be your grandfather!' Flora managed a smile.

William looked at her narrowly, then put his arm around her and gave her a little squeeze.

'Why on earth did Ralph have to pick on a poor little innocent like you?'

He kissed her hair and Flora leaned against him.

'Don't worry, Flora. I'll look after you.'

Fine words cost nothing. Flora wondered if he would.

Handing her the mushrooms, he took her across the fields to Falgrave. Flora was surprised that he was so certain of the way and wondered aloud if his mother had told him much about the place.

'Mum rarely mentions her early life. What little I know has come out in dribs and drabs over the years. I took my bearings from the church tower and that old cedar. I remember them from the day I brought you here in the Rolls.'

'That tree is growing in front of the Manor, where I had my first job.' Flora sighed. There would be no cooking for dinner parties and bridge afternoons now. 'Why don't you stay and have dinner with Dad and me, William? It'll be all right—as long as you don't say anything about—well, you know. . .'.

If she must cater for small numbers in the future she might as well get some practice in now.

'I'm quite happy to try for something at the pub,' he said affably, but Flora was horrified at the idea.

'You should hear what Dad has to say if a stranger strays into the Porter Stores on his own! The locals are very suspicious of strangers. I wouldn't want you to risk it.'

'It's all a bit different from London.' He squeezed her arm. 'It doesn't matter there if a chap has three heads as long as he stands his round. It's a bit like an officers' mess—a great social leveller, with everyone on first-name terms.'

'That explains why you fitted in so well up at Alvoe Court, then. I would have thought that any ordinary chap would have stuck out like a sore thumb.' Flora started to correct herself but William waved away her apology.

'It also explains our first meeting, Flora. I don't volunteer information about my home life easily, and as far as I know Ralph neither knows nor cares much about my family history. That doesn't mean to say that I'm ashamed of it, though. Quite the reverse. I was ashamed of arriving at Alvoe Court unwashed and unshaven after some trouble with the trains. A ten-mile walk followed by a lift on a milk cart is no recipe for sartorial elegance.'

'You always look very smart,' Flora said loyally. 'Too smart for farmyard visiting, that's for sure,' she added as they approached the village of Falgrave.

The footpath ran past the wall of the Barton farm-yard and she ran forward to look down into the yard.

'Dad! Have you got a minute?'

George Collinton emerged from the byre, wiping his hands on a piece of sacking. He was in his working clothes, respectable but soiled with honest work. As befitted the head dairyman, he was wearing his hat.

'I've brought William back with me, Dad,' Flora said pinkly as William joined her beside the wall.

'Ah.' George Collinton advanced and offered his hand to William. 'Glad to see you again. I've been thinking—you any relation to Gully Pritchard over at Westing?'

Flora and William shot a look at each other and Flora interrupted her father's train of thought.

'Can William stay to dinner, Dad? There will be enough—we've picked some mushrooms to eke it out a bit and there's plenty of potatoes in the sack.'

'Course he can stay. We can go down the pub afterwards, if you like.' George surveyed his new acquaintance appreciatively. 'Gully's working at the sawpits. At least, he was there yesterday. Thirsty work, so we'll probably bump into him down the Stores.'

Flora could imagine the scene. Gully Pritchard's hot temper, fuelled by the local brew and inflamed by the mention of a fallen woman of the village, would probably lead to a riot. She knew that William was well able to defend himself, but did not want to risk it. She caught hold of his arm protectively.

'William's going away soon, Dad. You wouldn't want to take up all his time, would you?'

George Collinton grinned and took a step back towards the byre. 'Of course not. Just you go carefully. And mind your manners, Flora!'

He raised his eyes meaningfully at William.

'I think that is what they call a fatherly warning,' William said as they strolled away toward the estate cottages.

'I shan't need that ever again.' Flora looked around the deserted village for any sign of eavesdroppers.

'I suppose that's the best way,' William said quietly.

Flora was unusually quiet all through dinner, but her father hardly noticed. He was far too busy talking to

William. When the meal was over they left Flora to the washing up and went off to the Porter Stores together like old friends. Flora didn't expect them to be gone long. As soon as William asked to marry her, that would be it. Her father would realise why, and come storming back to throw her out of the house.

No estate worker could risk associating with what Sir Hubert and many others would call a fallen woman. Standing by a daughter in trouble would mean loss of the tied cottage, and at his age her father couldn't risk that.

Time went on. Flora could not simply sit around waiting for the axe to fall. She made apple dumplings with some of the big yellow-streaked Emperor Alexander apples from the store. They would be good hot or cold, after she had been thrown out. As she was sure she would be.

She was just about to slide the dumplings into the oven when there was a sound outside. It was her father—laughing. Flora closed the oven door on the dumplings and went to the back door, frantically wiping the flour from her hands.

'Congratulations!' her father announced, enveloping her in a hug.

'You don't mind?' Flora managed, watching William's face. He was looking delighted too.

'Well, you hopping off to the other side of the world isn't so clever, no—but apart from that I'm thrilled for you, girl!'

India. Flora had forgotten that.

She looked at William, and wondered what on earth she had done.

The next few days went past in a blur. William helped her write a resignation letter to the Duchess, and went back to Alvoe with her that evening to stand by her as it was delivered.

The Duchess was furious. William offered to pay the fees of an agency cook until a new permanent member of staff could be found, but that suggestion only made things worse. The Duchess had been deceived, which was bad enough. After the compliments she had received for the catering at her bridge party it was Flora she wanted in the kitchens, not some untried amateur.

Flora kept her head down while William tried to diffuse the Duchess's fury. He was holding Flora's hand tightly, but now she wondered whether that support was enough. This awful scene was putting an end to her working life, and for as long as Flora could remember her work had been all that she lived for.

Strangely, the only thing that the Duchess did not accuse Flora of was falling for a baby. Flora was glad. She tried to push all thoughts of her troubles to the back of her mind, but the awful shame of it kept struggling up to wash over her. To have the Duchess discovering the whole awful truth would have been too much to bear.

Flora was also glad that her mother wasn't alive to see this awful day. Many years ago Flora had been given the dreadful warning that if she ever got into trouble she would be turned out of the house straight away—and she had believed it.

William arranged for Flora to leave Alvoe immediately. She went back to live at Falgrave until the wedding. The atmosphere at the big house would have been too much to bear, and there was a lot to get ready.

Soon after William's proposal he presented her with a list of things she would need for life in India. This began with six calico nightgowns and itemised the number and type of every piece of clothing Flora would need, right down to petticoats, stays and combinations. Flora didn't know whether to be glad or sorry that the list was written in flowery female handwriting. William must have got it from someone. She couldn't help wondering if that someone wasn't Cherie Barclay.

Flora was able to provide most of the things on the list, which surprised her. Nearly all the requirements seemed so ordinary—old-fashioned even: stout walking shoes and boots, thick stockings, a mackintosh and an umbrella. The real surprises came at the end of the list.

'"Four tennis gowns, one pair of tennis shoes and one riding habit."' She read out the last remaining requirements. 'Well, I shan't need any of those.'

'Yes, you will,' William corrected her. 'There's nothing much else to do out there for the ladies.'

Another shadow of foreboding fell upon Flora.

'William, I can't play tennis! And the nearest I've ever come to riding a horse is clambering onto Johnny Onion's donkey. And that was more than a dozen years ago!'

'You'll learn. I'll get someone to teach you.'

The determination that Flora had once found attractive now gave a sinister edge to William's voice. It was almost as though she would have no choice but to learn to do all the things an officer's wife was expected to do, and be expected to like it. Flora was sure that she would not.

'Don't worry,' he added. 'You'll soon pick it all up by watching the others. It's not as though anyone will be expecting you to get up to anything energetic for a while, anyway.'

The baby. Flora had almost managed to forget the

real reason for all this planning and packing. William was doing her a favour, after all.

'Yes, William,' she said, secretly wondering how she would manage to live in his debt for the rest of her life.

William took her to Gloucester to buy the last few things on the list. This included a riding habit, although Flora wondered whether it would still fit her in a year's time. All the expense terrified her, but she had at least managed to provide her own tennis and tea gowns. Cook at the Manor had come to the rescue there. Copies of *Punch* handed down from Sir Hubert and his wife had provided lots of sketches of what young women in society were wearing. Flora had proved to have a good eye for a pattern, and had made enough simple dresses to complete her India wardrobe.

Without a job and with all the circumstances surrounding it, Flora could not bear to make a splash over the wedding. With Alfred, marriage had been the thing to do before going off to war. Everyone had been doing it. With William it was the decent thing. An obligation.

The marriage itself was as quiet as it could be. Flora had been desperate that old Mrs Westbury should know nothing about it, so nothing had been said in the village. The cottage curtains in Falgrave twitched enough when Flora's father led her, William and Mrs McSweeney into his house in the middle of a working day, all dressed in their Sunday clothes.

Flora and Mrs McSweeney had put on a good spread between them. There was baked ham, salad, sandwiches made with real butter and filled with bloater paste or cream cheese, and even an iced sponge to do duty as a wedding cake. Flora had been up since four o'clock that morning getting it all ready, and now couldn't face any of it.

'Cheer up.' William put his arm around her, openly showing off his new position as her husband. 'You'll need a smile for the photographer.'

'Oh, no,' Flora muttered. 'Surely you don't want a photograph?'

'Of course. To remind us of the day.' William was still smiling. Flora couldn't imagine why.

'I'd like to send the Reverend one, as well.'

'Why didn't he come today?' Flora asked. 'I thought you were a favourite of his.'

William stopped smiling. Instead he exchanged a look with Mrs McSweeney.

'He couldn't get away,' he said diplomatically. 'That's why I particularly wanted him to have a photograph. To see how happy we are.'

Happy? Flora thought. She was Mrs William Pritchard now, which a few weeks ago would have been a prize beyond her wildest dreams. William had his arm around her, and her father was beaming at them both as he toasted their health with two-year-old parsnip wine. Everyone was smiling.

Yet Flora felt as though she was dying inside.

A cold hand had slipped around her heart. It began to tighten its grip as she said goodbye to her father and Mrs McSweeney and didn't relent when they stopped off in Bristol to have the photographs taken. She managed a smile for the camera, but William's hand on her shoulder felt more like a shadow of the fear that was gaining on her than the warm support that he had intended.

They walked from the photographer's across town to Temple Meads, where they boarded the train for Salisbury. The only time Flora had ever been on a train before was the annual Sunday-school outing to Weston-Super-Mare. That had been something to look forward to, but now it felt as though each rattling mile drew her closer to disaster. As she watched the sun sink towards a rim of rising ground outside of Salisbury she knew that the end was very near.

'Flora? Are you all right?'

William had been silent for so long that Flora jumped at the sound of his voice.

'I feel a bit funny. That's all,' she lied, unable to put her feelings into words.

'I'm not surprised. I haven't seen you eat a thing all day. Never mind. Mrs McSweeney packed us up a tuck box of party fare, so we won't starve. As long as the hotel staff don't requisition it, of course!'

The hotel. Suddenly Flora's fears had a form and substance. She looked away from him quickly. The sun was balanced on the horizon now, stretching evening shadows long and low. It would soon be dark. Time to go to bed.

'We'll be able to have a midnight feast,' William whispered, very close to her ear. He was leaning in towards her, almost pressing her into the corner of the carriage. Flora was glad then that they were sharing it with other people. Goodness knew what William might have done if they had been alone together.

Suddenly it was all too much.

'I can't—' Flora gasped.

William sat back. 'Can't what?'

'Breathe. . .'

He stood up and wrestled the window open before sitting down beside her again and taking her hand.

'It's all the excitement. And the worry,' he added swiftly. 'And leaving home on top of everything else. . . Take a few deep breaths. By the time we pull into the station you'll be as right as rain.'

Flora wasn't right at all. Her head was pounding and

her pulse racing so fast that she was sure he must be able to feel it, but when he took her hand to help her down onto the station platform he said nothing. Alfred had always been so furious at her nervousness, but William never even seemed to notice it.

Proof that he doesn't really care for me, Flora thought with growing dread. This is nothing but a marriage of convenience. If it wasn't for my disgrace I'd still have a job and we would both still be free.

All too soon they reached their hotel. While William supervised the unloading of their luggage from the taxi cab that had brought them from the station, Flora introduced herself to proprietress of the hotel. Mrs Coates was a comfortably upholstered lady in middle age who smiled broadly and often.

'I've got no need to ask for your marriage lines, have I? Not with you being such a little blushing violet, *Mrs* Pritchard!' She laughed, taking down a large brass key from the rack behind the reception desk.

'My husband has the certificate, Mrs Coates,' Flora said, pausing to wonder at how strange the word 'husband' sounded now. 'We were only married this morning.'

'Then we shan't worry if we don't see you down in the dining room for supper, then!' Mrs Coates nudged her playfully.

Flora felt a lurch of nausea. William would have done his worst by then. And found her wanting.

Mrs Coates led her down a creaking corridor on the second floor of the hotel. The dark runner of carpet and brown paintwork depressed Flora's spirits even further.

'Here's your bathroom.' Mrs Coates opened a grim-faced door to reveal a surprisingly light room beyond with a frosted window and light grey linoleum. The plumbing hissed expectantly, but there was a bright rag rug beside the high white bath and everything looked and smelled as clean as anything at Alvoe Court.

'You'll have it to yourselves as we don't have many other guests today,' Mrs Coates said before moving along the corridor to open another door.

'Oh!' Flora gasped as Mrs Coates revealed the room that William had reserved. The curtains had already been closed but electric lamps glowing at either side of the bed and on the dressing table showed a large airy room with clean, fresh decorations.

There was a large and colourful carpet covering most of the floor, showing only a narrow margin of polished linoleum around its edges. Flower-sprigged wallpaper and cream paintwork made Flora wonder how many servants were needed to keep it all so clean and neat. The open fireplace, also painted cream, must make a lot of dust.

And then there was the bed.

It was enormous. Flora felt her mouth grow dry as she stared at it, knowing what the coming night would bring.

'I've laid the fire, so you only need to put a match to it,' Mrs Coates was saying. 'I'm afraid there's not much of a view from this window, even in daylight. It looks out over the stable yard, but then with a good-looking young husband like yours you won't be spending much time looking out of the window, I'll be bound!'

'Thank you, Mrs Coates,' William said pleasantly, entering the room. He was carrying a large bunch of flowers—Michaelmas daisies in pink and blue, ice plant and a few late roses.

'For you,' he said softly, handing them to Flora. 'Perhaps you could press them somehow, to keep as a souvenir of old England.'

The clouds of apprehension parted for a moment as Flora looked at the beautiful flowers. 'Oh, William, they're lovely! Where on earth did you get them so late in the day?'

'I couldn't have you looking so downcast. I had to see you smile again.'

Silently Mrs Coates took an empty jug from the mantelpiece and went to fill it with water from the bathroom.

'I suppose I should have carried you over the threshold.' He searched out the last few grains of rice that had lodged about his uniform and threw them into the grate.

Flora was glad of the bouquet to hide behind, but Mrs Coates soon relieved her of that. Settling the flowers deftly into the jug, she left quickly, closing the door behind her. William let out a long, heartfelt sigh.

'I was beginning to think that we would never manage to be alone together,' he breathed, crossing the small distance between them to take Flora in his arms.

It was her turn to hold her breath.

'Any chance of a kiss, Mrs Pritchard?'

He was still smiling. That will soon change, Flora thought, but lifted her face obediently. She was a wife now, and had to do her duty. William had saved her from shame, and she had an obligation to him. While she had been living at home and William had been staying at the vicarage she had been safe. The most William had done during that time was to kiss her goodnight each evening before leaving her. His kisses then had been formal and restrained. But they were married now.

Flora accepted the first touch of William's lips with dull obedience. Then, as his arms enfolded her, something strange began to happen. Instead of the rigid,

muscle-tightening endurance that she had prepared for,
Flora felt herself begin to melt. It was the evening
under the old elms all over again. She closed her eyes
and slipped her arms around William's neck, feeling
the softness of his hair beneath her fingers.

'I don't feel like supper,' he breathed in her ear.
'Although you ought to eat something, Flora. Let's stay
here. I brought Mrs McSweeney's hamper in myself.'

He ran his cool, strong fingers the length of her jaw,
down her neck and to the collar of her blouse. 'Ever
since we first met at the lake I've wanted to do this. . .'

He was kissing her again, his fingers caressing her
shoulder then drifting down to move lightly over her
breast.

Flora sprang back at the touch.

'It's quite all right.' William chuckled softly. 'We're
married now!'

Alfred had never laughed. Not when he had done
that sort of thing—and especially not when she had
resisted.

'I—I'm still feeling queer,' Flora announced, and it
was true. A strange liquidity was overtaking her and it
was making her nervous.

'Oh, Flora. . .'

She tensed for the blow, physical or verbal, that was
sure to follow. It never came.

'And after I've been in a bate about it ever since I
proposed!'

Flora was incredulous. 'You've been worried about
it too?'

'Not *worried*.' William tried to make a joke of the
situation. 'But I do have a standard to live up to, don't
I? I don't want to be proved second best!' he finished
in a low voice.

Flora's heart stopped its steady thaw and froze again.

Even now the past was putting up barriers between them. William must still be thinking about Ralph, and what a good job he himself was doing to save the Morwyn family name.

'I love you, Flora.' William had taken her in his arms again and was murmuring into her hair. The words resounded in a way that Flora had never experienced before. William's hand was moving to her skirt, and she was alarmed to feel his touch sending shivers right through her body.

'William. . .I don't think I can. . .' Flora began, but he was engulfing her in more kisses. She heard his belt slither off and hit the floor, and the rustle as he worked off his jacket and braces, always keeping her close within the compass of one arm.

Despite the heat of his passion Flora's mind stayed cold and clear. Her hands went to the neck of her blouse in an action that was totally without feeling. Better to get the inspection over with first as last.

'Don't bother,' William said between kisses, pulling her hands away and edging her back towards the bed. 'It'll be more fun like this. More. . .*spontaneous*. . .'

The amazing thing about it was that he was still so eager, so uncritical. His grey eyes were so full of mischief now that Flora even forgot to close her own eyes as he took her in his arms again as they lay on the bed. All of a sudden he was filling her mind with his presence, kisses and endearments, thawing her frozen feelings until at last she melted beneath his touch again. She wanted to hold him close, then closer still, until at last, in a movement that surprised them both, they were united.

He stopped. 'Flora? Are you all right?'

She had to think about that.

'Yes. . .yes, I am,' she decided, then winced as he

moved again. To her confusion he neither swore nor hit her.

'It's been a long day,' he murmured softly, kissing her again as he adjusted his position. 'Shall I stop? After all, we've got all the time in the world for this sort of thing now we're married.'

A feeling shot through Flora, but this time it wasn't pain. She gasped, eyes wide, and saw him grinning at her in delight.

'Better?'

It was. Unimaginably so. The fluttering feeling began running through her again and again until she forgot everything but the desire for William's kisses and the touch of his fingers. Then his movements changed and she saw her own ecstasy reflected in his face as his expression was lit with the perfect joy of release. When he realised how intently she was watching him he laughed again.

'There, Mrs Pritchard! What did you make of that?'

'It was. . *unbelievable*. . .' She sighed.

'I'll pass muster, then?'

'Oh, much more than that.' Flora cupped his face in her hands and kissed him. 'I never knew that love could be like that.'

'It gets better, I can assure you.' He kissed both of her hands before pulling away a little and searching out a handkerchief from his trouser pocket. 'To tell you the truth, Flora, I was so concerned about living up to—'

He had been doing something out of her line of sight but now he stopped. Flora raised herself up on her elbows and saw him looking down in concern. He immediately moved to hide what he had been looking at, but not before Flora had seen a streak of scarlet standing out against the whiteness of his handkerchief.

'William?'

He looked at her, and he wasn't smiling now. Instead his face was unnaturally pale and concerned.

'I think you'd better lie down properly, love. Don't worry. It's probably nothing, but I'll get Mrs Coates to send for a doctor, just in case.'

William made her get into bed, just as she was. When he got back from seeing Mrs Coates, he sat on the edge of the bed and held her hand until the doctor arrived.

'I should have been more careful,' he burst out as the doctor was shown into the room. 'It's my fault. . . my wife is losing the baby.'

'I'm surprised you sent for me, sir, if your medical knowledge is so great,' the doctor announced. A large, florid man glowering over half-moon spectacles, he ignored Flora at first, speaking only to Mrs Coates and William.

'Hot water and towels, of course. The usual business. And you—' he raised his eyebrows reprovingly at William, who had remained at Flora's side '—off and do a smoke.'

'I've given it up. My wife doesn't approve.'

'Take it up again,' the doctor ordered gruffly through a cloud of smoke from his own cigarette. 'Nothing like it for clearing out the lungs.'

William went, but not until he had given Flora a kiss. She lay motionless, coming to terms with what had happened. 'Losing the baby,' William had said. Not our baby. *The* baby. That showed what he thought about it—or, rather, didn't.

Mrs Coates delivered the hot water then disappeared again. At the look on the older woman's face as she left the room Flora began to feel afraid.

'Now then, Mrs Pritchard.' The doctor shed his

brusque manner with his jacket and even stubbed out
his cigarette. 'Any regular pains?'

'No. No pain at all. At least, not exactly,' Flora
whispered. 'Although I am a bit sore.'

'Where?'

The doctor drew back the bedclothes that William
had arranged around her so carefully. Flora looked at
him suspiciously. He was the doctor, after all. It was his
job to know about this sort of thing, without her having
to put it into words.

'I'll need facts, not silence.' He sighed in exasperation. 'Slip your skirt off and I'll have a look.'

The doctor washed his hands at the basin then turned
back to the bed. Flora had used one of the towels Mrs
Coates had brought to cover herself decently, but the
doctor guffawed.

'I'm afraid a woman leaves modesty behind when
she gets pregnant, Mrs Pritchard!' Pulling the towel
aside, he then opened his Gladstone bag. Flora closed
her eyes.

The examination was uncomfortable, but swift. The
doctor said nothing, and Flora only risked opening her
eyes when she heard him return to the basin.

'Is everything all right, Doctor?' she asked at last.

'That rather depends.' The doctor dried his hands
again then strolled over to relight his cigarette from the
box of matches on the mantelpiece. 'Sit up and undo
your blouse and corset, please.'

Flora was beyond shame now. This, she supposed,
was what she would have to get used to. And worse.

She sat on the edge of the bed, shivering and
avoiding the doctor's eyes as he examined her and
asked all sorts of questions to which she had no answer.

'Well, Mrs Pritchard,' he said at last, flicking cigarette
ash expertly straight into the fireplace. 'In a quarter of

a century of general practice I thought I'd seen everything. But I've never come up against anything quite like this.'

His expression was totally unreadable.

'Am I going to lose the baby?'

'What baby?' the doctor countered smartly. 'There *is* no baby. As far as I can see, Mrs Pritchard, you are not now, nor have you ever been, pregnant. In fact, in my view you were still a virgin when your husband rather comprehensively made a wife of you just a short while ago.'

'But what about Master R—?' Flora remembered her promise to William just in time. And she remembered Alfred, too. 'My first husband—'

'How long were you married the first time?' The doctor stopped studying the end of his cigarette and looked at her keenly.

'Only two days—it was in the war. He was killed. . .'

'That might explain it. But what on earth made you think you were expecting a child?'

'There was another man. . .he assaulted me. He *hurt* me,' Flora said with a growing feeling of injured innocence.

'Not enough to do any harm.'

'Then. . .I'm not going to have a baby?'

'Mrs Pritchard, the last time that happened there was a star in the east.'

Delighted with his own diagnosis, the doctor snapped his bag shut and rose to leave.

'Will you tell Captain Pritchard, Doctor?'

The word 'husband' seemed altogether the wrong one now, after what she had put William through.

The doctor misunderstood her meaning.

'Certainly not! That's your job. Presumably you were

quick enough off the mark to ensnare the poor chap with talk of a baby in the first place?'

He was not interested now, dragging on his jacket and picking up his hat.

'Goodbye and good luck, Mrs Pritchard.'

'Wait!' Flora stood up, still fumbling with the hooks and buttons of her underclothes.

He stopped, and Flora realised that she did not know the right words to say.

'What is it, Mrs Pritchard?'

'The reason I thought I might be. . .expecting.' The word was doubly hard to say now. 'Things. . .haven't been happening as they should. . .'

'Oh, *that*.' The doctor drew on his cigarette distract-edly, already thinking of home comforts and a good dinner. 'Any number of reasons. Worry, the upheaval of getting married, that sort of thing. Nothing to fret about. It'll all come right soon enough.'

'But what am I going to tell William—my husband—when it does?'

The doctor shrugged. 'If I were you I'd tell him now, Mrs Pritchard. Right now. Put him out of his misery.'

He opened the door to go. Immediately Flora heard William's light footsteps advance along the hallway outside.

'Is Flora going to be all right, Doctor?'

'Ask her.' The doctor tipped his head toward where Flora had sunk down onto the edge of the bed in despair.

There was a muttered consultation about costs and Flora heard the jingle as coins changed hands. That it should come to this, she thought bleakly. I've betrayed William's future, and he's still paying for it.

The doctor left them, and William was at her side in an instant. Despite the shock, the indignity and her shame at getting into such a fix, a desperate plan was already starting to force itself into Flora's mind.

'Are you all right, Flora?' William's hand was very cold as he took hers, and he smelled of clean fresh air.

'Yes. . .' Flora said faintly. She was staring at the carpet, trying to steel herself for the dreadful lie. 'The doctor says there's nothing to worry about. Everything is all right.'

'And the baby?'

Flora could not bring herself to say it. She nodded dumbly, unable to look William in the eye. He sounded so concerned, his intentions so fine and noble even though he had lost his collar and the top button of his shirt was undone. His hair was tousled as though by sleep, although his movements were sure enough. He gathered her in his arms, pressing her head against his chest.

'Oh, thank goodness for that.'

Flora twined her arms around him readily. This part of the deception would be easy.

'I love you, Will,' she murmured, snuggling down into his embrace like a kitten. She could at least say that with some honesty. He was surely every girl's dream—young, handsome and successful.

Although I'm not really sure what being in love is like, Flora reasoned, it will be easy to convince myself that I love William.

Especially after the way that he had made love to her.

Flora felt a thrill at the memory of it, but knew it shouldn't be a welcome one. She was about to deceive William, and go on deceiving him for as long as it took her to fall for his own child. It will make me a cheat, she thought, hating herself for it, and cheats don't deserve pleasure.

'Oh, Will. . .' she murmured again, pushing her fingers through his hair. 'Let's go to bed properly. . .'

'Of course.' He patted her companionably. 'You need your rest, and we both need to be up early in the morning. You can use the bathroom first, while I unpack Mrs McSweeney's picnic. You're not going to bed until you've had something to eat.'

He stood up, kissed her nose then moved away to the picnic hamper standing in the corner of the room. Flora watched him with growing dismay. This wasn't what was supposed to be happening at all.

'William?'

He looked up, immediately concerned.

'Aren't you going to come to bed. . .now?'

He strolled back to her side. 'I think we've had a narrow squeak, love. It might be best to take things carefully for a while, don't you think? I don't want anything happening to you, do I?'

He kissed the top of Flora's head and stroked her hair—but then he went straight back to the picnic hamper.

Chapter Ten

Flora's mind was in a turmoil. Alfred had never been content to let matters rest. That was why she had been wary of any intimacy with William. Now she knew that William's care and patience was a world away from the inexpert fumblings of her first husband. Suddenly she was feeling the need to put that new knowledge into practice in ways she would never have imagined possible with Alfred.

She brought herself up short at that thought. It had always been very painful to think of Alfred. Now it felt disloyal as well.

William was unpacking the picnic hamper with relish. 'The Branxmere parish outings must be fine days out if they get as much as this,' he was saying as he took two sets of cutlery from the collection fixed to the inside of the hamper lid and set them out on the small table that stood before the fire. 'Although I did think to add something myself.'

He withdrew a large, heavy bottle with a foil cap from one of the straw-lined compartments which usually held bottles of barley water or lemonade.

Flora had seen bottles like that before. It was champagne. Champagne had a compartment all to itself in

Mr Perry's wine cellar at Alvoe Court, and he had shown it off proudly on Flora's first visit. Each bottle, he had told her, would cost at least a month of her salary.

'Nothing like a drop of the finest medicine ever invented.' William set the bottle down, then looked out two glasses. 'You won't mind drinking it out of ordinary glasses?'

Flora shook her head. He obviously didn't realise that she had never tasted champagne before — not even the champagne she had used in sorbets and sauces for the Morwyn family.

William finished setting out the supper things then went to the fireplace. Taking a spill from the holder, he lit it, then touched the fire alight.

'By the time you're ready to eat there'll be a jolly blaze in here.' Going to her side, he kissed her indulgently. 'You go and get ready for bed, my love. Take your time. I shall be quite happy organising our supper.'

Flora went to the bathroom. When she had locked herself in she sat on the hard wooden chair that had been provided, alone with her thoughts. The bathroom felt less like a sanctuary than a cold, bright cell where there could be no hiding from her worries.

She tried turning each tap on and off several times, just to see if the water really would gush out every time, even though they were on the second floor. It had been meant as a distraction, but nothing could take her mind off what she had to do. If William wasn't going to risk making love to her for a while a decision had to be made.

She could tell William the truth straight away, which would be only right and proper.

Or she could tell him that she had lost Ralph's baby after all.

The first way would be the best. It was honest—but Flora was sure she would then have to spend the rest of her married life having her innocent stupidity thrown back in her face at every opportunity. She was sure to have ruined William's prospects. All his friends were bound to look down on him for marrying a servant. Marrying a *stupid* servant would be even more unforgivable.

Flora knew that her second idea had an even worse drawback. To say that she had lost the baby might gain William's sympathy, but it would be a lie. Flora could have no respect for herself or William if she was prepared to lie and go on lying.

Falling for William's baby as quickly as possible was the only real alternative to the truth. It would make things unbearably complicated, but it seemed like her only option.

Flora spent a long time trying to work out how it might be done. She had a hazy recollection of a baby being born too early to a young wife in Falgrave, although it had only been spoken about in puzzling whispers at the time. Perhaps the opposite might also be true. Babies might come late.

The only trouble was, Flora didn't know how long it might take to fall for a baby in the first place. Especially if William was going to try and be considerate. She didn't know how late such a baby might reasonably arrive, either. Not only that, but using an innocent little life to cover up her own mistake felt like another betrayal.

Flora sat in the bathroom for a long time, thinking around the problem from every angle. There was no painless solution. In the end William came and tapped on the bathroom door to make sure she was all right. Stirred into action, Flora bathed quickly, but getting ready to go back into the bedroom took a lot longer, Her new dressing gown covered her from neck to ankles, but she still crept back into the room as though hoping William might not see her.

The room was lit only by the crackling fire and the two dim lights at either side of the bed. William was seated at the table. Firelight rippled over the cutlery he had laid out, and Flora saw that he had put some pie and salad on her plate. As soon as she slipped into the room he stood up and held out a glass of champagne.

'To us,' he said softly as she joined him.

Flora murmured a reply and tasted the champagne. It was quite unlike the sips of wine the cook at Falgrave Manor had let her taste. Soft and fragrant, it slipped down almost too easily, the bubbles bursting deliciously on her tongue. Suddenly Flora realised that she was ravenously hungry.

'Eat up while I go and get ready. I'm afraid I was so inspired by the standard of the picnic food I've finished all mine,' William said a little apologetically.

Flora was beginning to enjoy the champagne. 'I'm glad you like it, William.'

'At least you won't have to slave away at any cooking in India,' William said. 'It will all be done for you. You'll be a real lady of leisure.'

Until that moment Flora had thought her troubles couldn't possibly get any worse. Now she realised that they were only just beginning.

'But I *like* cooking,' she said as William collected a towel from one of their trunks.

'Ah, but there are other things to do now that you don't have to do it for a living.'

Flora wasn't convinced.

'What sort of things?'

William paused on his way to the door.

'Oh. . .I don't know. The ladies always seem busy enough. Card parties, tea parties, social evenings, all that sort of thing. And not forgetting your tennis and horse-riding, of course!'

He opened the door to leave, and missed Flora's horrified expression. Parties and social evenings were the sort of thing that the Duchess of Alvoe got up to. It was a cook's job to do the catering, not take part.

Flora looked at the cold chicken pie on her plate and wondered if she would ever see a boiling fowl again. It sounded as though the nearest she would get to birds now was when she was expected to poke their feathers into her hat.

Marriage to William was feeling more of a life sentence with every passing moment.

Flora finished her meal, then pushed her chair back from the table and stared deep into the fire. All she could do was concentrate on her feelings for William, and support him as a dutiful wife should.

That ruled out telling him that there wasn't going to be a baby. A gentleman trapped into marriage by a servant was sure to lose every scrap of respect among his fellow officers, Flora decided.

William came back from the bathroom and it was Flora's turn to rise and greet him. She could afford none of his restraint now and put her arms around his neck as soon as he was within reach.

'I'm so happy,' she breathed into his ear, and it was true—as long as she only thought of him and him alone. As soon as her mind started to wander onto the circumstances and effects of their marriage the ogre of guilt began to grow again.

'If you're happy, then I'm happy,' William whispered

back, not knowing that this would confirm all Flora's misgivings.

'Make love to me,' she ventured, forcing herself to be unnaturally forward. William held her very close for a long time.

'Not for a while,' he said softly, although the touch of his hands betrayed his true feelings. 'Not until we know everything really is going to be all right.'

Flora laid her head against his chest, but it was a gesture of despair rather than acceptance.

He was wrong. Nothing was going to be all right. Things were only going to go on getting worse.

Embarkation day arrived all too soon. The dock reek of fuel oil and tar infused the smell of ozone like a fog that shrouded the whole of the coast. There were men everywhere: stevedores tossing great trunks and cases about as though they were toys, soldiers in full kit carrying packs on their backs like snails, and through it all the truck drivers inching their unpredictable steeds between pedestrians, mules and machinery.

William shepherded Flora on board in plenty of time, before the last rush of latecomers. At first she was grateful for his kindness. Then, as they leaned on the ship's rail to watch the furious activity along the dockside, she realised why he had been so eager to get settled in.

Ralph Morwyn and his covey of friends were the last to arrive. They straggled up the gangway, fielding good-natured banter from their companions who had boarded in good time. Flora looked up into William's face, but he was already taking her arm and turning away from the rail.

'Come on,' he said stiffly. 'I don't want you subjected

to that fathead Ralph's fawning attempts at ingratiation.'

They took a turn about the deck. Looking out toward the open sea, Flora began to feel apprehensive. Six weeks afloat. How on earth would she survive? The words of a hymn rushed into her mind—rock and tempest. For those in peril on the sea. It was all very well to sing those words in the snug little land-locked church at Falgrave, which must be as far away from the sea as it was possible to get.

The annual trip to Weston-Super-Mare was the nearest she had been to the sea, and that wasn't saying very much. There was a world of difference between a distant grey line glimpsed beyond miles of mud and this swelling, oily slop that had to support them all the way to India.

'Don't worry,' William murmured, as though reading her thoughts. 'I'll look after you.'

Flora had started out with no illusions about married life. She had expected the journey to be unbearable, too. Expecting nothing from either, she was surprised. Everyone was kind to her, the sea was almost calm and the food, while not quite home cooking, wasn't the inedible mess that her brother David had endured in the trenches.

Flora and William had a cabin to themselves, although once past Port Said it became too hot for sleeping below. They took mats out onto the deck each evening, along with everyone else, and slept beneath the stars. During the day they could watch flying fishes dart like needles over the surface of the sea, while during the evenings there was a band and dancing on deck until the small hours.

William proved to be an ideal companion, friend and

confidante—in every matter except one. Flora could not persuade him to make love to her. He was affectionate and passionate in every other way, but his kisses and caresses were no longer enough. Having once tasted paradise, Flora now found herself locked out.

That was the most painful thing of all. If she had been as frightened of William and his attentions as she had been of Alfred, everything would have been all right. But things were so different for her now. She wanted William's body, but that was the only thing that he would not let her have.

In every other matter William was a perfect husband. He never overwhelmed her with a lot of instructions about how to behave, but was always ready with advice. He taught her the rules of tennis. He engaged two of his men to help teach her to play bridge and whist.

These new skills meant that she could understand what Colonel Primm's wife was talking about when she told the ladies of all her great triumphs throughout the Home Counties. Flora wasn't sure where the Home Counties were, but she learned to nod knowingly and remember all these puzzles to ask William when they were alone together.

Despite the press of people aboard the troopship, William and Flora managed to be alone together a great deal. Not that it advanced Flora's plan one inch. Most of the time they talked or read. William was always attentive and affectionate, but he would never risk letting things get out of hand.

As the climate grew hotter, Flora's agitation increased. She had hidden the truth from William for so long now that telling him would be impossible. He would feel deceived in a way that he wouldn't have done if only she had been given the opportunity to fall for his own child. But there was no possibility of that. Not when he was being so considerate, and reminding her every night of what had happened at Salisbury.

The whole thing was a disaster. Despite all his care and attention Flora was sure now that she should never have married him. William had thought it was the right thing, but Flora's innocence had meant that she had married him under false pretences. If there was any right thing that should have been done, it was to have told William the truth straight away, as the doctor had suggested.

It had been too difficult then. It was totally impossible now.

Worry consumed Flora's every waking moment. She did not know what to do. Worse, there was no one that she could possibly confide in. She was besieged in a hell of her own making, and had no one to blame but herself.

The married quarters at Karanpur were a collection of low thatched bungalows set along one side of the barrack square. Flora was horrified when she and William were shown into their new home. Its thick walls were made of mud, the windows were small and shuttered and the floor was bare, beaten earth. The Home Farm cows live better than this, Flora thought in disgust.

William didn't seem to notice any of it. He had already supervised the delivery of their belongings and was now setting up a large wooden screen across one corner of their main room.

Although the house had been aired there was no escape from the cloying heat. Jolted, jarred and over-heated by a week-long journey overland in rattling trains and army transport, Flora had a headache that

ran from the roots of her teeth to the roots of her hair
and held every point in between in a crippling grip. All
she wanted to do was to lie down, close her eyes and
sleep until their time in India was over.

William had other ideas.

'We'll have to look sharp, Flora. The Colonel is
hosting a drinks party this evening to welcome us all
home—if anywhere could ever be considered to be
home for a soldier.' He looked around the whitewashed
walls of their spartan but functional rooms.

'Never mind. We'll soon make this home, between
us.' He slipped one arm around Flora's waist.

It can't be long before he guesses, she thought
bitterly.

'I—I've got a bit of a headache, Will. I don't suppose
you'd mind going to the Colonel's party on your own,
would you?'

He clicked his tongue. 'Well. . .I know it's an awful
bind but I do think you'd better show your face, Flora,
if it's only for five minutes. I've never been the type for
this kind of do at the best of times, so it'll be an ordeal
for me as well. We'll show the flag for one quick turn
of the hall, then come back for an early night. All
right?'

Flora could hardly refuse. She felt guilty enough for
tying William down in the first place, without handicap-
ping his career as well. She washed and changed in the
little partitioned area that served them as a bathroom,
splashing plenty of lavender water over her pulse-spots
to try and cool down. The effect was only short-lived,
but at least it smelled nice.

William looked so smart in his uniform that Flora
gazed at him in wonder, hardly able to believe that she
was accompanying the best-looking man in the regiment. Then she remembered that everyone else was

sure to disbelieve it too, and her nerve almost failed her.

'William. . .I can't. . . All your grand friends, all those ladies—'

'And you're more than equal to any of them. Remember what Kipling says about the Colonel's lady. You're all sisters under your skins.'

You can choose your friends but you can't choose your sisters, Flora thought bleakly.

'Here, take my arm.' William laid her hand on his sleeve. He felt warm and vital and his strength of purpose allowed Flora to rally a little.

They reached the hall at exactly the right time: after the commission-hunters and before the charge-sheet regulars. Suspicious of any mixture labelled 'punch', Flora listened to what the other women were requesting from the stewards. Gin and Indian tonic seemed the favourite, so when William asked her what she would like to drink she was ready.

'Are you sure?' He looked at her with new eyes before calling a steward.

Flora was not sure, but she could hardly be the only person standing in the Colonel's party without a drink.

It was difficult to know which hit the pit of her empty stomach harder—the gin or the tonic. When a steward offered her a refill she asked for plain Indian tonic, which filled her glass but had the reassuring word 'water' in its name. Unfortunately the taste was far too bitter for Flora. While William was talking to men she did not know about places she had never heard of, she smiled encouragingly at a waiter, who was only too pleased to top up her glass with gin.

'And this is my new wife,' William was saying, drawing her forward into a knot of his companions. 'Flora, this is Colonel Primm.'

Flora curtsied automatically, then looked at William in case it was the wrong thing to do. Even if it had been a slip-up, no one seemed to have noticed.

'Ah, yes. The demon whist player.' All waxed moustache and whisky fumes, the Colonel leaned over her solicitously. 'My wife has told me all about your triumphs, my dear.'

'Beginner's luck,' Flora said, wondering what the gin was doing to her. 'I don't think I shall risk playing again, Colonel.'

'A diplomat as well as a beauty, Pritchard? You've done well there. May *will* be pleased when I tell her your good woman is quitting the field of battle!'

William squeezed Flora's hand, but the conversation had already swung him back to logistics and stratagems. Pleased with herself for the first time in weeks, Flora summoned another drink. If she could talk to a colonel she could certainly talk to William.

She would tell him tonight.

She held onto his arm tightly. She should have told him before they set off for India. That would have been the right thing to do, she repeated to herself as she had done so often over these past weeks.

But then he might have left her behind.

That would have been unbearable. She knew that now.

Almost as unbearable as his horror would be when he finally realised that he had been duped into marriage.

She was vaguely aware that William was making their excuses and looking down indulgently at her. She drank her remaining gin and parked the glass on the nearest table. Unobtrusively William picked it up and transferred it to a steward's tray, then led her out into the night.

'Well done, Flora. I'm proud of you.'

Flora didn't answer him. The rush of fresh air after the heat of the hall was making her dizzy. William didn't seem to notice. All the way back to the married quarters he kept up an idle, one-sided conversation: identifying the various buildings that made up their station, pointing out the constellations visible high above them and pausing to pick some sprigs of pink and blue toadflax from the flower bed that Colour Sergeant Barclay had drilled with such precision.

'I'm surprised these are still here,' William said with a laugh. 'Poor Barclay tended them so carefully, thinking they were a real eastern exotic. When he got home he found out that toadflax is a real weed back there!'

'William. . .'

He had got so used to her calling him Will that he stopped and looked at her, puzzled.

'I've got something to tell you.'

Wordlessly he handed her the bunch of flowers, waiting. He was destined to wait for a long time.

She could not say it.

If ever there was a time and place less suited for the ending of dreams it was in that warm, still evening with the light of stars scattered over the sky like pinpricks in black velvet.

'I—I love you, Will,' she managed at last.

'Well, thank goodness for that!' He took her in his arms and hugged her, which made things still worse. 'I didn't know *what* was coming! I was expecting something dreadful!'

'Yes,' Flora said thoughtfully, pressing her face against the rough fabric of his uniform until it hurt. She did not speak again

When they reached their bungalow, William took a

pitcher of water behind the wooden screen and prepared to wash and change.

Flora sat down on the bed. The gin had made her
light-headed and numb. She gripped at the edge of the
bed with either hand to try and get some sort of grip
on reality. From the other side of the screen came
sounds of water bubbling into the basin and the rustle
of Will pulling at his clothes.

'I thought that went quite well,' he called across
affably from behind the screen, as though he really
meant what he said. Flora parted her lips to reply but
could make no sound.

'How is your headache?'

Sounds of William undressing were replaced by the
splash and fritter of water and soap. When Flora did
not reply the sounds stopped, suddenly and completely.

'Flora? Did you have a good time? Or at least not a
bad one?' This time his words were a little louder, with
a little more edge. 'I didn't know you liked gin.'

'I—I don't,' Flora managed eventually.

'You want to watch that stuff. Mother's ruin, they
call it.'

Flora stood up. The gin had been intended as a
support but it was proving a false friend. The floor was
sagging slightly beneath her feet. She made it across
the room toward him, but as she reached the screen
she had to steady herself against it.

He was stripped to the waist, lithe muscles gliding
easily beneath the thin, fine surface of his skin. Hearing
a slight noise, he turned to face her. A smile began to
lift his features but stopped as he saw the look in her
eyes.

'Will—I'm not expecting a baby.'

The words burst out suddenly, falling into stunned
silence. William closed his eyes and exhaled softly.

'You needn't have married me after all,' Flora went on, numb with the horrible inevitability of his reaction. 'I could have kept my job and stayed at home and not come to this awful, hateful place and—and—'

He crossed the distance between them and gathered her in his arms. Flora's feeling of detachment, of numb disbelief dissolved into horror. He wanted her, pressing her against the warm plane of his body. His face was buried in her hair, droplets of warm water on his freshly washed skin mingling with the light dew of terror that was still rising within her.

He wanted her now, urgently. She could feel it, the desire rising in him that wanted to sweep everything away. In her confused panic Flora forgot Salisbury. The awful memory of what Alfred had inflicted upon her and his revenge filled her mind and made her oblivious to everything else.

'Let go! Let go of me!' She levered herself away from William's caresses. 'I should never have married you! I never wanted to be married again!'

He let her go. His withdrawal was so sudden, so total that she stumbled and had to grab at the screen for support again. Shivering at the impact, the screen discharged a fine powder of the ever-present dust upon them.

'I wish I'd never come to this hateful place! It's hot and dirty and—'

'It pays my wages.' William's lips were a thin, hard line of disapproval. 'I'm lucky to have such a good job.'

It was the worst thing he could possibly have said. Fired by the heat, the dust and the three glasses of gin, Flora felt all the wrongs that had ever been done to her magnify and distort the whole scene out of proportion.

'*I* was lucky once too! *I* had a good job. But I had to give it all up to marry you *and look where it's got me!*'

Tears of rage and disappointment and pain at the unfairness of it all were pouring down Flora's cheeks. Recovering from his initial surprise at her outburst, William tried to put his arms around her again but she flung them aside. The gesture was so savage, so alien that it ignited real fury in him for the first time.

'Don't you come the downtrodden little waif and stray with me, madam!' he roared at her. 'If I can drag myself up from the gutter you can damned well do the same!'

'Don't make me laugh!' Flora spat back. 'The nearest your sort ever come to a gutter is when you step over some poor unfortunate lying there. Cast out when your sort have had your bit of fun—'

'Like my mother was, you mean? Or like you would have been?'

A wall of horrified silence fell between them.

'Your. . .mother,' Flora said slowly. That at least had registered.

Colour was rising in his face and he looked away, unable to face her.

'I married you to save Ralph's child from the sort of life I've had to endure and to give you some sort of life, and what do you do? Throw it all back in my face. What is everyone going to think now? You've ruined any illusions I might have had about the future, that's for sure. I should have stayed a poor bastard in the East End. There's an admission! Satisfied?'

Flora stared at him in horror. What was he saying? That marrying her had been just another step in his efforts to be accepted?

His features hardened with barely suppressed rage as he snatched up his shirt. Pulling it on over his head, he pushed past her.

'Don't worry, Flora. I shan't stay where I'm so obviously not wanted.'

Striding across the room, he went out into the night, slamming the door behind him so violently that it bounced open again. Even the incessant, mind-destroying whisper of insects was crushed into insignificance by the furious intent of his footsteps as he marched away.

Chapter Eleven

'Lovers' tiff?' Ralph grinned as William stormed into the otherwise deserted officers' mess. 'Or are you laying down the rules of engagement early on? You want to watch out, Will. I could hear you two arguing from right across the square. You and Cookie are going to end up like my ma and pa if you're not careful. Sparring like professionals.'

William rounded on him, the pain of rejection still too raw.

'Flora only married me because she thought she was going to have *your* baby!' he spat furiously.

The words struck Ralph far harder than any physical blow had ever done. All the colour left his face and his jaw dropped.

'My God,' he breathed eventually. 'You mean she thought—that business at the pavilion?'

He sat back, then drew on his cigar. Exhaling at length, he gave William a slow grin.

'Well, I always knew I was good, but I didn't realise I was *that* good.'

'You weren't.' William was quick to quash him but Ralph's mind had already moved onto something else.

'My God,' he repeated with growing horror. 'You

mean she would have saddled you with my brat? No wonder they say the working classes have such a reputation for survival. Wait here, Will. This won't take long.'

He grabbed his jacket, but William blocked his route to the door.

'Where are you going, Ralph?'

'To pay her off, of course.'

'*What?*'

Ralph took a step backwards, out of reach.

'Don't look at me like that, Will.' He smiled ingratiatingly. 'It's perfectly simple. It was my slip, so I'll pay her off. No need for you to have got yourself stuck with that, old sport.'

William stared at him, incredulous. 'I've underestimated you, Ralph. After all these years you can still surprise me.'

Ralph didn't appreciate the irony in William's voice. His smile widened. 'Thank you, Will. Only trying to help. No hard feelings now?'

'I'm sorry I thrashed you—'

'Don't worry about it,' Ralph began with justifiable modesty. 'At least we can go back to being mates again—'

'I should have *killed* you instead, while I had the chance,' William concluded.

Ralph stopped smiling. 'Will?'

'If you *ever* go within one hundred yards of my wife in future without my express permission, I really will kill you.' William compressed all his pent-up fury into the words and left Ralph in no doubt that he meant every single one.

'Fine,' Ralph said uncomfortably, subsiding into a chair and summoning a steward. 'Want to discuss it over a drink?'

'No.'

William watched Ralph ferret through his jacket, pulling out matches and cigarettes which he offered nervously.

'Here, Will. Do a smoke. Stay here for a bit. We've got a lot to catch up on. Let Cookie sweat it out for a while. It pays to be a bit dusty toward them now and again.'

Sweat and dust. Another raw spot.

'Go on, have a cigarette,' Ralph wheedled. 'It'll calm your nerves—'

'There's nothing wrong with my nerves,' William growled.

Ralph's temporary tide of courage receded a little.

'Do a smoke anyway. Have a drink. Go back smelling of the twin evils and that'll make her *really* mad!' he suggested with glee.

'Flora doesn't care what I do any more. If she ever did,' William added bitterly.

His head was swimming, but he put that down to the unaccustomed cigarette. Leaning forward, he rested his elbows on his knees and stared at the floor. His black silence was only interrupted when the lengthening tip of ash on his forgotten cigarette shattered and fell to the floor in a grey smudge. Absently, William moved his foot to rub the ash away.

'That's the sort of thing the men would do.' Ralph sniffed with disapproval and hailed a waiter to clear up the mess.

'Yes. Well.' William sat back in his seat. Then he ground the unwanted cigarette forcibly into the nearest ashtray.

'Can I stay with you tonight, Ralph?' he asked suddenly.

'Of course.' Ralph grinned, not realising that laughter was the last thing on William's mind at that moment. 'It'll be just like old times!'

Flora lay on the bed and cried until she had no tears left. Even then she could not stop. Only when she had no strength left at all did she drift into restless sleep.

William had married her more out of thought for the child than for her. To advance his status in the regiment and to save the Morwyn family from scandal. A virtuous sacrifice on the altar of Ralph's friendship.

William had been surprised at his reaction to Flora's announcement. Relief had been tinged with a touch of selfish disappointment — until she had made her own feelings so clear.

In long hours of dark reflection that evening William realised how much saving a child from the disgrace that he had once suffered would have meant to him. He knew what it was like to sit on the sidelines, listening to other boys' tales of outings with 'Father'. Mr and Mrs Fielding had always been there at the Mission for him, but it had never been the same. The Sunday-best appearance of two missionaries at sports day and prize-giving had been no substitute for the glamour and dash of a real papa and mama to share in all his achievements.

It was only now, after all these years, that William was beginning to admit these long-buried feelings to himself. He would have died rather than show anything but loyal thanks to the Fieldings. They had looked after his mother so well, too.

All the same, visions of an ideal family life had been forming in his mind over the past few weeks. Now he felt cheated.

Ralph went out at midnight to do a spot check,

leaving William to his own devices. There could be no question of going back to the bungalow to fetch a book. Besides, translating Virgil wouldn't be much of a substitute, and rereading *Far from the Madding Crowd* would be ten times worse. Reading of an honest working girl abandoned by a soldier who only discovered the depths of his passion when it was too late would hardly be relaxation tonight.

William began to wish that he had stayed at home in England. A transfer to a desk job would have meant more money and less risk. It would have been a more suitable job for a family man, too. He and Flora could have set up home in some rose-covered country cottage in Dorset, and started married life away from the pressures of living on the strength.

He could have gone off to work each morning like proper husbands did while Flora spent the day tending cabbage roses and fat, sun-browned babies in the garden. Inside the house, servants would have freed her from all the tiresome duties. She would have been able to take her ease to perfection, everyday clothes replaced by the fondant confections of a lady.

He knew now that he must have been mad ever to raise his voice to her. A fantasy started to form in William's mind, softening all the hard words that had come between them.

The coils of Flora's auburn hair would be laid out over silks and lace rich with the floral perfume that caressed the air whenever she moved. He thought about her moving now—raising her hand to brush a curl back from her face, a froth of creamy lace falling back from the fine pale skin of her wrist—

'All leave cancelled.' Ralph clattered into the room, shattering William's concentration. 'This is no time to be lying about! They want volunteers for a night patrol.

The rumour is that there's to be a big push across the border tonight. Young Amanullah's men will be taking advantage of all that trouble in the Punjab to try and get across the border. No Afghan gets past here until further notice.'

There were always rumours, alarms and rumours of alarms. William did not think that this latest excitement would be any more genuine than others had ever been, but he did wonder about calling in on Flora to make things up in case things started to get hot.

'There's no time for that,' Ralph said gaily, pressing a revolver into William's hands. 'Come on, there'll be nothing to it!'

With a sigh William strapped on the revolver and went out to report for action.

There was no warning that this evening alarm would be particularly serious. Colonel Primm had been unable to get a line on his field telephone earlier that afternoon. In the heavily wooded hill country around them there was always the chance that a falling branch might foul the surface lines, but a regular patrol had returned with no faults to report. It was thought that the problem must lie in underground cables laid along the local tracks and roads. That meant miles of rough terrain to be checked for landslip or other disturbance.

It would be a tiresome business, but the Afghans had been keeping to their own side of the border for a number of days. This often happened at times of religious festivals and a repair team had been sent out in the hope that this was one such occasion.

Coils of cable and enormous battery packs had been slung over the saddles of pack mules, who had viewed the proceedings with narrow-eyed suspicion. They were right to be cautious. The repair team had sent back one inconclusive report, but since then there had been silence.

Within minutes of the alarm, the station at Karanpur was under attack. A liquidity of men flowed from the surrounding hills, covered by sniper fire and intent upon crossing the border. Weeks of guerilla warfare had failed to unnerve the British, so now the Afghans had decided upon an all-out attack.

They had staked everything on a confrontation, but they had underestimated their enemy. Intermittent action had only served to sharpen the British reflexes. The station was virtually impregnable. Well supplied and staffed with men fresh back from home leave, there could be little danger to the residents. Flora and the other ladies living on the strength were in the usual flutter of anxiety, but they were well shepherded by May Primm, the Colonel's wife, who came into her own at such moments.

The British soldiers were more than ready and willing for a fight. Ralph was in his element for the first time since leaving home. Face glowing in the crude flare of incendiaries, he ducked below the outer wall of the station to reload his gun yet again.

'Four brace and a couple of runners,' he yelled to William above the din. 'What's your bag?'

'I haven't kept count!'

'You'd do better to use a rifle. Makes a better job than a revolver. Nip back and fetch it — I'll keep your place warm till you get back. It'll give me a chance to keep up my average while you're gone!'

'I'm all right with this,' William said during the next gap in the firing. He was privately relieved to see the Afghans starting to retreat. He had no interest in either tallies or averages. To fell a tribesman bent on murdering him, man to man, was one thing. Calmly picking off men like partridges was quite another.

'That's given them something to think about,' Ralph said as the attacking fire became intermittent then drew further off toward the east. He dried his palms down the sides of his trousers before wiping the butt of his gun on the corner of his jacket.

'Right—now to send out and find what's happened to the repair party. Poor devils.'

William looked at him quizzically. 'Not yet, surely?'

'Why not? I'll send somebody out before anybody else gets the same idea. A bit of glory for the family escutcheon!'

'Ralph, be serious. The Afghans are still too close. They'd like nothing better than to draw some of us out there. You'd be mad to try it.'

'It's the ones that give the orders gets the glory.' Ralph made a sweeping movement with his gun as though following the flight of an English pheasant. 'I take it from your expression that for once in your life you're not going to be volunteering, Will?'

'I might be keen, Ralph, but I'm not tired of living. If you've got any sense you won't risk yourself, or anybody else just yet.'

Ralph put on a comically false expression of concern.

'What about the poor repair team lying out there ambushed—injured—?'

'If they were ambushed by Afghans there's no hope for them anyway. They'll be dead. If by some miracle the locals never got to them and they're still alive then they'll be safe. They know how to lie low and how to survive. They can wait until it's perfectly safe to come back.'

'Ah, yes—but where's the glory for us in that? I've spent all my life living in the shadow of others. Now

it's my turn to make my mark. I'm surprised you're not
more keen yourself, Will. Especially now you've got
that crafty little wife of yours to impress. Didn't your
friend Cicero reckon that glory in war exceeds all other
kinds of success?'

'Cicero ended up with his head and hands nailed to
the Forum in Rome,' William said succinctly.

There was a longer lull in the firing. Two flares were
sent up and in their brilliant light the slopes around the
station were shown to be littered with dead and dying
like autumn leaves. William turned his head away.

'Well, if you're not interested in covering yourself
with glory, Will, I'm quite sure some of your regular
cronies will be.' Ralph scanned the small knots of
soldiers already relaxing into conversation with the
easy confidence of a job well done.

'Atkins? Mackenzie?' Ralph called out.

'It's Arnott and Mackenzie,' William murmured as
two of the men obeyed Ralph's order to approach.

'I'm looking for two volunteers to go out and look
for the line party. Captain Pritchard suggested you two
as likely-looking lads.'

William drew in a sharp breath at this. Arnott and
Mackenzie looked at each other, then at him.

'Major Morwyn should make it perfectly plain that
this is an entirely voluntary exercise.' William tried to
convey his apprehension without undermining Ralph's
authority. It was beyond him. He had to fall back on
appealing to the better nature of his men. 'I should
think your youngsters would prefer a live dad to a dead
hero, Arnott.'

'Yes, sir.' The older of the two soldiers lost his
suspicions and would have smiled if it had not been for
Ralph.

'I *was* detailed for saddlery duty tonight, sir,'

Mackenzie said when Ralph probed him. He was a rather sensitive character and William suspected he used volunteering as a method of testing himself. This foolhardy mission would be the ultimate test, William thought, quite understanding Mackenzie's unusual reticence. In this sort of job, enough was far more than a feast.

'That's quite all right, Mackenzie. We understand. I've been meaning to get someone to do something about the nearside girth on my first saddle. It's wearing a bit. See to it tonight, would you?'

'Wait a minute!' Ralph had been watching the exchange with disbelief and could restrain himself no longer. 'There could be men out there suffering in awful agony and you're more concerned about your blasted saddlery?'

'It's my view that the line-repair party are either hidden and perfectly safe, or more likely they are dead, sir.' William was careful to use formality in front of his men. 'If we wait until morning, the coast will be clear and the search will be much easier in daylight. Besides, if there's any hope for the repair men at all they'll be back here as soon as the Afghans are well out of the way.'

'Well, it's *my* view that somebody ought to go out and check. Now.'

Ralph stared at Arnott and Mackenzie. Hard. There was no mistaking the look. He had chosen his volunteers. Arnott, Mackenzie and William would simply have to live with his decision.

The two soldiers saluted, turned and marched off to prepare for their mission. William expected a reprimand for trying to stop his men from volunteering, but Ralph was not sensitive to ulterior motives.

'You worry about the men too much, Will.'

'I'll try to remember that,' William said carefully. 'Sir.'

'Come on. You know better than that, Will. There's no standing on ceremony between the two of us. Unless it's in front of the men, of course.'

He drew William away from the wall and toward the officers' mess. 'We'll have another drink or two, a game of cards and who knows? By that time Atkins and Mackenzie—'

'Arnott and Mackenzie.'

'Whatever—they might even be back with the line men before we're finished.'

William shrugged. The whole idea seemed madness to him. The best he could hope for was that his two men would return safely.

William was keen to make things up with Flora again, but there were things to do before he could take time off to visit her. He would carry out the ritual of gun-cleaning in Ralph's room, which would give him time to think about how he would approach her.

The sickly smell of rifle blueing hardly had time to catch in William's throat before the alarm sounded again. He went to the door immediately, but Ralph was more interested in grumbling. He didn't want to use his gun again so quickly after cleaning it.

The Afghans were returning. Flares were already arcing across the night sky and an enfilade of shots was already spattering out from the ragged rustlings of the forest night.

By the time Ralph was ready to take up his position at the outer wall William knew that Arnott and Mackenzie were still outside, in search of the line men. He called for his horse.

'Where do you think you're going?' Ralph called from the walls.

'Arnott and Mackenzie haven't been gone long. I should be able to catch them up soon enough.'

William was already riding across the parade ground, leading a spare horse in case of accident.

'Will, you're mad! Come back!'

'Is that an order, Major Morwyn?'

Ralph was laughing, already intoxicated by the thought of another engagement.

'Of course not, you idiot. You're not seriously going out there?'

'Yes.'

Ralph's laughter followed William toward the gates.

'In that case, keep your head down. We'll keep you covered.'

The station gates swung open. There was no time to think—which was just as well, William reflected as the horses reached the yielding surface of the forest track. It was safe to gallop here, and William was quick to take advantage of the conditions. Flares to the right of them, flares to the left of them, covering fire from behind and a sprinkling of sniper fire from the surrounding darkness—it was bad enough for William, but terrifying for the horses. At least he was leading them away from the worst of the noise.

William tried to ignore the intermittent whine of sniper fire and pressed on. Suddenly, he realised that a series of double shots to his left had a different sound from the Afghan guns. Not only that, but the fire was directed away from him and the station.

'Arnott? Mackenzie?'

With overwhelming relief William recognised the two voices that answered. He knew that the ground sloped into a ravine to the left of the track, which would be giving the two men some shelter from snipers in the forest.

'Are you both all right?' William spurred the horses on into the darkness. 'Keep down. I've brought —'

He never finished. The world exploded in light and pain, streaked through with agonising darkness as he tumbled into an enveloping void.

Chapter Twelve

William floundered back to consciousness through a sea of pain. A tide of oblivion washed over him time and again, but at last he began to make some sense of his surroundings. Pain was roaring through every inch of his body, right into the enamel of his teeth. Eventually, the enveloping darkness receded, and he could make out a low ceiling above him. And a presence somewhere close to his left shoulder.

In the silence he heard soft breathing pause, and became conscious of a familiar perfume.

'I only stayed because they thought you wouldn't wake up.'

'Flora?'

Another wave of pain engulfed him as he tried to turn his head to look at her. He moaned and closed his eyes again.

'I'll go.'

Her voice was small, subdued. He heard the scraping back of a chair and the rustle of her dress as she stood up.

'No. Wait. I'm all right,' he whispered, although that couldn't be true. He tried a laugh, but there seemed to be a heavy weight pressing down on his chest, making it difficult to breathe.

'Flora, don't go. What happened? The kitchens haven't been using river water again, have they? They ought to have remembered from the last time they did it that it's the quickest way to get everyone into the sick bay—'

'Don't you remember?'

Although William sensed that she was standing close beside his hospital bed he could not see her face. The dwindling of her voice was bad enough. Things must be pretty desperate. Thoughts slipped through his mind, but it was difficult to grasp any of them for long. Finally he managed to lay hold of one fleeting image, helped by a localised, gnawing pain in his left shoulder.

'I must have been shot. Is that it? I can see I shall have to be more careful next time.'

A stifled sob from beside him drowned the attempt at humour and hauled back other, far darker images.

'I wasn't thinking. That stupid argument— Oh, Flora. . .what can I say?'

He tried to roll over to face her, but nothing happened.

'Flora?'

'They say I'm not to worry—'

'Am I going to die?'

'I don't know. . .' she managed eventually.

'Let me apologise. I can still do that. Oh, Flora— what must you think? I was cruel and thoughtless—'

'It doesn't matter now.'

'Not even. . .' he swallowed painfully '. . .shouting at you?'

'Of course not.'

There was a long pause before he spoke again. 'Even though I went straight out from ruining your life and did my best to ruin my own?'

'You haven't ruined my life. That was Master Ralph.'

Flora tried to sound firm, but the threat of tears diluted her words.

William managed to chuckle softly. 'All right, pedant! But what about me? What's the damage?'

He heard her sit down again, drawing the chair close to the bed. Then he felt a strange sensation which he decided must be her hand closing over his.

'I heard the doctor say he thought it was concussion of the spine.'

William stared up at the ceiling, wondering what to say.

'That happened to Ralph's uncle,' he managed at last. 'On the hunting field.'

'Yes,' she said quietly. 'Master Ralph's been here. He told me all about it.'

'Remind me to thank him for that some time,' William murmured before closing his eyes again.

Flora sat beside the high iron bed in silence, expecting some outburst which never came. Eyes closed, William was breathing so faintly that she began to wonder if he had slipped away into sleep again.

'How long have I got left?'

The unexpected sound of his voice made her jump, but she never let go of his hand.

'Master Ralph didn't expect you to last this long.'

William laughed. Of all the sounds in that busy abattoir of an infirmary it was the strangest and most unexpected.

'It makes me sound like one of your fish fillets, love!'

The oppressive atmosphere of the little side room where he had been placed closed in around them again. Flora looked at the strong, vital body laid out in its prime. She thought of the nights that they had spent together, all wasted. The time at Salisbury came back to her at last, sharp in every detail. William's caresses and the sinuous grace of his limbs.

She had been more than half afraid of him then. Now the time for fear was long passed. She would never be frightened of him again.

Reaching out her other hand, she stroked William's brow. Damp strands of hair stuck to his skin with the perspiration that he could not wipe away.

'How long have I been here, Flora?'

'Three days.'

This seemed to satisfy him for a moment, then he frowned.

'How long *exactly*?'

The time was burned into Flora's mind like a brand.

'Three days, three hours and twenty-five minutes.'

His frown eased. 'I remember Ralph saying that his uncle had his accident on the Friday afternoon, and he died just before evensong on the Sunday. That's— say. . .fifty-two hours. If I've already managed seventy-five hours and twenty-five minutes. . .'

His voice died away before returning with the very thought that had been torturing Flora.

'Mind you, Ralph's uncle was about three times older than I am. Three times fifty-two—'

'Stop it!' Flora leapt to her feet and for the first time William caught sight of her face, white and drawn with worry.

'Flora! My love, you look dreadful. Haven't you had any sort of a break in all the time I've been here?'

'Of course not.'

'Oh, love, you must go and get some sleep—'

'And leave you here on your own?'

'I'm not exactly sparkling company at the moment.'

'I don't mind,' Flora said loyally. 'The staff don't have time to come and sit with you, and I didn't want

you to be on your own. . .' She faltered, then rallied in
a rush. 'Oh, Will, I love you so much—'

'Is that true? Despite everything?'

'Oh, *Will*. . .' Flora bent and pressed her cheek
against his face, feeling his lashes brush her skin. 'Any
minute spent away from you now will be wasted. I can't
leave you—'

'I know. And I don't really want you to, but right
now I've never felt less like dying,' William murmured
softly in her ear. 'Go home and get some sleep, love.
They'll send someone over to you fast enough.'

Feeling the warm solidity of him, Flora began to
relax, struggling against sleep.

'Are you sure?'

'This is your husband speaking,' William growled
companionably into her ear. 'Go—and obey.'

Flora did leave him, eventually. The matron promised to send for her if there was any change and in the
end she was persuaded to go off and get some sleep.
As she walked across the barrack square the warm
Indian dawn enveloped her with lassitude until even
the hated insect chorus became a lullaby.

Flora hardly had the strength to unlock the door of
their bungalow, let alone get undressed for bed. She
fought her way in between the yards of mosquito
netting, collapsed on the bed and knew no more for a
long time.

When she woke, sunlight was streaming in low
through the bedroom window. It felt like early evening.

Will! Anything could have happened to him while
I've been sleeping the clock round, Flora thought in
panic. Pulling on the dress she had discarded the night
before and scooping her tousled hair under a regulation
topi, Flora ran out into the yard. Hardly noticing the
well-wishers who called to her on the way, she dashed

to the infirmary and into the little side room where William had been.

It was empty.

She was too late. He had gone, and she hadn't been there—

'Mrs Pritchard?' A nurse, immaculate in starched white cap and apron, was smiling at her. Smiling. . .

'We've moved your husband out into the ward. It's a bit more interesting out there for him—'

Flora didn't hear any more. Already halfway down the corridor, she called back her thanks to the nurse and burst into the ward.

There was a shock in store for her. William was in a bed beneath a window, awake, and with the full attention of one nurse all to himself. She was blonde and very pretty—and she was feeding William pieces of fruit from a small bowl. Both were apparently enjoying the experience.

'Flora!' William grinned broadly as she reached his bedside. 'Have you met Nurse Cherie Barclay?'

'No, but I'd like a few words with her before she leaves,' Flora said meaningfully, with a narrow glance at the pretty blonde.

Flora waited until Nurse Cherie Barclay met her at the door. Then she turned her back so that none of the patients could see her expression as she spoke, or hear her words.

'If anyone is going to feed my husband, then it is going to be me, Nurse Barclay,' she said firmly.

'Of course, Mrs Pritchard.' Nurse Barclay handed Flora the fruit dish with a smile so full of innocence that Flora's mind was almost put at rest.

Almost, but not quite.

'Perhaps you might like to give your husband a wash,

Mrs Pritchard,' the pretty nurse went on. 'It's such a relief in this heat. I was about to do it myself, but—'

'That's quite all right, nurse. I shall manage,' Flora said before she had time to wonder how. She gave Nurse Barclay the benefit of a very hard stare before returning to William's bedside with the dish of unrecognisable fruit pieces.

'She's very kind—' William began, but stopped when he saw Flora's expression.

'Not *too* kind, I hope?'

'Not since I met you,' he said carefully.

Flora took her seat beside his bed and they shared the fruit together. It was warm, but sweet and not unpleasant.

'I don't think I can be as badly off as we thought,' William confided to her in a low whisper. 'The worst pain seems to be settling into just a couple of places now, instead of all over. The rest is reduced to something like pins and needles.'

'Can you move?'

'I don't like to try. The staff always look so grave, I thought it best not to. Ralph said the family reckon that the reason his uncle died was because he was moved after his accident.'

The dull rumble of a trolley stopped their whispered conversation. With another innocent smile Nurse Barclay arrived with hot water, soap and towels. Parking the trolley beside William's bed, she pulled the curtains around it to give them some privacy. Then she left them alone together.

'I've done it now,' Flora said softly.

'Are you going to do the honours yourself, then?' William sounded faintly surprised.

'I didn't want a strange woman washing my husband,'

she said primly, but the laugh William gave was anything but restrained.

'Cherie isn't a strange woman,' he began, then realised that a little tact might be necessary. 'She is a very good nurse.'

Flora had been looking at the bowl of hot water with growing dread. Then she gritted her teeth, stood up and went over to the trolley. She was certainly not going to let Nurse Cherie Barclay beat her on this, or anything else.

There was a stiff white square of towelling beside the basin, peg-marked with military precision. A hard cake of yellow soap sat so smartly to attention in its white china dish that Flora felt half afraid to get it wet.

'Shall I ask one of the other nurses to do it for you?' William asked quietly.

'No.' Biting her lip, Flora made a sudden grab for the soap and flannel, soaking them both in the bowl before she had a chance to think better of it. Then she realised that she hadn't pulled down the sheet covering William's body. She had to put down the soapy flannel and dry her hands before uncovering him, betraying her nervousness. She tried to hide this with a rapid efficiency, hoping that he would take her amateurish attempts as proof of her innocence.

'How are you doing?' he whispered at last.

'I don't know. I've got my eyes shut,' Flora confessed.

He laughed. 'You're not joking, are you? Why? Am I so badly shot up?'

'I don't think there's much to see. Except for your shoulder,' she added slowly.

'Could you bear to have a look elsewhere, do you think? I can't see anything but the ceiling, and they never tell me anything. I'm only the patient, after all.'

The sheet was already folded down as far as his waist. Flora had seen men stripped that far in the hayfields, but seeing a husband in that state of undress was quite another matter. Her fingers went on working through the flannel in furious embarrassment and an uncomfortable silence.

'Don't worry,' he said at last. 'I'll ask Cherie next time.'

In an act of sudden daring Flora pulled away the sheet. It nearly proved too much for her. For, in the heat of the infirmary and the apparent hopelessness of his situation, William had been laid on the bed naked.

She clutched the sheet to her as though for protection, but there was no escaping one fact. William was beautiful. And, apart from the damage to his shoulder, a neatly stitched wound stretching almost the length of his left shin and a few bruises, he looked quite undamaged. The skin ran in smooth, sculpted planes across his taut muscles, a thin line of dark hair running from the broad expanse of his chest down to a richer, darker luxuriance and—

'Oh!' Flora breathed, then blushed and laughed as she looked back to his face in guilty shame.

'What's the matter? I can't look too bad if the reward is a smile like that, surely!'

William was laughing, too. The ease of his familiarity almost overcame Flora's fear, but her shyness remained.

'You have a gashed leg, and a bad shoulder, of course, but everything else looks—perfectly good. . .' she said shyly.

'*Everything?*' he pressed, grinning, and she had to turn away.

'I'm sorry, Will. It's just that—well, I've never seen— you know—' One hand gestured ineffectually toward him, but he could only guess at her blushes. He stopped laughing.

'Not even Alfred?'

'Certainly not!' Flora snapped around to look him straight in the eye. 'What a suggestion!'

'It's just a part of me. Like fingers and toes. And like them it probably doesn't work any more, so you've got no worries *there*.'

No. Suddenly there was a flat desolation in his voice that Flora had never heard before. She had no medical knowledge, but she realised that the care of William's mind was going to be as important as the care of his body. There could be no place here for her own petty fears.

Wringing out the flannel, she carefully rinsed away the soap from his chest and arms. This time she didn't close her eyes. Neither spoke until she had finished. Both were wondering if she would continue with the wash.

'I wish I could help,' he said with real longing.

As he spoke his right hand closed with a sudden convulsive movement.

'Will! Are you all right?'

'Getting better by the minute, I think.' His head moved a fraction but a grimace of pain soon stopped him. As Flora watched he tried to close the fingers of his left hand but again his expression spoke of too much pain.

'That's a lot more than I've been able to do so far,' he said at last, breathless with the effort.

'Shall I fetch the doctor?' Flora was staring at him, water dribbling down unnoticed from the flannel in her hands.

'Not yet. Goodness only knows what torture they would start giving me! You could try going down to the foot of the bed, though,' he murmured, concentration focusing his steady grey eyes on the ceiling. 'I think they try and see if I have any feeling in my feet, but it's a bit hard to tell as I can't see what they're up to.'

Obediently Flora went to the end of the bed. Unsure of what a doctor would do, she did the only thing she could think of. She held the wet, rapidly cooling flannel against the soles of his feet.

He sighed heavily. 'I don't know. It doesn't feel like your hand touching me. It feels—I don't know... strange. Cold. A sort of generalised increase in the pins and needles...'

'But you can feel something?' Flora asked as she took the flannel away.

'Not now, no.'

He sighed again.

'I'll finish here, then I think you really ought to see the doctor again.' Flora went back to his side and soaped up the flannel again. After only a moment's hesitation she took up the wash where she had left off, trying to act as though she did this sort of thing every day but blushing furiously. Through the thickness of the flannel she felt him, warm, soft and after a while interesting in a way she would never have thought possible.

Until another involuntary twitch deep within his muscles made her stop with a gasp of alarm.

'My goodness,' he breathed softly. 'I certainly felt *that*.'

The next few days were very frustrating for Flora. The nursing staff seemed to look on her and her questions as nothing but a nuisance. They never told her anything, but then, they never told William anything either. There were a lot more tests and muttered consultations between the doctor and his nurses, but Flora and William were left to wonder. Despite the grave expressions around them they allowed themselves a small ray of hope, which grew stronger each day as first feeling then a little movement inched its way back into William's body.

After a week he could hold her hand. After a fortnight, installed in a special bed that had been transported all the way from Delhi, he drew her hand to his lips for a kiss.

Flora held her breath, restrained by the gnawing guilt that she had been the root cause of his accident. If she hadn't picked that stupid quarrel—

'Well?' he asked softly, still unable to turn his head to gauge her reaction. 'What do you say to that?'

Flora exhaled in a sigh of relief. 'I don't think there's anything *to* say,' she breathed, bending to kiss him gently on the forehead.

'Can't you do any better than that, Mrs Pritchard?' William whispered as her lips touched his skin. 'After all, we are man and wife.'

With a smile she moved round slightly so that they could enjoy a proper kiss.

'Flora. . .' he murmured eventually. 'Let your hair down.'

She drew back, puzzled.

'I want to touch it,' he explained softly. 'I might be a bit restricted, stuck in bed like this, but if you were to let your hair down so that I could feel it. . .'

With a giggle Flora looked around at the spartan efficiency of the hospital ward, the well-starched nurses acting as handmaidens to the lofty and unapproachable doctor.

'What on earth would they all think, Will?'

'They'd realise I must be on the mend. With luck it

would make them want to get me out of here double quick, so that I didn't make the other chaps wild with jealousy.'

'Then you don't really care for me at all.' Flora tried to look severe. 'It might as well be Cherie Barclay for all you care!'

'Draw those curtains, Flora, and I'll show you just what I think of you.'

His words were slow and considered, as though he had been looking forward to this opportunity for a long time.

Obediently, Flora did as she was told. They were now in a world of their own, cut off from everybody and everything. Only the heat remained, closing in upon them like a blanket.

'It's going to be too hot to stand this for long,' Flora said, going to the locker beside his bed. She raised her arms to unpin her hat, then snapped them back to her sides.

'What's the matter?'

'Oh. . .I—that is. . .'

'Everybody gets hot out here, Flora. It comes with the climate,' he said gently. 'Besides, you don't have to be shy with me.'

'But I *am*. . .'

He smiled. 'All right, then. I'll close my eyes.'

Flora waited until she was sure he wasn't looking, then raised her arms again and unpinned her hat. Placing it carefully on the locker, she then uncoiled her hair from its neat bun, letting it drape loose about her shoulders.

'There.' Hands clasped demurely in front of her, Flora stood ready for inspection.

'Beautiful,' he breathed. He was looking at her with such intensity that it was almost frightening. 'Now, if you were to sit on the edge of the bed, I could touch it. . .'

Flora did as he said, finding the padded edges of the special bed much more comfortable than the iron-hard army-issue ones. She leaned forward so that the water-fall of her auburn hair rippled over William's hand and arm. With a small movement he caught a skein and let it run through his fingers.

'Exquisite. The Indian girls dress their hair with some sort of oily concoction so that it—' He stopped abruptly.

'Yes?'

'I was about to be indiscreet.'

'Why?' Flora looked at him with such an absence of guile that he had to chuckle. 'Since I've been on my own such a lot, I've found out that I like discovering things about life here,' she persisted. 'It's better than sitting about in that prison cell they call the "hen house".'

'Or the officers' mess,' he agreed.

'Go on, then. Tell me about the Indian girls.'

William hesitated, nipping his lip before replying.

'Some of them can make the most delightful companions for a single man. I believe,' he said carefully.

This puzzled Flora, who had only ever seen soldiers escorting British ladies about the station.

'Do any of them ever get to marry their soldiers?'

'Oh, no!' William said rapidly. 'But then, of course, the soldiers don't marry the British girls out here that carry on like that, either.'

The unguarded reply told Flora more than William had intended to put into words. One of the many perks of being a cook was being allowed to read the *News of the World*—even if it was only while the young kitchen maids were safely shielded behind a mountain of washing up.

'Don't look at me like that, Flora!' William went on in exasperation. 'Wherever there are single men and single women there are going to be...well, *opportunities*...'

She raised her eyebrows, enjoying the unusual sight of his embarrassment.

'For you?'

'I was always kind and careful. After what happened to my poor mother you could hardly expect me to be anything less. Anyway, you must know how it is with men. You having been married, and all,' he finished sharply.

Flora sat up, confused at his harsh tone. Realising then that he had alarmed her, William reached out tentatively.

'Oh, I'm sorry, Flora. I shouldn't have said that. It was unforgivable.' His hand touched the silken curtain of her hair, parting it with gentle fingers. 'Do you think we might start again, you and I? From the beginning?'

Flora smiled. 'Do you remember that first outing, in the Rolls?'

'I don't ever want to forget it.'

'When you asked to put your arm around me, and said you'd wanted to do it when we were in the picture palace?'

William watched her expectantly, waiting for her to go on.

'I think I might be feeling a bit like you were feeling then, Will.'

'I doubt that,' he countered, but softly. 'I'd like to put my arms around you now, but you'll have to get quite a bit closer for that—'

'Like this?'

In a sudden movement Flora bent forward and slid her arms between his body and the gently yielding surface of the bed. Her head pressed against his chest, she shut her eyes tight with the fervent prayer that he wouldn't tell her to stop.

He didn't. Instead, she felt the light touch of his hand work its way up her arm to her shoulder and so to her head. Here it rested for a moment before starting to stroke her tenderly.

'I really do love you, Flora. If only I could get out of this wretched contraption and show you properly. . .'

Flora pressed her cheek still harder against his chest.

While he was still lying here like this there was no chance that he could hurt her.

'I love you too, Will.'

'Even if. . .?'

The broad expanse of his chest rose beneath her as he took a deep breath.

'Even if I don't recover enough to—you know—give you children?' The last words were muttered indistinctly, but Flora's reply was clear enough.

'*Especially* if.'

He was silent for a moment.

'You can't really mean that, Flora? Not after Salisbury?'

The feeling of being so utterly safe with him was leading to all sorts of new sensations. After all, it wasn't as though he could hurt her now, so any revelation would be easy.

Especially as he could not adjust his position to look at her as she spoke.

'I do. To tell you the truth I hated all that sort of thing when I was married to Alfred, and I'm glad we won't be troubled by it any more,' she said in a rush of relief.

'Oh, *Flora*! Why on earth didn't you tell me that before?' His fingers drew her hair back as he tried to get a sight of her face. Flora closed her eyes again.

'Would it have made any difference?'

'Of course!'

'Even that first night, in Salisbury?'

'Especially then.'

'I can't see how.'

'Because, unlike your dear departed Alfred, I knew we had all the time in the world. And, if I might be allowed the sin of speaking ill of the dead, Alfred also sounds like the sort of chap who had a lot to prove. I don't. Especially not now.' He tapped her cheek gently with one finger. 'So may I have another kiss?'

Slowly, Flora raised her head. William was looking at her so lovingly that she had no hesitation in moving forward to kiss him full on the lips. The heat and intensity of the moment cleared her mind of all thought, sending a cascade of unrecognisable feelings rushing through her body like warm oil.

'Making love is the most wonderful thing in the world, Flora,' William breathed at last.

'It never seemed to be like that for Alfred.' Flora grimaced suddenly at the memory. 'That sort of business only ever made him fighting mad.'

'And you?'

'It's only ever led to tears.'

'Well, my mother might agree with you there, but that shouldn't be the way.'

William had been stroking her hair, but this lightest of touches now began to move down over the curve of her cheek. Gradually it drifted across the line of her throat. Then, as though exhausted by the effort, his hand fell back to the bed. A slight frown furrowed

Flora's brow. The touch of his hand had been pleasant, and she was sorry to lose the sensation.

He read her expression and lifted his hand again, this time to her lips. She responded with a kiss, and he traced the outline of her mouth with a touch as light as thistledown. It was such a delightful sensation that Flora reached out to do the same to him, touching the smooth, firm surface of his lips.

'There,' he murmured softly. 'Now what in the world could there be to dislike about this?'

'Nothing.' Flora felt his hand slip from her cheek to the back of her neck, but no longer felt afraid. Instead that faint but undeniable longing had begun to stir deep within her again. 'Except that I wish it could go on for ever.'

'Well, I think it had better come to an end right now,' William said softly. Puzzled, Flora raised her head and was treated to another long and lingering kiss.

'Because I must be quite a bit better than even I thought, and I don't want this to get out of control,' William continued. His eyes, large and dark with desire, suddenly lightened with a return of the old merriment. 'Not until I'm in a position to do rather more about it, that is!'

William's recovery was rapid after that. When he learned that Ralph was to go back to England he was quiet for a time, but Flora did her best to take his mind off it. Within days the doctor allowed William to be pushed out onto the veranda, where, with the special bed cranked almost upright, he could watch Colour Sergeant Barclay practising his shouting out on the square.

Flora spent as much time with William as she could,

but with Christmas approaching she couldn't always escape May Primm's working parties. To her surprise Flora found that helping with the Christmas catering was the one job that all the ladies hated. She was the first and only one to volunteer for kitchen duties, but that suited her.

'Too much like hard work for some of them,' she confided to William, bringing him some of the first mince pies. 'They'd rather sit about in the "hen house" cutting out paper snowflakes and having a good gossip.'

'Are you going to make any decorations for our rooms?' William wondered idly.

Flora shook her head. 'I've made the place feel a bit more homely but I won't be going that far. There doesn't seem to be much point. Not when I shall be there all on my own for Christmas.'

'I think you should,' he said firmly. 'After all, you don't want to take delivery of my Christmas present in a room as unfriendly as a Bethlehem inn, do you?'

Flora did decorate their quarters in the end, although her heart wasn't in it. She even made a pretend Christmas tree. Arnott cut her a branch from a tiny-leaved evergreen bush growing in the ravine. Grated white Windsor soap mixed with a bit of water made some kind of substitute for snow when dabbed over the branches.

Her work in the kitchens provided more than distraction from William's recovery. One day she had the task of cutting up a large cake that the Primms had received from England. The cake tin had been wrapped in pretty silver and gold paper, which Flora quickly requisitioned for herself. She was sitting in the bungalow cutting out gold and silver paper stars to decorate her little tree when there was a knock at the door.

Visits from the other ladies were always a trial for

Flora, but she always tried to put a brave face on it. After all, they were all a long way from home and with Christmas coming. . .

She opened the door with a polite smile carefully pinned in place, but then she stopped. For standing unsupported and alone on the step was a tall, handsome soldier in full uniform. The very last person she had expected to see.

It was William.

Chapter Thirteen

It took Flora a second or two to take it all in. Then she threw her arms around his neck, showering him with kisses.

'*Will!*'

'Steady on! Let me get over the threshold. I shall need a sit down.'

Fielding all her questions amiably, he went over to the chair and sat down, leaving Flora to rush about tidying cushions and worrying about his escape from the infirmary.

'May Primm isn't the only one who has been glad of all the time you've been spending in the kitchens.' He smiled as Flora knelt on the newly carpeted floor beside him. 'I wanted to get out in time for Christmas. I've been practising, with all the staff sworn to secrecy. I wanted to surprise you.'

'You did.' Flora could still hardly believe it. 'Are you back for good? Can you stay here?'

William looked guarded. 'Well. . .I'm not quite sure about that. I went over to see Colonel Primm before I came here.'

'All that way?' Flora was aghast.

'That's nothing. I walked as far as the gymnasium

yesterday and got back safely. I've seen plenty carried out of there in my time, and I wasn't going to be the first one carried *in*!'

He looked around the room, which Flora had tried to make more homely. Muslin had been pinned up to make a false ceiling, obscuring the thatch above, while the new carpet provided a touch of real luxury. Across the room the little substitute Christmas tree stood in a large paper-covered container, which looked suspiciously like an old bully-beef tin filled with sand. Pots of poinsettia represented the red and green of absent English holly. The place was almost cosy.

'Do you like it here, Flora?'

Torn between truth and loyalty, Flora carefully avoided giving him a direct answer.

'I'm getting used to it,' she managed at last.

'The termites and white ants will make short work of the carpet. They've already finished off the only piano here that the elephants hadn't smashed. That wouldn't happen in old England.'

'The men put down a sheet soaked in something that's supposed to put them off,' Flora said, trying to forget the way that all their books on the brand-new shelves had been nibbled by something overnight.

'How would you like to go back to England?' William said suddenly. 'If you could bear to leave this place, that is. . .'

It was a miracle. The Christmas present to end all Christmas presents. Flora jumped up and hugged him again, almost speechless with delight.

'Oh, Will! When? And for how long?'

'For always,' he said slowly. 'If you like.'

Flora stopped and looked at him closely. 'You're doing this for me?'

'And me,' he said firmly. 'It's no life here for you,

Flora, and I'm going off it rapidly too. The thought of
making you happy finally made up my mind for me.'

'You always make me happy,' Flora murmured,
nuzzling his ear.

'I do try.'

He slid an arm around her, drawing her close. Flora
noticed that he looked pale and was instantly
concerned.

'Are you tired, Will?'

'That rather depends.' A slow delight pushed the
exhaustion from his eyes and he bent his head to rest
his cheek against her hair. 'I might let you persuade me
into bed, Nurse Pritchard. If you promise to be gentle
with me, of course.'

Flora had always loved Christmas, but the thought of
going home more than made up for missing Christmas
at Karanpur. She could not get packed fast enough.
When the time came to leave she tried to put
on a grave face and look sorrowful when William
said goodbye to all his comrades, but her heart was
singing.

She had sent a letter to her father asking if they
might stay with him until things were settled. William
had disguised this home leave as a convalescence to
begin with, but during the trip back to Bombay he told
Flora that he had all but made up his mind to leave the
army. He had been offered an administrative post in
England, but that wouldn't hold him for long if the
right job came along.

Flora did sometimes wonder about all the plans she
had once had of setting up in her own business, but it
hardly seemed right to think about them now. William
was clever, and successful. In the circles in which he

would be moving there would be no room for a working wife.

There was time for a lot of talking on the journey home to England. Flora began to realise that there wouldn't be time for her to run her own business in any case. She would be busy enough loving William, and helping him to build their new life together. It wasn't that she had lost her ambition: all her energies were now going to be channelled to an equally important end.

'I could definitely get to like sea cruises,' Flora said as she reclined on a steamer chair in the deep shade of the starboard deck. William was beside her, a three-week-old copy of the *Bombay Times and Herald* lying unopened on his lap. They were still holding hands.

'You could have one every few years if I stayed in the army,' William said with gentle humour.

Flora bit her lip. 'I don't know if I would ever get used to being an army wife. I don't think I should ever have got to like India. It was all so different to Falgrave.'

'That's certainly true.' William smiled at her. 'You liked Delhi, though, didn't you?'

'Yes. . .but I thought the English ladies there were a bit overdressed.'

'And you liked the kitchens at Karanpur. Apart from the white ants.'

He was teasing her again, and she liked it. She reached over and stroked his cheek.

'There were lots of things I liked about India.' She thought carefully. 'In fact, the only things I didn't like about it were the heat and the dust. The people were friendly, the flowers were beautiful and the food was— well, I was getting used to the way the food was cooked toward the end.'

They exchanged a knowing look.

'But to tell you the truth I was always afraid that one of those sacred cows might run amok in the streets, or a tiger might spring out at me from the undergrowth, or—'

A steward materialised in front of them, stiff with formality and a neatly pressed uniform. He bowed from the waist and held a tray out to William. Flora regarded the tray with a professional eye, wondering if it was real silver or only EPNS.

'A communication for you, Captain Pritchard,' the steward intoned gravely.

Flora felt a cold lurch of fear. It was the same feeling experienced by everyone who had sat out the Great War at home, waiting for news. Anything other than an ordinary letter meant bad news.

Sensing her fear, William tried to make light of the delivery.

'The game must be up! Somebody's tracked me down by radio telegraphy, like Dr Crippen!'

He unfolded the message quickly to put Flora out of her misery, but it was a cryptic message and it made him frown. Flora immediately sat forward, grasping his arm. He patted her but it was a preoccupied gesture and did nothing to calm her.

'What is it?' Flora burst out, unable to contain herself any longer.

William shook his head in disbelief.

'I don't know—but it's from the Duke of Alvoe, of all people. Listen to this—'

The steward cleared his throat meaningfully before William could begin reading. William immediately remembered himself and began searching through his pockets for a tip. The delay was more than Flora could bear. She turned the paper so that she could read its message, but it made her none the wiser.

'Request presence at Alvoe Court immediately on arrival in England—transport arranged,' Flora read silently, her expression slipping from fear to disbelief. 'Will? What on earth does it mean?'

'I don't know,' William said thoughtfully, watching the steward walk away along the deck. 'Ralph must have reached home by now. Unless, of course, he couldn't face his people. Going home was made to look like his own decision, but he told me that he wasn't given much of an option. The Duke and Duchess will have picked up on that fast enough.'

Relieved that at least it wasn't bad news about Will's family or her father, Flora rallied enough to pat his hand. She was looking earnestly into his face and noticed that there was grave concern in his eyes despite his attempts to conceal it.

'I know—they're blaming me for Ralph's disgrace. After a show trial they will hold a summary execution. I shall be up against the kitchen garden wall with a blindfold on before the next pheasant shoot—'

'Don't joke about it.' Flora shuddered. 'It was bad enough when we handed in my notice. I never thought I'd have to go there again. Oh, Will—whatever can it be? Trouble, that's for sure—'

'Don't worry, love!' William silenced her with a kiss. 'Look. The Duke would hardly end his message "Regards" if there was any trouble, would he?'

Flora returned his kiss, but she was uneasy. She sensed that William was more concerned about the message than he would admit. For the first time since they had met she felt that he was keeping something from her.

Flora didn't know what it could be, but she knew that it was going to cast a long shadow over them both.

Thereafter William never referred to the Duke's summons himself. Whenever Flora raised the matter he was quick to put her mind at rest, but she noticed that he often looked troubled. When Flora asked him about it again he offered to send a message to Alvoe Court asking for more details, but she wouldn't hear of it. The whole idea of giving a week's wages to the telegraph office for something that might never reach its destination seemed madness to Flora.

When at last in mid-February they reached the docks, Flora was the first to spot James, the chauffeur. He was leaning against the Alvoe Rolls and enjoying a smoke, but he was quick enough to toss his cigarette aside when he spotted William and Flora approaching. At any other time Flora would have been conscious of the chauffeur's scorn at her advancement by marriage, but she had no time to be embarrassed now. She allowed William to shepherd her into the car, but as soon as he was settled beside her she pretended to remember a handkerchief she had left in her hand baggage.

She got out and went round to where James was stowing it away. When she returned to William's side she was still without her handkerchief but she had heard such a staggering piece of below-stairs gossip that she could only gaze at him in wordless disbelief.

'What is it? Flora? Are you ill?'

'N-no. . .I'm fine,' she managed.

'Are you sure? You're as white as paper!'

'I'm perfectly all right. I've just had a bit of a shock, that's all.' Flora's voice sounded unconvincing, even to her own ears.

'Come on, love. What is it?'

Flora looked into William's steady grey eyes, seeing genuine concern for her reflected in his expression. She searched his features, returning his loving look with one of growing amazement.

'Tell me, then! You look as though you've lost a florin and found a farthing!'

'The other way about, more likely.' Flora took his hand. She looked down at the strong brown fingers encircling her own, so that he wouldn't be able to see her expression.

'A—a newspaper-seller on the quay was advertising a bad motor car accident,' she said eventually. 'It made me realise how far it is to Alvoe Court and how dangerous the journey could be—'

'Rubbish!' William chided her gently. Slipping his hand out of her grasp, he put his arm around her instead. She was drawn close to the warm stability of him and held there like a precious prize. But for how long? she asked herself, with a terrible premonition of disaster.

'I know a lovely little pub on the Salisbury road.' He spoke softly into her ear in a way that usually made her shiver with anticipation. 'I've asked James to get us there in time for morning coffee. We can look forward to sharing a snack on dry land, and forget all about any sensational newspaper headline.'

He leaned forward as James got into the driving seat in front of them.

'You've got a nervous lady traveller here, James. Take care.'

James looked back and smirked at Flora. She no longer cared what he thought. She had somebody far more important than a mere chauffeur to worry about.

Flora struggled with her inner turmoil all morning. It was impossible to tell William what the chauffeur had told her. For one thing, gossip below stairs was notoriously unreliable. Look at the silly story that had gone the rounds about Queen Alexandra. A royal would never try to commit suicide, whatever the provocation. It was unthinkable. Flora was sure *that* rumour couldn't have been true, and she hoped against hope that this rumour about the Duke of Alvoe was just as fanciful.

By the time they reached the outskirts of Falgrave her appetite had grown, and she suggested stopping off at her father's house for something to eat. William sent James off to the Porter Stores and for once Flora was too busy with her own thoughts to wonder how a stranger—and a stranger in a fancy uniform, too—would get on in the tiny village pub.

Her father was away at work, as she had known he would be. Flora made herself busy by putting the kettle on the fire, getting the old frying-pan out from beneath the sink and fetching some fat bacon from the meat safe.

'Will,' she said slowly as soon as her back was turned toward him. 'Would you really have got around to marrying me in the end, even if my. . .mistake hadn't happened?'

'Of course. I've told you before—your fright only hurried things up a bit, that's all.'

'Are you *sure*?'

He was stunned that she could still doubt him.

'Of course! There were lots of reasons why I would have asked you to marry me eventually, but at the time the thought of a baby seemed the most important. I had already convinced myself that I was in love with you. I liked your looks, your company, and it's just gone on getting better and better since then, hasn't it?'

Flora went to the kitchen table. She put the frying-pan down carefully.

'Are you sure?' The chauffeur's version of Downstairs gossip was still simmering away in her mind. 'I thought you ought to have preferred a girl who would have done your career some good.'

William looked at her steadily. She was edging around some concern, but he couldn't think what it might be. Her misty green eyes were clouded with worry, and more than anything else he wanted to relieve that worry, whatever it might be.

'I married you because I wanted to, Flora. Nobody forced my hand. No thoughts of advancement ever crossed my mind. All I ever wanted to do was to keep you safe, and to support and care for—' his eyes flickered momentarily to her waist '—for *you*.'

'Oh, Will.' Cooking forgotten, Flora's hands dropped to her sides. 'Then I didn't trap you into marrying me?'

'You did me a favour,' he said, trying to lighten the situation. 'Spurred me on. I might never have had the nerve to ask if it hadn't been for—well, what nearly happened. I'm only sorry that marrying me rather put paid to *your* career.'

She picked up the teapot and went to the hearth. The kettle was nearly at the boil, and she filled the teapot mechanically as she spoke.

'As long as I could have your love then I could find pleasure in other things in life apart from work, Will. Besides, I don't suppose there's much else for a captain's lady to do apart from having babies.'

'What happened to your ambitions? To be the best cook?'

'That wouldn't have been much use in India.' Flora stirred the tea then sat down at the kitchen table.

'Flora,' William said slowly, fingering his teacup without lifting it from the saucer. 'I've been giving a bit of thought to what I could do once I leave the army.

I'd never really liked the thought of working women until I met you. The war has changed things, and I'm beginning to think that everyone should have a chance to prove themselves in a job that they are good at. I'm good at administration and organising—you're good at cooking. How about going into business?'

'With you?' Flora could hardly form the words.

'Of course. I've got a bit of money put by—enough to set us up. I know you're the best there is at your job, but you'll need money to get going. If you wanted to take up catering again on your own account, I could help you set up your own empire. It would make a lot more sense than wasting my time trying to stop the King's empire falling to pieces.' He grinned at her. 'You could do all the donkey work and let me worry about all the money and the living in luxury.'

'I love you, Will.'

'I should hope so too, Mrs Pritchard.'

If only his idea could come true. If only the next few hours were the first and not the last they would spend together. Flora flung herself at him, wanting his arms around her for what she was sure would be the last time. William responded, holding her close as they kissed and caressed in the silence.

Outside a blackbird flew to the top of the jasmine in a flounce of fanning tail and threw a snatch of song to the late winter wind. Desperate to feel the full power of William's love just once more, Flora twisted in his arms and sat down on his lap, twining her arms around his neck as his kisses became more urgent.

'Let's go upstairs,' she whispered.

At that he pushed her away gently so that he could look deep into her eyes.

'Well, you're becoming forward and no mistake!' he murmured softly, smiling. Flora shifted her weight slowly and expertly in his lap and his smile became broader, more knowing.

'Please, Will?'

She knew he could never resist that.

'I'm still supposed to be convalescing. As my nurse you ought to be aware of the dangers of anything but the most innocent kiss,' he said with mock gravity.

'Is there such a thing as an innocent kiss between a nurse and her patient?' Flora said, her hand slipping between the roughness of his light tweed jacket and the warmth of the waistcoat within.

She could feel the faint thunder of his heart beating rapidly beneath her hand and excitement began to overwhelm all of her concerns.

The pupils of William's eyes were larger and darker than Flora had ever seen them. The grey was a mere misty halo about them now.

'Take me upstairs.' Flora's voice was low with longing, the words almost drowned by the waterfall of song the blackbird was pouring from the outhouse roof. She felt William's heart rate increase, the warm, vital strength of him barely restrained by their surroundings.

'This is going to be the best ever,' she murmured as he lifted her up and carried her gently up the stairs toward her old, familiar room beneath the eaves.

And the worst, she added silently to herself before William's love overwhelmed her with a tide of passion.

Chapter Fourteen

Flora and William loved with an abandon that neither had ever experienced before. Her hunger for his body and his enduring love roused them both to such heights of passion that even the frantic hammering on the partition wall from old Mrs Westbury next door went unheeded.

When it was over William collapsed, laughing, at Flora's side.

'That's given her something to think about!' He bent to kiss Flora again but she shook her head.

'No, Will. What about the Duke of Alvoe? He'll be waiting for us, and—'

'Let him wait.' William silenced her with the touch of one finger against her lips.

Slowly, Flora sat up and looked straight into the darkness of his eyes.

'Will, there's something you should know—'

Faced with his unsuspecting gaze, Flora could go no further.

'Yes?'

She bent to retrieve the coverlet that had slipped to the floor, rather than look straight at him.

'Oh. . .it can wait until after you've seen the Duke. It's probably nothing, anyway.'

'Is it the same "nothing" that's been haunting you since the car picked us up from the docks?'

Since the truth had come out about the phantom baby William had become very sensitive to any trace of unease in Flora. For a moment she considered telling him everything that she had heard, but superstition stopped her. The very act of telling the tale might make it true. Then she would lose him for sure. If there was the smallest chance of even half an hour more of William's love before any truth came out. . .

'Yes! Will. . .I wasn't quite honest about what happened when James picked us up, but it's probably nothing. Below-stairs gossip picked up from him, that's all.'

William looked doubtful. 'Are you sure you don't want to talk about it, Flora? The Morwyn family don't owe you anything now, you know.'

No, she thought painfully. And they won't want to, either.

'The staff aren't telling tales about that delicious little cook who seduced one of their house guests, are they?'

Slyly William reached forward and ran his fingers quickly up and down her ribs. She tried to wriggle out of his reach but he continued unmercifully until they were both laughing again. In the confusion of giggles William's arms went around her waist. Dragging her back across the bed toward him, he kissed her.

All Flora's struggles stopped. William's kisses always made her forget everything. Only the cool firmness of his lips and the touch of his hands mattered as he caressed her. The warmth of him and the close fragrance of soap whispering over his skin absorbed her totally as she clung to him.

'Will. . .' she murmured at last.

'I think we'd better get to Alvoe Court. Fast.'

He kissed her forehead in what was supposed to be a parting gesture but Flora drew him back to her lips once more. This time when they reluctantly drew apart a thought managed to struggle into Flora's mind. Anything to delay the awful moment of parting, which was sure to come as soon as they reached Alvoe Court.

'Perhaps we could call in on the vicar and Mrs McSweeney on the way.'

'I'm sure they'd love that.' William stroked a stray auburn curl away from Flora's eyes. His touch continued the caress across her shoulders and down to the small of her back. 'Let's go now, shall we? After we've called in at the Manor to see your father, of course.'

'What about that bacon sandwich you wanted? I'm more than satisfied now but if you're still hungry. . .'

'Not for food.' William pinched her gently. 'Come on. If we don't make a move now we'll be here all day. Old Mrs Westbury will be sending for the constabulary. Let's go and find your father. If your ex-mother-in-law hasn't already done so, that is!'

They separated slowly, both reluctant to let go of each other, even for the few moments it took them to dress.

As they left the cottage the blackbird flounced up to the chimney with a cackle of alarm but soon settled to singing again. Flora and William walked across the home meadow lost in a silence that was companionable on William's part but troubled on Flora's.

Eventually William stopped walking and put his arms around her again.

'Look, Flora, are you going to tell me what is upsetting you, or am I going to have to go on worrying?'

'It's nothing. . .'

'It *can't* be nothing. "Nothing" doesn't dim that smile of yours. You know what we agreed at Karanpur. No more secrets! Tell me, Flora. What are they saying back at Alvoe Court that has upset you?'

It was too much. Flora shuddered with the fear of what was to come and the desperate struggle of trying to keep William's love until the last possible moment.

'You'll give me up!' The words tore from her with an agonising cry. 'You really will wish we'd never got married! Once you're back there with all your fine friends—'

'*Nothing* and nobody will make me give you up now, Flora,' William said gently. 'Ever. Not after all we've been through together. Understand?'

He stroked her cheek gently as though she might break at the lightest touch.

Flora tried her best to smile.

'Don't worry. I won't hold you to it, Will.'

'What on earth can be any worse than what we've been through already?' William was running his hands up and down her back now in distraction.

'Something that will come between us.' Flora shook her head.

'Nothing will ever do that.' William gave her a little shake of reproof, then had an inspiration. 'Ralph! I'll *bet* it's something to do with Ralph. He'll have been giving his parents some colourful story about us, and the staff have overheard and got everything out of proportion. When we get to Alvoe Court I'm going to give him a piece of my mind.'

'If you're sure that you can spare it!' Flora said with an attempt at mischief.

'Come out with cheek like that, Mrs Pritchard, and I shall have to give you a good talking-to,' William said with a look in his eyes that belied the sternness in his voice.

'I won't need anything like that.' Flora took his hand again and they walked on. 'For as long as I have you, Will.'

Flora's temporary happiness was given a jolt as soon as Mrs McSweeney opened the vicarage door. The house-keeper's carefully practised politeness fell away as soon as she saw William. She stared at him in open disbelief for some seconds. Flora immediately stepped forward to find out what was wrong, although she had a horrible feeling that she knew. The news from Alvoe must have reached Branxmere already.

'Mrs McSweeney?'

The housekeeper looked from William to Flora and seemed to come out of her trance.

'Oh, my lord! Stay there, the pair of you. I'd better go and warn him.'

'What's the matter?' William started to follow her into the vicarage but Mrs McSweeney was already down the hall and into the vicar's study.

'It sounds as though something has happened to him,' William began, his face ashen. Flora took his arm.

'No, Will, I don't think it's that.'

She didn't have time to say any more. Mrs McSweeney was already coming back along the passage, the study door left open in her haste.

'Go straight in, Master William, before he's had a chance to get into a fluster. Flora, you're coming with me.'

Mrs McSweeney pulled her over the threshold into the house and slammed the front door shut behind her. Flora went to follow William into the vicar's study but Mrs McSweeney took her arm, leading her down the passage toward the kitchen. This is it, Flora thought. The separation has begun. I shall never get William back now.

'I'd be grateful of your opinion on a cake I made yesterday, Flora. It's a recipe from the *Woman's Weekly*. I'll copy it out for you, if you like it.'

'But—'

'No arguments. There's likely to be enough of them in there.' Mrs McSweeney cocked her head toward the study in passing. Its door had closed behind William with a thud of awful finality.

'What has been going on here, Mrs McSweeney? Is it something to do with the Duke of Alvoe?'

Mrs McSweeney pursed her lips, and Flora knew that the rumours must have been right.

'I'm not at liberty to say. Not even to you. *Especially* not to you. I've only recently managed to persuade the vicar to come to terms with you and Master William getting married,' Mrs McSweeney said grimly. She led Flora into the kitchen and sat her down at the table for the obligatory cup of tea. Flora's spirits sank still further when she found that the tea set before her was both strong and sweet—the sovereign remedy for shock.

It really must be the end.

'It's about the rumours James, the chauffeur, told me, isn't it?' Flora persisted as the clouds of dread swept in over her again.

Mrs McSweeney was rolling out pastry to line a pie dish and crimped her lips as tightly as she was crimping the pastry.

'Rumours aren't always to be trusted,' the house-keeper said in a dreadful tone that Flora could not bear to question.

She watched Mrs McSweeney finish her pie-making

in silence. After wiping her floury hands clean on a dishcloth and putting the pie into the oven the house-keeper sorted through her selection of storage tins to bring out a fruit cake. It looked as impressive as anything Flora might have presented at Alvoe Court. It probably tasted as good as it looked, but Flora could not tell. She barely picked at the slice she was given. Manners meant nothing now. She was losing William, and didn't care about anything else.

After an eternity the kitchen door opened slowly behind her. Then William was standing at her side, one hand on the back of her chair.

'Flora. . .the Reverend has sent a message over to Alvoe Court, telling them to expect us.'

'I hope you're taking Flora with you,' Mrs McSweeney said rather stiffly.

'Of course.' William's hand moved protectively to Flora's shoulder. She looked up at him quickly, and that same well-loved light was still in his eyes.

'It'll be all right, Flora,' he said softly. 'Nothing is going to part us.'

'I suppose there's no point in asking you if you'll have anything to eat or drink before you go?' Mrs McSweeney said wearily.

'There's nothing my wife and I would like better than a cup of tea and a slice of your excellent cake, Mrs McSweeney.'

'But what about the Duke?' Flora was still studying William's face closely and was rewarded with a kiss.

'He's waited this long, my love. He'll just have to wait a bit longer.'

Flora looked back at William steadily, gradually gaining strength from his quiet support. There were a thousand questions that she wanted to ask, but only one that she could put into words.

'What about Master Ralph?'

Despite the fact that William had been put in an impossible situation, Flora could still feel some sympathy for Ralph Morwyn. He had ruined his own career through his own actions, but life was about to deal him another surprise.

William addressed the vicar, who had entered the kitchen and closed the door.

'I don't want this to cause any more trouble for Ralph. I used to be the only friend he had, and I shouldn't like him to think that this awful business is going to change things.'

'I think the matter is out of your hands now, Will,' the vicar said softly. Flora couldn't tell if he had really forgiven William for the hasty marriage, but it was the first time she had seen him mellowed by anything approaching emotion.

'I told Jethro to go to Falgrave and send the Alvoe car here, Mrs McSweeney. He's despatched his boy across the fields to Alvoe Court at the same time. The Duke will be expecting us.' The vicar tried to hurry things along as though trying to conceal his momentary lapse into sentiment. 'I'm sure Will and Flora won't mind if I accompany them in the Alvoe motor car?'

There was an uncomfortable silence that Flora felt too confused to question. She forced down a last morsel of cake and put down her fork with relief.

'That was delicious, Mrs McSweeney.'

The housekeeper's starched apron rustled noisily in the awkward silence.

'Would you like the recipe, Flora?'

'Indeed I should.' Flora tried a smile, but it was without conviction.

'I'll have it written out by the time you come back,'

Mrs McSweeney said, turning away before the difficult conversation could be extended.

She expects me to come back straight away, Flora thought with a return of her old desolation. Then William took her hand, and she began to hope that everything might be all right again.

It was some time before a growling spatter of gravel on the drive outside had the vicar striding to the door.

'Don't forget your coat, Reverend!' Mrs McSweeney called. 'There's still a chill in the air.'

'Particularly when travelling in the Alvoe Rolls, I suspect. Come and see, Mrs McSweeney. A grand car for a grand family, don't you think?'

The vicar spoke without awe or affection as he looked out of the open kitchen door but his housekeeper made up for that.

'You'll have to wrap up especially warm. I don't hold with all this speeding around the countryside, Vicar. It's bad enough when you get up on that great big horse —'

'You sit in the back with the Reverend, Flora. I'll sit in the front,' William said gently.

'I'm the one with an unlimited supply of coats and scarves to hand, William. You're the one with the new wife. Sit in the back with her.'

It had been a statement of fact, hardly a blessing on their marriage. All the same, Flora saw a glimmer of hope that at least the Reverend accepted that they were a proper couple.

William stayed by Flora's side. When he had first arrived in the kitchen he had been taut with a suppressed fury that Flora recognised from that one dreadful night back in Karanpur. Now his initial anger had subsided, but it had taken with it his usual good humour.

'I'm sorry about all this, Flora.' William's voice was full of regret, but he managed a smile for her.

'Is it true, then?'

William looked from the vicar to Mrs McSweeney, then took both Flora's hands in his. After taking a deep breath he closed his fingers protectively around hers.

'Yes, love. It seems that the Duke of Alvoe is my father.'

Flora was quiet for a long time, listening to James nursing the waiting engine outside.

'What about Gully Pritchard?'

'He is my mother's father. She left home as soon as she knew that the Duke had got her—' he hesitated, unable to use the painful word in front of Flora '—into trouble.'

The only crumb of comfort Flora had been able to salvage from the rumours was that William would be relieved to find out who his father was, after so many years of uncertainty. She had been sure that he would be made to reject her, but at least he would have a family at last. One look at William's face now showed that the opposite was true. Whatever feelings the news had evoked in him, relief wasn't among them.

William helped her into the car, then settled the Reverend into the front seat with a blanket. His face was closed and grim. When he sat down next to Flora in the back of the car it was some time before she could summon up the courage to speak.

'William, what can I do?'

The car had started to move. William tore his gaze away from the countryside and tried to smile for her again.

'Nothing.' Putting his arm around her, he gave her a reassuring squeeze. 'Except understand that what happens next means a great deal to me.'

The Rolls flew down Branxmere Hill, past gnarled fruit trees where pearly white mistletoe berries would ripen later in the year. Pearls for tears, Flora thought.

'Does it feel like coming home?' she said as they swept through the winter-washed countryside.

William's answer was considered, but abrupt.

'No.'

The main doors of Alvoe Court opened as the Rolls prowled up to the house. William's urgency was visible but he helped Flora down from the car in taut silence and waited until the vicar had joined them on the front step before addressing the butler.

'Where is he, Mr Perry?'

'His Grace awaits you in the study, Captain Pritchard.'

William handed the butler his hat and immediately went into the house, straight to the blank face of the mahogany door of the Duke's study.

'Perhaps Mr Perry could show us somewhere to wait?' the Reverend suggested.

'I should like you both with me.' William reached out his hand for Flora and she went to him. 'For moral support.'

William went forward even before Mr Perry had finished formally announcing the visitors. Flora and the Reverend followed his lead with the proper deference expected of the lower orders.

'Is it true?' William was saying even before the butler had left the room.

The Duke of Alvoe had been sitting behind the safety of his desk but now rose to his feet to face William across it.

'Yes,' the Duke said, his heavy features hovering

between uncertainty and nervousness. 'You look as though you regret the fact.'

'Don't you?'

The Duke had no answer to that.

'How did you find out?'

'A certain vanity. . .' The Duke fingered his tie tensely. 'You look as I fancy I should have done back in the early nineties. In those days I used to be very close to one of the parlour maids here. Daisy Pritchard.'

William moved restlessly, but his silence made the Duke continue.

'Your name, your age. . .it wasn't difficult to put it all together, even for me. Then all I had to do was put the right questions to the right people—'

'Not me,' the Reverend interrupted sharply.

No, Flora thought. Not with Mr Perry always hovering around the post baskets and Will sending regular letters off to Kilburn.

It wasn't only the Duke who would have been able to come to a conclusion. Mr Perry and Mr Stacey both looked old enough to have been working at Alvoe in Daisy Pritchard's time. There was never a shortage of long memories among domestic servants.

'William. . .' Flora said, apprehensive of the look he was levelling at the Duke. He heard the concern in her voice, but misunderstood its reason.

'Why have you chosen to make all this public, your Grace? I hope you don't think it gives you the right to meddle in my private life.'

'I respect you too much for that, William,' the Duke said gravely.

Momentarily put off his stride, William took a step back from the Duke's desk. Flora watched the way they were looking at each other, sizing each other up with a sort of wary regard.

'If you would like to take a seat...Captain Pritchard...' The Duke had hesitated, uncertain of how to address his newly discovered son. 'Perhaps we can discuss this rationally.'

'You'll forgive me if I don't feel very rational at the moment, your Grace.'

'I thought you wanted to find your family, Captain Pritchard. Hasn't that always been the real reason behind your friendship with Ralph, whether you realised it or not? To visit this area and search?'

William had taken a seat but almost rose again at that.

'I wouldn't use a friendship like that. I hope that I could never be accused of using *anybody*.'

William's eyes flashed and Flora reached forward to him. With a reassuring squeeze of her hand he took his eyes from the Duke for a moment to settle her.

'It can be no real defence, Captain Pritchard, to tell you that I did not know of your mother's condition when she left here. She was the one who abandoned me. We were in love, which was foolish. There could have been no future in it for either of us, but I could have helped her. I was married, Daisy was working here below stairs—'

'I didn't even know that much.' William shook his head. 'When I was a child I remember she once mentioned that she had worked in Alvoe, but she never said where. I knew she had been in service, but apart from a terrible pining for the countryside she never mentioned what had happened here. She must have been made to feel terribly ashamed.'

He looked his natural father full in the face, trying to redress the wrong done to his mother.

'Not by me,' the Duke said quietly. 'If I had known why she disappeared then I would have. . .' He stopped.

'What? What *could* you have done?' William raised his hands and let them fall again in desperation. 'Divorced the Duchess and tried to set my mother up in her place? In the circles you move in? Oh, I'm *sure* that would have gone down well with the Widow of Windsor!'

'I would have made sure that Daisy was properly provided for.'

'There is still time, your Grace,' William said with icy venom.

'Quite. That is why I was so eager to see you, William. I want to help your mother. And with my boys gone, I want to help you, too.'

William leapt on that.

'What about Ralph?' he asked almost before the Duke had finished speaking.

The Duke smiled with open and undisguised pleasure. 'I had someone check all the records. As I am sure you are aware, William, you are five months older than Ralph.'

Flora and the vicar gasped at that. The Duke looked triumphant, but William's face was unreadable.

'I see,' he said at last. 'Poor old Ralph always said both his parents disliked him.'

I can see why, Flora added silently. Now that the Duke has taken a fancy to William he won't be able to elbow Ralph aside fast enough.

'Are you hoping to slide me in as your heir rather than Ralph, your Grace?'

The Duke's smile slipped. 'Sadly, I can't, William. It was my first thought, of course, but the unfortunate circumstances of your birth mean that you could not inherit the Alvoe title. That will have to go to Ralph, but then titles are empty things. There are far more useful things in life, like money, property... Rest assured I intend to do as much as I possibly can for you and your mother, William.'

'It's a pity you never thought of that thirty years ago,' William said harshly. 'When you were so distraught at losing touch with my mother that you took comfort in your wife's arms.'

'Will!' Alarmed at such talk and the sudden harsh tone of William's voice, Flora turned to him, but the Duke had known what to expect.

'I realise this must be a shock to you, William.'

'Not half as much of a shock as the Mission would be to you, if you'd ever bothered to find out about it before, your Grace,' William said in a low voice full of contempt.

'I may not have been able to help you in the past, William, but I can start making it up to you now.' The Duke lifted a book from the drawer of his desk and took a pen from the ink-stand before him. 'And to Daisy.'

He wrote something out, then turned it face down on his blotter before handing the single sheet of paper to William. William took it between finger and thumb, looked at it with undisguised contempt then held it out where Flora could see it.

'Two hundred pounds?' she said faintly. The size of the cheque astonished her, but there was another surprise to come.

'Not much,' William said dismissively. 'But I suppose it's a start.'

'*William!*' Flora whispered fiercely, but he was already tucking the cheque into his notecase.

'And now, your Grace, since you summoned us here without a thought to any plans we might have had in

mind, I think it's about time you had a taste of
pandering to us. I had some urgent business to attend
to in Gloucester which I had to postpone to come here,
so I would like to borrow the Rolls and attend to that
now. I'm sure that my wife and Mr Standish would like
nothing better than to be fed here while I'm away, so I
shall leave you to make sure that they are entertained
properly.'

There was an unspoken warning in William's words,
and panic rushed to the Duke's face.

'William. . . .Ralph doesn't know about any of this
yet. . .'

'Then I think it's about time you told him, don't you,
your Grace?'

William bent and kissed Flora, whispering in her ear
as they parted, 'Don't worry. I won't be long. It's time
this family started treating you properly. Enjoy your
lunch!'

He winked at her with some of the old mischief, and
then he was gone.

'Well!' the Reverend said when he could put his
alarm into words. 'I never expected *that* from William!'

'I wanted him to be glad,' the Duke whispered
quietly but he looked white, too. 'When I found out
the truth a few weeks ago I wanted to do so much for
him and his mother. I really did love her, you know,
Standish. I don't suppose you believe that now. You
didn't believe it then. Daisy was so much more lively,
more interesting, more affectionate than—'

'Your wife?' Flora said coldly.

'I was going to say girls of my own class, Mrs
Pritchard.' The Duke used her new title without a trace
of bitterness. 'I'm sorry, Standish. This must be bringing back a lot of painful memories for you.'

'Daisy never cared for me in the way that I cared for her, your Grace. You should have known that.'

The Duke turned to Flora. 'Standish loved William's mother enough to find her a place of safety away from the wrath of her parents, Mrs Pritchard. And to keep the secret of where she had gone, and why.' The Duke looked at his old sparring partner with a certain admiration. 'No wonder you always hated me so, Marcus.'

'Daisy wouldn't let me tell you, and she wouldn't marry me because she still loved you. Is it any wonder that I have hated you with such violence all these years?'

The vicar was mellowing. The Duke sensed it, and found a smile from somewhere.

'Hate in a true Christian man, Marcus? You *do* surprise me.'

'I did not feel so very Christian at the time, your Grace. It was painful. I watched the woman I loved ruined while you enjoyed all the rich fruits of prosperity. No vengeance I ever obtained seemed great enough in those days.'

Something of the vicar's old pugnacity surfaced again. Flora saw his hands grasp the arms of his chair as though ready for another confrontation. The Duke noticed nothing. He rang the bell beside the study fireplace then sank into a comfortable chair.

'Let's settle all this once and for all, Marcus. Like civilised men. Isobel's gone to bed with one of her heads so we can adjourn to the drawing room for a drink before eating.' He went on, 'Although the standard of food around this place seems to have taken a tumble recently.'

The Duke didn't seem to make the connection between Flora leaving Alvoe Court and the decline in cooking standards. She felt annoyed, but said nothing.

'William was right, I suppose,' the Duke began after a pause so long that even he realised that his guests were in an impossible situation. 'I ought to have put Ralph right about the situation first. I know—I'll do it now before they serve our tea.'

Flora couldn't stand the thought of being a witness to that. The grimace that crossed the Duke's face whenever he mentioned Ralph's name made it clear that he was not the son that the Duke would have chosen to inherit the Alvoe title.

'Excuse me, your Grace. . .' She stood up and backed away toward the door. Sitting in the Duke's study was bad enough. To see Master Ralph shamed—however much she hated him—would be too much to bear. She walked quickly from the room, without knowing where she would go or what she would do, but was brought to a sudden halt in the great hall.

A hunched shape was sitting at the bottom of the great marble staircase. Its back was toward Flora and although it was silent and still there was no mistaking Ralph Morwyn.

William must have told him. Nothing else would have stopped him and shut him up so completely, Flora reasoned. She wondered if there had been another fight. If so, Ralph had been the loser, to judge by his appearance.

Flora edged through the hall, hoping that he would ignore her. She fully intended to ignore him. Then he spoke.

'Hello, Cookie.' His voice was flat and dull, which was the most shocking thing of all. Flora stopped and looked at him. With his sandy hair and pale blue eyes Ralph Morwyn never did have much colour, but now he looked grey and lifeless. 'I suppose I'll have to stop calling you that.'

Good heavens, Flora thought suddenly. I suppose he's my brother-in-law now.

That did at least give her a sense of security. She went toward him.

'William has told you?'

'Mmm.' Ralph studied the end of his unlit cigar with a frown. 'He *said* that everything is going to be all right. That nothing will change...but that I ought to enjoy making the old man sweat—'

The Duke's sudden appearance in the study doorway distracted them both.

'You need say nothing to Ralph, Mrs Pritchard. I will explain everything to him. Right now. The drawing room, Ralph. If you please.'

'Well—I can at least keep *my* half of the bargain,' Ralph murmured to Flora as he stood up and walked off toward the drawing room.

Flora stayed where she was. The Duke was ushering the Reverend along in Ralph's wake and as they passed her he urged Flora to follow them.

'Are you sure, your Grace?' she asked as the Duke beckoned her into the drawing room. 'Don't you think you'd better speak to Master Ralph alone first?'

'Don't see why.' Andrew Morwyn looked genuinely puzzled. 'You and Standish know it all already!'

Flora wondered how to suggest that he ought to be taking Ralph's feelings into account, but she was saved from speaking out of turn by an equally unwelcome voice from up on the landing.

'Are we to begin letting all and sundry into the great hall, Andrew?' the Duchess of Alvoe announced as she swept along the balcony and reached the head of the marble stairway.

'Mrs Pritchard isn't "all and sundry", Isobel. She is William's wife.'

Andrew Morwyn advanced toward Flora. To her surprise and the outrage of the Duchess he took her arm. 'Mrs Pritchard has been good enough to hear me out already. Now it is Ralph's turn. I don't intend repeating myself again so perhaps you would be good enough to join us too, Isobel.'

The hideous double indignity of being deceived by a house guest and losing an excellent cook at the same time was still fresh in Isobel Morwyn's mind and she was glaring at Flora.

Flora met the look stoically. 'I'll take my meal in the kitchens, your Grace,' she said to the Duke without taking her eyes off the Duchess.

The Duke didn't seem to notice the looks the two women were exchanging and patted Flora's arm reassuringly as the Duchess descended the great stair-case and went toward the drawing room.

'I shall entertain you in the way that William intended, Mrs Pritchard. Cheer up! I'm the one who is in disgrace, not you!'

The Duke went into the drawing room. Flora hung back to follow in behind the Duchess, as her ex-employer would expect. She felt no need to try and make a point now.

Inside the drawing room, the Reverend was already seated, looking appreciatively at a well-filled drinks trolley. The Duchess stopped dead as she saw him and darted a furtive look at her husband. For his part the vicar was visibly trying to avoid looking at the Duchess. Ralph had to tread heavily on the vicar's toe in passing to remind him of his manners. The Reverend looked at Ralph in confusion, then dutifully rose from his seat until Flora and the Duchess had taken their places.

The Duke remained standing, eventually motioning to Standish to sit down again. The vicar was avoiding the Duchess of Alvoe's stare in a way that Flora found embarrassing. She could see how angry the Duchess was already, without a word having been said. Her face was white and her lips tightly pursed.

The Duke cleared his throat for an announcement.

'I'll be brief, as this is a painful matter but a necessary confession. Your mother, Ralph, knows that I had a love affair before you were born.' He went to his Duchess and took her hand. Isobel Morwyn was refusing to look at anyone now, as though trying to hide her embarrassment at such a bald revelation. Ralph was suddenly uncomfortable too, looking at his father with an embarrassment that was only just camouflaged by curiosity. Flora wished she had William at her side to support her, but the family were so consumed by their own feelings that they were paying no attention to her.

'What neither of us realised at the time was that the poor, unfortunate girl went on to bear my illegitimate son,' the Duke continued, and the Duchess gasped. A split second later Ralph did the same. This sort of thing was not the usual topic of conversation in the Alvoe drawing room.

'The tragedy touched the Reverend's life too, for he and I had both been in love with the same girl,' the Duke went on. 'While I might have seemed the winner in that particular contest, poor Daisy Pritchard was definitely the loser.'

'*Pritchard?*' Ralph queried with theatrical thunder. 'Father! Surely this can't mean that Will is your—'

Flora could not look as the Duke held up his hand for silence. All she could do was stare down at her hands, clasped white and tense in her lap, as the Duke continued his story.

'Acting like a true gentleman, the Reverend stifled

his justifiable loathing for me by helping poor Daisy and her child in every way that he could—'

'*Stifled?*'

The Duke, Ralph's feigned dismay, the vicar's cringing, Flora's embarrassment on their behalf—everything ground to a halt. The Duchess had spoken, rising to her feet in a swirl of ivory silk. Throwing off the Duke's hand, she took two steps toward the vicar. Immediately the Reverend was transfixed, his face slack with a horror that Flora could only wonder at.

Worse was to come.

'Stifled?' the Duchess repeated, her voice ringing through the room. 'That's what he told you, was it? I'll tell you how this "gentleman of the cloth" was paying you back in kind while he was paying off your fancy piece, Andrew Morwyn. Shall I?'

Flora slipped away unnoticed from the explosion of furious recriminations. No one was interested in her now. The Duchess's own revelations had given them more than enough to argue about. She had to find William.

Flora wondered what he would say when he heard what had happened. Learning that he was the result of the Duke's adulterous liaison had been bad enough. Now that it turned out that his half-brother—no, Flora corrected herself. That wasn't right. Not any more.

The most important thing was to find William. Flora didn't know what he was up to but she needed him. He had been loyal to her before. Now she needed that reassurance again, to convince her that she had done the right thing.

The carrier had already left, so there was no other way to leave Alvoe except on foot. Flora was stuck on the estate. She could not face going down to the kitchens. They were all bound to have heard that the rumours were true by this time. Flora knew that the news wasn't going to make any difference to her, but she had the horrible feeling that the staff wouldn't believe that. The truth was that Flora no longer knew what she could say to the staff who had once been hers to command. They might think she had returned to gloat or throw her weight around.

It was cold and cheerless out in the grounds of Alvoe Court. To try and warm up Flora went for a brisk walk, visiting all the places that William might take sanctuary in if he returned to find the atmosphere that she had left behind in the drawing room.

After endless circuits of the grounds she paused at the door to the kitchen garden. She hadn't dared to enter it before, but now something led her toward the smartly painted wooden door. Her fingers were almost too stiff to lift the latch. Mrs McSweeney had been right about this treacherous cold. At least no one would be working in this weather.

Flora opened the garden door, expecting the grounds beyond to be deserted. Instead she was confronted by quite an audience. Resplendent in a navy blue three-piece suit and matching tie, Mr Stacey, the head gardener, was supervising the garden boys as they wheeled barrows of manure out onto the frozen ground. At least, that was what they had been doing. At the first sign of this intrusion Mr Stacey and the boys had stopped. They were all looking toward the door. And at her.

'Oh. . .I'm sorry.' Flora backed away, but to her alarm Mr Stacey smiled at her. He *never* smiled, and it gave him an unintentionally sinister look.

'Your husband is over in the summer house, Mrs

Pritchard,' he said without the slightest hesitation over her unfamiliar name.

He was still smiling. The boys were smiling too, until Mr Stacey caught them at it. Flora felt duty bound to smile back at them all, but it was a poor effort.

'Thank you, Mr Stacey.' She revived her best cook's manner and entered the garden. Without looking to either left or right she marched straight along the gravel path that led to the little summer house. The sound of iron barrow wheels on the frozen earth did not fool her for a minute. Every one of the garden staff was still looking at her. She could feel it.

The summer house was built on a turntable so that it could be moved to face the sun at any time of day. The glazed front was facing away from her, but William recognised her footsteps and called out her name.

Flora felt her heart jump with anticipation at the sound of his voice and quickly went to find him. He was sitting inside the summer house but rose to open the glass doors for her. There was a glass of hot chocolate steaming in a silver holder and a plate of cake and biscuits standing on a small wicker table before him.

'Oh, Will, I'm so glad you're back!'

He took her in his arms, smiling.

'That's the sort of welcome I like! I was on my way in to find you, but I took refuge in here for a minute to thaw out before facing the Duke again.' He led her to a seat beside him. 'Have a drink of chocolate. It's very good. I'll send Mr Stacey into the kitchens for another—'

'Oh, Will, he'll never stoop to running errands!'

'He didn't seem to mind last time.'

Flora took a sip of the creamy chocolate, wondering why William had never mentioned any business in

Gloucester to her, and whether he would tell her why he had gone there.

'I'm sorry I left so suddenly,' he began slowly, 'but I really did have something to do in Gloucester. After the Duke's news I needed time to think, too. Your father has always seemed a sensible sort of chap, so I called in there before returning.'

'You must be hungry, Will. What's wrong with the refreshments?' She looked at the untouched plate of cakes.

'Your father produced some bottles of porter that he'd kept from Christmas. He had some bread and cheese, too, but he told me to tell you that both were fresh, and *not* left over from Christmas. The only thing that was missing from the feast was you.'

He kissed her hand, and for the first time in what felt like a lifetime Flora laughed.

'Wait—you haven't heard the best bit. After that we went and had a drink at the Porter Stores. *And* another helping of bread and cheese each.'

Flora looked puzzled. 'You *must* be honoured. The Stores only lay on food for high days and holidays...' A horrible thought struck her. 'Oh, Will. You never told them about this business with the Duke, did you?'

It was William's turn to look astonished. 'No fear. I wouldn't have got out of there alive! No, I think it was more to do with what I said to Gully Pritchard.' William laughed as Flora's hand flew to her mouth.

'Your mother's father? You've seen him? Did you tell him who you were?'

William's expression eased still further. 'Not in so many words. There were some men logging by the side of the road, and once your father had told me which one was Gully I couldn't help my eyes straying toward him all the time. Eventually he came over and asked me why I was staring at him.'

'That sounds too polite for Gully.'

'Those weren't his exact words.' William smiled to himself again. 'All I could think of to do was to introduce myself and say, "I believe you once knew my mother, Mr Pritchard?" He backed off at that, which is just as well. I wouldn't have known what to say if he'd greeted me like a long-lost relative. And neither, I suspect, would any of his cronies. Your father seemed quite impressed. Let's hope the Alvoes are as impressed with my peace-making.'

'You may not need to do any,' Flora said cautiously. 'When I left them they all had too much to think about. Ralph, the Duchess, your father. . .' The Duke's new title sounded odd, but it needed to be said.

'I've already told Ralph that he's got no need to worry.' William shrugged, offering Flora a piece of cake. She studied the selection with a critical eye, then chose a piece of Genoa cake. It was surprisingly good for an unsupervised effort. Flora decided that she would call in at the kitchens and congratulate the girls. That would break the ice, and give them all something to talk about.

'Ralph's the legitimate heir, and there's no changing that. He's welcome to it all as far as I'm concerned,' William said without malice. 'All this wretched business will make no difference to me.'

Flora put down her piece of cake and rested the plate on her lap.

'Then you'll be happy to live off the Duke?'

'Certainly not!' William looked at her narrowly. 'I'm surprised that you would think that of me! I know my worth, Flora, and it's a lot more than two hundred pounds, I can tell you. I've thought out a plan, but I want to get your opinion before I put it to the Duke.'

William was so animated at the thought of his plan that Flora could not bear to raise an objection. She listened in silence.

'I know that there are quite a number of unoccupied cottages on the Alvoe estate, including the one that belonged to the estate manager before the war. We need a home, and I need a job. Alvoe has homes, but it doesn't have an estate manager—something the Duke was always complaining about when I was staying here.

'The Duke can look after my mother, and employ me. I've worked for my living all my life, and I'm not going to change now. I don't intend living off the Duke's guilt. Ralph has his inheritance and everything that goes with it, and he's welcome to it. As long as I've got you, and a job, and my mother is going to be provided for, that's all I want. Nothing more.'

'Ah.' Flora put her cake plate back onto the table. 'There's more to it than that now, Will. A lot more was said here after you'd left. Whatever else might happen, Ralph won't be able to inherit his father's title. The Duchess was determined to get her own back on your father by having an affair herself. When she realised she had fallen for a baby she went back to the Duke and made out that Ralph was his.'

William took her hands in his, his eyes thoughtful.

'The Duchess might only be saying that in the heat of the moment.'

Flora shook her head. 'I don't think so. It seems that Ralph's natural father had his suspicions he might have made the Duchess—' The word was still impossible to say. Flora gesticulated feebly, talking quickly to cover herself. 'That the Duchess might be going back to her husband in an interesting condition, but of course he could never prove it.'

William had stood up. He was looking toward the bulk of Alvoe Court, rearing above the walls of the kitchen garden. Flora wondered if he was thinking what it would be like to be master of it all.

'Why on earth would the Duchess choose to say such a thing? Unless, of course, it is true. . .' The idea was so unthinkable that William's voice died away for a moment.

'I could understand if she wanted to hit out at me,' he went on eventually, 'but surely this way is more painful for Ralph and the Duke, because now there is no legitimate heir to Alvoe. What on earth will happen?'

Flora went to his side. 'I had an idea while we were all taking in the Duchess's news,' she began slowly. 'There were no staff in the room while she was saying her piece. It was only me, the Duke, the vicar and Ralph who heard it. Everybody knows how keen the Duchess is to be well thought of, so as soon as I could catch her eye I took her aside and told her that it might be as well if she kept quiet about her lapse—'

'You did *what*?' William was incredulous. 'It didn't take you long to stop seeing the Duchess as your mistress, did it?'

'She's no better than she should be.' Flora pursed her lips despite William's laughter.

'There's nothing wrong with marrying above yourself, Flora!' He tweaked her cheek playfully.

'That's not what I mean. Acting like a common hussy and carrying on with a *vicar*, of all people, and her a married woman. And a Duchess!' Flora added with the moral outrage of a woman who still read the *News of the World* in secret.

'I told her that if she ever repeated what she had said, or tried to make trouble for the Duke, or Ralph, or the vicar, she would lose whatever reputation she might have left,' Flora went on. 'Women like that are always made to look bad in the witness box. There would be no more visits by Lady Molly Berkhamstead or anybody else if that happened,' she finished firmly.

'The Duchess would lose everything,' William agreed thoughtfully, 'and so would Ralph. If they all keep quiet as you suggest then Ralph could still inherit the Alvoe name. I believe the Duke has no other relatives at all. Did they agree to your idea?'

'I don't know.' Flora touched the tip of her tongue against her teeth. 'I don't know what else they *can* do if they want to avoid a terrible scandal. I left them to sort it all out between themselves.'

Seeing her shiver, William offered Flora his arm and they went down the summer-house steps. They walked back through the kitchen garden wordlessly, passing all the garden staff, who took care to touch their caps respectfully. William appeared not to notice, his steps quickening as they neared the house.

'Are you still going to tell the Duke that you want to work here?' Flora risked asking at last.

'Of course. That hasn't changed, although I will see Ralph first. He must be feeling dreadful. I know how you must hate him, Flora, but for him to learn such a truth in front of you all. . . . How on earth could the Duchess be so hurtful?'

'It's not Ralph she wanted to hurt, Will. It's Ralph's real father. When she heard how desperately he had hated the Duke she realised how she had been used. It was his way of getting back at the Duke—your father.'

William stopped walking.

'Then the Reverend must be Ralph's real father.

He's the only man I can think of who actively dislikes the Duke.'

Flora nodded silently. William exhaled, the late-winter chill condensing his breath into wisps of steam.

When he did not move for a long time Flora slipped her arms around him.

'Did you really have business in Gloucester? Or was that just a way to escape?'

He looked down and smiled. 'I did need to go to Gloucester, but I needed time to think out our plan, too.'

'What if the Duke and Duchess won't agree?' Flora stroked his hair, still half afraid of losing him even now.

'That's their look-out. I've done very well for myself so far without their help. It's going to get even better with you as my wife. If they won't let me work here for my living—' he nodded toward the great bulk of Alvoe Court '—then we'll be off to make our fortunes some-where else. We'll set you up as a caterer, as we intended.'

Suddenly he took hold of Flora's hand and started leading her away from the house and toward an old garden seat that stood in the shelter of an ancient shrubbery.

'Before we go and talk terms, I have some unfinished business to attend to, my love.'

Flora was very quiet as they trailed through the points of crocuses and snowdrops on the way to the garden seat, wondering what William might mean. She need not have worried. After making sure the seat was not damp he let her sit down, then withdrew a little parcel from his waistcoat pocket. It was wrapped in coloured paper and tied up with a pink ribbon.

'This is why I had to go into Gloucester. We got married in such a hurry that I never had a chance to give you an engagement ring, did I? I wanted to put that right.'

Warmed by his love, Flora forgot the frosty chill around them and took the parcel from him. She began to open it, then hesitated.

'Will?'

'Yes?'

'You didn't use the Duke's money on this, did you?'

'Certainly not! That's going to the Fieldings. Every penny,' he said firmly, but with a smile.

Within the crackling folds of wrapping paper was a small square box. Flora turned it about in her hands, savouring the moment of anticipation. Then suddenly she lifted the lid. The last afternoon shreds of weak winter sunshine danced blue fire over an extravagance of diamonds.

'Well? What do you think?' William said with the faintest hint of uncertainty.

'Will, it's beautiful. . .'

'Why don't you put it on, then?'

'I'm waiting for you to do the honours.' She nudged him playfully.

'Oh, of course.' He reached for the ring and, taking Flora's hand, slipped it onto her finger above their wedding ring.

'Goodness! And I was worried that my hands were shaking!' she teased him gently.

'It was quite an ordeal for me, I can tell you,' he said as they admired the ring that now glittered on her finger. 'All those understanding smiles from the jew-eller and giggles from his girl assistant when I said it was a present for my wife. I'm sure they thought I was making an excuse.'

Flora put up her hand and stroked William's hair. The electric glitter of the diamonds in her new ring flashed in the fading sunlight, but Flora hardly noticed. She was more concerned with receiving William's caresses in return.

He kissed each of her fingers, admiring the ring again with a certain amount of pride.

'Perhaps I'd better wait in the kitchens while you sort everything out with Ralph and the Duke. Not to mention the vicar,' Flora said as they walked hand in hand across the damp grass of the park. 'And what on earth will the Duchess say when she sees me wearing a beautiful ring like this? She really will think I've got my claws into what passes for the family now!'

'It's not the Duchess I care about, or Ralph, or the Duke, or any of this.' William threw a glance in the direction of Alvoe Court across the lawns that were starting to become brittle with frost. 'It's you, Flora. You're the only thing that matters to me; I'd give everything I've *never* had to keep you!'

'I know,' she said simply as he stopped to kiss her in full view of the house. 'I know that now.'

Historical Romance™

Coming next month

THE EARL OF RAYNE'S WARD
Anne Ashley

Rebecca Standish *refused* to comply with Drum
Thornville's outrageous demand... Since she was twelve
years old her best friend Drum had tried to curb her wild
ways. When he'd left to join the army she had been freed
from his domination, but seven years later he was back!
He was still as overbearing, arrogant and authoritarian as
ever—and very handsome! She vowed to ignore him, but
that proved impossible when she was forced to stay at
Rayne Park, Drum's residence, while her grandfather
travelled! She soon discovered that he had *every* right to
boss her around, but he had *no* right to let her fall in
love—with him!

GABRIELLA
Brenda Hiatt

Gabriella Gordon knew that she would have to agree
to a London Season sooner or later or her Society
sister would plague her to death. So when the celebrated
Duke of Ravenham came to call, supposedly owing to the
outcome of a wager, the duke was obliged to lend
Gabriella his escort and consequence. Gabriella's sister
was in raptures, but Gabriella most definitely was not. She
was determined to be as difficult as possible but found that
was easier said than done...

FROM MAY 1997

New York Times bestselling author

JAYNE ANN KRENTZ

Full Bloom

Part bodyguard, part troubleshooter, Jacob Stone
had, over the years, pulled Emily out of countless
acts of rebellion against her domineering family.
Now he'd been summoned to rescue her from a
disastrous marriage. Emily didn't want his
protection—she needed his love. But did Jacob
need this new kind of trouble?

"A master of the genre...nobody does it better!"

—Romantic Times

**AVAILABLE IN PAPERBACK
FROM MAY 1997**

FREE!

FOUR FREE
specially selected
Historical Romance™ novels
__PLUS__ a FREE Mystery Gift
when you return this page...

Return this coupon and we'll send you 4 Historical Romance novels and a mystery gift absolutely FREE! We'll even pay the postage and packing for you.

We're making you this offer to introduce you to the benefits of the Reader Service™– FREE home delivery of brand-new Historical Romance novels, at least a month before they are available in the shops, FREE gifts and a monthly Newsletter packed with information, competitions, author profiles and lots more...

Accepting these FREE books and gift places you under no obligation to buy, you may cancel at any time, even after receiving just your free shipment. Simply complete the coupon below and send it to:

MILLS & BOON READER SERVICE, FREEPOST, CROYDON, SURREY, CR9 3WZ.

READERS IN EIRE PLEASE SEND COUPON TO PO BOX 4546, DUBLIN 24

NO STAMP NEEDED

Yes, please send me 4 free Historical Romance novels and a mystery gift. I understand that unless you hear from me, I will receive 4 superb new titles every month for just £2.99* each, postage and packing free. I am under no obligation to purchase any books and I may cancel or suspend my subscription at any time, but the free books and gift will be mine to keep in any case. (I am over 18 years of age)

H7XE

Ms/Mrs/Miss/Mr _____

BLOCK CAPS PLEASE

Address _____

_____

_____

_____ Postcode _____

NEW YORK TIMES
BESTSELING AUTHOR

Anne
Mather

Dangerous Temptation

He was desperate to remember... Jake wasn't
sure why he'd agreed to take his twin brother's
place on the flight to London. But when he
awakens in hospital after the crash, he can't even
remember his own name or the beautiful woman
who watches him so guardedly. Caitlin. His wife.

She was desperate to forget... Her husband
seems like a stranger to Caitlin—a man who
assumes there is love when none exists. He is
totally different—like the man she'd thought
she had married. Until his memory returns.
And with it, a danger that threatens them all.

"Ms. Mather has penned a wonderful romance."
—Romantic Times

AVAILABLE IN PAPERBACK
FROM MAY 1997